MIDNIGHT BAZAAR

A Secret Arcade of Strange and Eerie Tales

MIDNIGHT BAZAAR

A Secret Arcade of Strange and Eerie Tales

SIMON CLARK

ROBERT HALE · LONDON

Robert Hale Limited
Clerkenwell House
Clerkenwell Green
London EC1R 0HT

2 4 6 8 10 9 7 5 3 1

Typeset in 10/13½pt Sabon
by Derek Doyle & Associates, Shaw Heath
Printed and bound in Great Britain
by Biddles Limited, King's Lynn

CONTENTS

1

LANGTHWAITE ROAD

What comes before

When I look out of my room window I see the road. It's a road that runs broad and straight until it reaches Annie Tyndall Wood. There, it makes a sharp left.

I see it in my imagination, too. I can run my mind's eye over it like you can run your finger over your lover's arm. There's the road: with one lane for traffic into town; the other lane takes the traffic away into the world beyond the wild wood. There's the road sign. Here's the bridge where a river flows to the sea.

Langthwaite Road runs all the way to the city of York. I like to think about that at times likes this. I see myself riding up safe and high in the cab of a truck. The road bridges muddy fields, a span of firm asphalt that supports the turning wheel. The line of white dashes along its centre guides the driver home.

To rest one's gaze on its surface you would see its blue-black skin; one that feels a thousand tyres across its back in any one day. On hot summer evenings one might catch the tar rich scent of asphalt. To press ones mind's eye to the surface would take you deeper into the road. Through the cool, crisp shell of asphalt into compacted limestone beneath. Below that is a firm, supporting bed of red shale that rests on God's own sweet earth.

I've stood at this window and watched the road ever since I was able to pull myself up from my infant bed. For me the road's always been there.

I hear the sound of its pulse at night. Passing cars, trucks, hearses, buses, ice cream vans, ambulances.

When I was eight I saw a car tearing the length of the road's strong back. The car jumped. I ran out of the house, then down the driveway to the road. The car lay belly up on the black top. Already Langthwaite Road had begun to eat. I saw the driver hanging by the seatbelt. There were bite marks on his face. The road had chewed the meat from his arms. The asphalt had started to drink the life blood that poured from him.

It's happened quite a bit since then. Every few weeks one sees another car deliver the road yet another meal.

For a while I tried to explain to my mother. She'd smile and pat my head. 'My goodness you have an imagination, young man. Now go out and play, Leo. Mummy's meeting a new friend tonight.'

So Leo ran and played.

Leo made friends with the road.

But then the road and Leo fell out.

Happens sometimes, you know?

(From Life Bites by Leo)

One

My name's Vic Blake. This is the place to start it as much as anywhere. I've thrown newspaper cuttings on to the bed. You can stick your hand in and pull them out at random.

Like this:

ACCIDENT BLACKSPOT CLAIMS ANOTHER LIFE

North Sutton's notorious Langthwaite Road was the scene of a fatal accident yesterday. A car driven by Daniel Franks, a local man, was in collision with a stationary tractor.

Another:

Police are appealing for witnesses after a hit and run left a mother of three critically ill in hospital. Kathleen Wilson, 43, had been cycling

8

toward North Sutton along Langthwaite Road when. . . .

More:

. . . around thirty local people gathered outside the town hall to protest about Langthwaite Road, the notorious accident blackspot, which has claimed eighteen lives in the past five years, and left more than thirty people seriously injured. Council officials stated that they would investigate. . .

And:

Police are appealing for witnesses after a stolen van was involved in a head-on collision with a car on Langthwaite Road. All three occupants of the car were pronounced dead at the scene of the accident. The victims were named as Mary Douglas (56), her daughter Kate Delgardo (35) and granddaughter, Chloe, aged eighteen months.

More? You better believe there's more:

The Coroner, Mr Stanley Hope, recorded the accidental death of 8-year-old Robin Slater, who was a passenger in the car driven by his grandfather. In closing, Mr Hope stated that, 'I find it tragic that this, the third inquest I've presided over involving a fatal vehicle accident this year, has yet again occurred on Langthwaite Road. Drivers must remember that speed restrictions are mandatory for a reason. Those who drive too fast endanger not only their own lives, but. . . .'

There are plenty more where that came from, I can tell you, though you'll be thinking that people who collect newspaper clipping are obsessed. I agree. It gets you like that. But first, I should explain something. In the early hours of a Sunday morning five weeks ago my friend was killed on Langthwaite Road. From tyre marks the police concluded that his car swerved to avoid hitting 'some unknown obstruction' and spun off the road. It landed upside down in a field. He was strangled by his own seatbelt.

Dead on arrival, as the saying goes.

I'd known Paul Robertson since nursery school. He was a big softie then. After his mother left him in class he'd wind up on the nursery teacher's knee as the rest of us sat cross-legged on the carpet to sing 'The Wheels On The Bus' and 'Wind The Bobbin Up'. He'd soon stop crying (or 'rawping' as we call it round here, an old Viking word our history teacher used to tell us). Every now and again, the nursery schoolteacher would hold a big handkerchief to Paul's face so he could blow his nose.

Paul Robertson was 24 (the same age as me), played in the same pub football team. More or less did the same kind of stuff. But when he left school he went into the army, while I joined my dad on the boat. Paul became a big, tough artilleryman. He could bend six-inch nails with one hand. No one messed with him. Then he went and ran his car off the road and strangled himself with his own seatbelt.

After the funeral, his mother gave me this Tesco carrier bag full of things '. . he would have liked you to have,' she said. Without looking at what was inside I dropped the lot in the wheelie bin.

It's funny. I grew up, like you, thinking that grief made you feel sad. It doesn't always, does it? Sometimes it makes you angry. Even so, I wanted nothing to do with bloody Langthwaite Road. I certainly wasn't going to collect damn newspaper cuttings about the thing. There was nothing I could do about Paul Robertson, good friend though he was. Like everyone else in his life, once the funeral was over, the bereaved had to get on with their own three score and ten.

Two weeks after he died a letter came.

> *Vic,*
> *Leo Carter thinks you should know.*
> *Paul Robertson saw it happen once.*
> *So Paul Robertson was murdered.*
> *Leo.*

I started collecting newspaper clippings.

'Vic, who are you talking to?'

'Nobody.'

'I heard a voice.'

'I was thinking aloud.'

'You know what they do with people who talk to themselves?'

'Yeah . . . I know . . . lucky them. Three free meals a day and as much television as they can watch.'

'Mr Grumpy Boots.' Faith walked into the bedroom. There were towels round her body and her head. 'You'll have to get that shower looked at; it keeps running cold.'

'It'll need a new thermostat.'

'Oh God, Vic. What's this all over the bed?'

'Just some clippings.'

'I need to sit down at that end to dry my hair.'

'I'll move them . . . hang on, your hands are wet. They'll get ruined.'

'It's about time they did.'

'I'll decide when to throw them out.'

'It puts you in a bad mood every time you look at them.' Faith pulled the towel free of her head. 'Will you plug the hairdryer in for me?' She began to comb her damp hair. 'Never mind, I'll do it.'

'No, it's OK . . . just let me shift these off the bed first.'

'You haven't done anything with that letter from Leo, have you?'

'No.'

'If you take it to the police you'll end up a laughing stock.' She reached out to touch my arm. 'I don't want people taking you for a fool, Vic.'

'They won't.'

'So you're not going to take that letter any further?'

'No. Now, what do you want with the chicken? Noodles or salad?'

'I thought we were going out for an Indian?'

'I don't think I can eat one tonight.'

She glared. 'See? Those bloody newspaper clippings and the bloody letter!'

'I'm just not hungry enough for a take-away.'

'They're preying on your mind, aren't they?'

'No, Faith, they're not.' I put the clippings into the shoebox, then pushed it into the wardrobe. Leo's letter was on top.

Bloody poison, that letter.

'So what do you plan to do after supper?' she asked.

I shrugged. 'Nothing much.'

'So I take it you won't be going out for another of your walks again?'

'I don't know what I'm doing yet. Or have you written out a damn

timetable for me? Supper at seven. Television at eight. Bed at ten—'
'Vic—'
'Lights out ten fifteen.'
'Vic.' She pointed the hairdryer like it was a gun. 'Stop it. This has gone far enough.'
'Damn right.'
'Vic. Listen, I'm on your side.'
'You've got a funny way of showing it sometimes.'
'That's because this has got me worried. Do I like to see you lying awake at night raking it all over? Paul had an accident, that's all. It was tragic, but it was just another accident out on bloody Langthwaite Road.'
'I know. So why keep going on about it?'
'Because you keep going on about it.'
'I don't—'
'You might not be talking about Paul, but you're thinking about him. Then you know full well you go walking up the road until you get to . . . you know. I don't have to paint you a picture, do I?'
The bedroom was hit by one of those silences that can go either way. Into blistering argument . . . we'd had plenty of those, I can tell you. Or to apologies, followed by kisses. And kisses sometimes followed by bed.
Big pause.
I heard the traffic going by in the rain outside.
'I'll get a new thermostat tomorrow,' I told her.
'It'd be nice to get under without freezing my boobs off.' She smiled. 'See?' She opened the towel. 'They get all goosy.'
'I'll do salad,' I told her.

Downstairs I rolled a tomato backwards and forwards on the table.
Faith came in. She'd dressed in jeans and a sweatshirt. She walked through to the lobby. I heard her pull her shoes from the cupboard.
I asked one of those questions that's intended more as a prompt than anything. 'What're you doing, Faith?'
'Going out.'
'What about supper?'
She looked at the tomato. 'Doesn't look quite ready yet.'
'Soon will be. The chicken will microwave.'
'How'd the catch go?'

'A couple of lobsters and around a dozen crabs.'

'Better than nothing I suppose.'

'There'll be more tomorrow. It was running a swell today. Lobsters don't like waves.'

'So they stayed at home?'

'It'll be all right next time. The forecast's for light westerlies. Faith?'

'Uhm?'

'Where are you going?'

'Where?' She pulled on her coat, then looped the scarf round her neck. 'I'm going out walking with you. We'll do a turn on Langthwaite Road first.'

'Then what?'

'Then we're going up to Leo's.'

'Leo's?' This caught me by surprise.

'Leo's,' she said firmly.

'But he won't be in.'

'He's always in.'

'No, I mean. . .' I tapped the side of my head with a finger. 'He won't be in.'

Two

It's funny, isn't it? The decision you make in the next ten minutes could result in you dying. Doesn't have to be a big LIFE or DEATH decision. You might choose to take a bath. You slip on the soap: break your neck. You might decide to fix the downspout on the guttering. Only you fall off the bloody ladder. In our case it was the walk.

I led the way. Streetlights burned with that orange light that makes you think the world's gone rusty in the rain.

'I'm not an Olympic athlete, Vic.'

'What's that?'

'Can't you slow down?'

'I'm not walking fast.'

'Fast enough,' Faith complained. 'I'm breaking a sweat.'

'Here.' I held out my hand. She took it. Her palm felt hot.

'Cold hands, warm heart?' She smiled at me.

'Yeah . . . toastie.'

She rolled her eyes. 'Your mother always said you were a moody bugger.'

'You had fair warning then.'

She shook her head with one of those long suffering sighs that she did so well. 'I know this isn't you, Vic. You are moody at times, but you've never been like this before.' Then talking to herself she hissed, 'Bloody letter.'

'Bloody Leo,' I said. 'Maybe it's time he was locked up.'

'I used to feel sorry for him. Not anymore.'

We walked hand-in-hand. When I started walking faster Faith squeezed my hand, then pulled me back with a smile as if to rein me in. I looked up at the sky. The cloud was thinning nicely, letting a bit of moon peep through.

'It's coming from the south west. The sea'll drop soon.'

'Fancy taking a look at it?'

'The sea?' I shook my head. 'I'll get enough of it tomorrow.'

'So, it's Langthwaite Road after all, then?'

'Yep.'

'Lovely . . . a moonlit night; the company of the one you love . . . and a stroll to a notorious accident blackspot. You know how to show a girl a good time, Vic.'

'You didn't have to come.' We turned at the junction leaving the houses behind.

She said, 'Call me, daft, but even after this long together I still like your company.'

'What me? A moody bugger?' This time I did smile.

It was the usual mid-evening you get in November. Dark. Wet underfoot. In the distance you could make out the sound of surf. If it ran an easterly the surf ripped at the beach. Then you could hear the sea when you were in bed. Tonight the sound was soft. So, maybe we were set for fair fishing tomorrow.

This road was a feeder for the estate so it was mainly cars with one optimistic ice-cream truck. It's only when you reach Langthwaite Road that you get the real speeders. And there are the usual heavyweights: the oil tankers pounding the highway toward the refinery in North Sutton. When they leave full they're pulling a lot of weight up the slight incline.

It slows them down, so that's when you get cars overtaking.

That's what could've have happened to Paul. He might have risked passing a slow truck then spun off. Bastard trucker never stopped if that was the case. A farmer found Paul still strung up by the seatbelt in his car. Poor sod must have been there all night.

I wondered if Paul'd been conscious when he'd started to choke. God only knows why the daft idiot couldn't reach the seatbelt release button.

'Hmm? What's that, Faith?'

'You haven't been listening have you, Vic?'

' 'Course I have.'

'What did I say, then?'

'About Christmas.'

'What about Christmas?'

'Shopping?'

'Vic.' She did the sigh again. 'About Christmas Day. Do we go to your mum and dad's for Christmas dinner or to mine.'

We left the feeder road. Now we were on Langthwaite Road. Or at least the pavement that runs alongside it. The road's broad and straight. Streetlights are few and far between here. The road surface is black. In the dark, it always makes me think of deep water. For some reason I shivered when I walked along the road. But then for the last few weeks I've always shivered when I'm on Langthwaite bloody Road. Flaming stupid, isn't it? A grown man of twenty-four. I see that bit of road and the hairs stand up on my arms.

Faith looked up at me. I couldn't see her face in shadow. Her eyes glinted though. 'Cold?'

'No, I'm fine.' I curled my toes inside my seaboots. She'd heard the waver in my voice.

Sure, she registered the sound. She had the sense, though, not to pass comment.

I walked, keeping myself between Faith and the road. The oil tankers were roaring by tonight, flinging spray into our faces. Faith leaned into me as she walked, keeping warm, or maybe just wanting to maintain a closeness with me.

'So what's it to be then, Vic?'

'What's what to be?' I asked. Maybe I'd missed another question?

'Your family or mine for Christmas dinner?'

15

'Neither, we'll picnic on the beach.'

She knew I was joking. 'Yeah, I should cocoa. People already think you're odd.'

'I must be . . . I'm married to you.'

'You swine.' She had a smile on her face as she pulled away from me then made as if to thump my arm. I stepped back as she moved forward.

Normally, I'm the clumsy one, but Faith tripped. Her whole body gave a dip as her balance shifted; her trying to recover only made it worse. She sort of boosted herself forward, both arms reaching out.

I remember making a grab for her as she fell, but although my fingers made contact with her coat I couldn't grab the fabric. She tumbled forward on to the road, landing flat on her stomach, arms stretched out. Palms down.

She looked back at me. First, there was surprise on her face at the suddenness of the fall, then an annoyed expression as if she couldn't believe she'd just gone and tripped over her own feet.

I looked down at her. One of those split second things where I told myself: it's OK, she'll get straight back to her feet. The sound came as a rush at first before becoming a roar. I looked to my left to see a wall of light rush at her.

'*Vic!*'

The note of panic did it for me. I pounced, grabbed her arm. Heard her grunt because it hurt her, then yanked her back off the road.

The truck swept by. Slipstream dragged at our hair, clothes, even our faces. Spray blinded us, got in our mouths, road grit scratched against my teeth.

Damn thing didn't even sound its horn. Just tore by us like we didn't even exist. The lunatic was probably talking on a mobile phone or even pouring himself a coffee.

'Faith, are you all right?'

She brushed her hands down the front of her coat. 'Damn it,' she said under her breath. When she held her wrist up to what light there was it revealed a graze across the heel of her hand. 'Damn,' she said again.

'Faith?'

'I'm all right.' She looked down at her coat. 'I hope that mark isn't oil.'

I watched her straightening her clothes, pushing back her hair from her face, checking the graze again. Some blood. Not much.

16

Like I said. Decisions. Decisions. . . . Make the wrong one and that could be the end of everything for you. If I'd decided she could make it to her feet by herself Faith would have gone under the truck's wheels. Another one up for Langthwaite bloody Road, eh?

She marched away along the path.

'Where are you going?' I asked.

'I'm finishing the walk. Why?'

'Don't you want to go home?'

'Not on your life. Not until we've done what we set out to do.'

Three

Faith held my hand tight as we walked after the near accident.

Accident be damned. That old road just wants to gobble folk up. Yeah, couldn't you just see it as some Gothic animation? The road, the big black road that has all the menace of deep water. Dozens of swellings appear like blisters . . . they break open to form mouths that snap. Cat's eyes glinting all greedy and evil. The mouths dart at passing cars. The teeth rip the rubber to shreds. Punctures galore. Cars spin out of control. Crash and burn. The snapping mouths lunge out at pedestrians. There's screaming, there's running—

'Vic?'

'Uh?'

'You're not listening again.'

'Oh.'

She put her arm around my waist as we walked. 'That was quick thinking. Thank you.'

'You are OK?'

'I am now. But what if you hadn't been fast enough?'

I could feel tremors running through her body.

She gave a nervous sounding laugh. 'I'd have been dead, wouldn't I?'

'Best not think about it.'

She sighed. 'Just be thankful you won't be in the nightmare I have tonight.'

I was trying to think of something reassuring when we reached the spot.

'So it was here?' she said.

I nodded. 'You can't see much. There's broken branches on the bush over there.'

'The car almost went right over the top of it.'

'It must have taken off like a rocket when it left the road. There weren't any marks in the field until about thirty yards out. The car didn't even hit the fence.'

Faith gazed out into the dark field. 'He must have been going fast, Vic.'

'You should have seen the state of his car.'

Here, the road stood on a causeway a good five feet above the surrounding fields. The ploughed earth looked mushily soft. Even so, when Paul's car hit it must have felt as hard as concrete.

Traffic streamed by us, still raising clouds of white spray. Tyres hissed like a bunch of mad snakes. Above us, the moon went in and out of cloud. There was nothing much here but fields. There were no other pedestrians about. Not many people are stupid enough to stroll along a busy road on a dreary November night. Faith crouched to look at the flowers that friends and family had laid on the grass verge. They were bedraggled specimens now, going to mush in the wet. Cellophane wrappers fluttered in the slipstream from trucks. If you had a mind to, you could still make out a few words on the cards tied to the bunches.

We love you, Paul . . . God bless. . . . Can't believe you were taken from us . . . RIP, love Auntie Mary xxx. . . . From your mates in C platoon. . . . All my love. Dad.

Funny thing is, every time I saw the bunches of flowers lying there I felt a real, burning urge to kick the flaming things into the ditch. I glanced at Faith. She'd turned away from the flowers now. She faced the only house on this stretch of highway. It was an old stone farmhouse that stood on a piddling bump of a hill. It didn't look much but what it had going for it were clear views of Langthwaite Road. A light shone from an upstairs window.

Faith turned to me then nodded back at the house. 'Looks as if Leo's still up.'

'You don't have to go if you don't want to.'

'Oh, I want to all right. Ready?'

I nearly said to her, *Now take care crossing the road*. Instead, I kept my mouth closed. We had to wait for a while for a break in the traffic, the trucks were coming thick and fast tonight, roaring like monsters. All noise and lights and spray. All motorized aggression in spades. I gripped my wife's hand as at last we crossed the road to Leo's house.

Four

'Yes, of course Leo's in . . . *Leo? Leo! You've got visitors*!' This last bit was thrown up the stairs. Leo's mother looked pleased. She probably didn't make this kind of announcement often. 'Leo. Some of your friends have called to see you.'

Friends, huh.

She shot me a near wolfish grin, her eyes sparking. 'It's Vic, isn't it? And. . . .'

'Faith.'

'Leo?' she called up the stairs again. 'It's Vic and Faith . . . they're here to see you.'

She smiled back at us. 'He won't be long. He's working.'

Working. Jesus. What as? A cracked teapot?

'I'm sorry,' Faith said. 'We should have phoned first.'

'Oh, that's no problem.' Leo's mother smiled brightly, delighted someone had made the effort to see her son at all.

Miss Carter had Leo when she was sixteen. She was the type that towns like North Sutton love to hate. My mother and my friends' mothers weren't slow in filling any gaps in her life down through the years. By the time I was twelve I had the whole case history. Miss Carter had been a wild child. Expelled from school for messing with drugs. A shoplifter ('Brazen as anything', Mother told me. 'Walked out of Woolworth's with a pile of records that high'.) A teenage runaway ('Left on Christmas Eve with a man twice her age'.) Eventually she returned pregnant with Leo when she was sixteen ('She's nothing but trouble to her parents . . . well, she's pregnant now . . . that's her life ruined for good'.)

Miss Carter rented a market stall. She sold stuff she got from jumble sales as antiques. By the time Leo started high school she had three antique shops in towns along the coast ('Some people can't but help fall on their feet', grumbled the gossips. 'She can't have made all that money herself. A man must be giving it her'.) That'd make men in the pub smile in a knowing way. Whatever. She bought this big farmhouse and drove a new BMW. She must be doing something right.

Now Miss Carter chatted pleasantly. Forty, if she was a day; she still looked good. She was slim, attractive. Her hair was curly, and in a style that wasn't fashionable in North Sutton. To my neighbours she was some combination of tart and snob, but men always took a long, lingering look at her when she glided by.

She was as popular as a fly in a sugar bowl. But she had style. And she made your skin tingle when she looked at you.

Her charisma sparkled as she talked. 'Vic, I haven't seen you for ages. What are you doing with yourself now?'

'I'm on the boats.'

'With your father?'

I nodded.

'How's he keeping?'

'Oh, he's all right.'

'Faith, I know your mother. She works at the travel agent's in Wood Street.'

'She's gone part-time now. My Dad had a thrombosis last year, so she has to look after him now he's not so good on his feet.'

'Oh no, I am sorry to hear that, how awful.'

'He's a lot better than he was. But he had to give up work.' Faith wasn't too sure about the charisma treatment. Miss Carter leaned close to you when she talked. Her eyes searched your face as if you'd mucky marks on your cheeks. For men it sent up their pulse rate: it made women uneasy.

As she talked to Faith I couldn't help but notice the slender shape of the woman's body. She was wearing a black lace top that hugged her figure. Her trousers followed her curves in the right places. On her feet were sandals that seemed to be all criss-crossing straps that left her toenails showing. They were painted a vivid red. Her neck was very long and pale. There was something aristocratic about it and I remembered my grandmother used to refer to Miss Carter as 'that little duchess'. She didn't mean it as a compliment either.

I got the feeling that I was beginning to stare, so before Miss Carter and Faith noticed I looked round the hallway. Victorian in style, it had heavy purple curtains and there was lots of dark wood. Pieces of chunky antique furniture. A grandfather clock with a TICK . . . TOCK loud enough to drive you crazy if you had to sit with it for long. The stairs, with a heavy banister in more of that dark, muscular wood, loomed down out of the darkness.

'Leo's taking his time,' Miss Carter said. 'He probably wants to make an entrance. . . . Oh, I know, I'll make a pot of tea. You can have it in his room. Do you both like chocolate cake?'

Faith smiled. A polite one rather than a warm one. 'That would be very nice. Can I give you a hand?'

'Yes, please. The kitchen's this way . . . oh?' She looked upstairs as a light came on. 'Leo's opened his door.'

I didn't move or say anything. She obviously knew her son's routine by now.

She rested her finger on my arm. 'He's ready now, Vic. Go on up. First door on the left.'

Five

The man with the guitar's all right.
The man with the guitar's all right, all right, all right!

By Heaven . . . the times we'd walked home from the pub at midnight singing that one. It had been a summer hit the year I left school. Like the man said: catchy enough to do your head in.

Paul Robertson and me used to yell our bloody heads off with it as we walked along the sea front with enough beer inside us to keep our bellies afloat. *The man with the guitar's all right. . .* Only this one isn't, I can tell you.

I'd gone upstairs just as Miss Carter suggested and crossed the landing carpet to the open door. I'd thought it would be a bedroom but it was done out as a lounge. There were no lights on. Three chunky candles did the best they could to chase away the shadows. A spicy smell took your nostrils by storm. Incense, I guess. There was a big leather sofa. Sitting on it cross-legged, with a black acoustic guitar like he was just about to play, was Leo.

'Knock, knock, anyone in?'

Leo sat staring into thin air. It looked as if he was trying to remember the chord before he began. Only he didn't start to play anything. He sat there: a white, middle-class Buddha. Staring at the wall. Not noticing me. Not moving.

'Knock, knock. . . .'

Nope, Vic, old son. Nobody's home.

I stood there feeling a right prat. Not knowing whether I should go out again. Maybe I should *really* knock on the door? If I knuckled on wood hard enough it might snap him out of it. Then again, he might be getting his thoughts back together. So maybe I should wait a bit longer? I waited. I used the time to run my eyes over the room. Even though it was furnished with antiques, with more heavy purple curtains at the window, it had a hippy feel to it. There were paintings on the walls of hippy heads with sunlight bursting out their scalps. Leo's? I guessed so. He hung out with the art set at school. There were more guitars – Strats and a curvy Les Paul; a Marshall amp stood against the wall like a tomb-stone. Next to that, a hi-fi system with a kind of flower design on the speakers. I guess Leo must have decorated it with his own fair hand.

And Leo – the man himself. He was thin enough to be gaunt. Long hair, hollow cheekbones. Eyes that stared all the way to outer-space. Unblinking. Dead-looking.

Much more of that, mate, and your eyes'll dry up and drop out . . . That's just one of the thoughts going through my head as I waited for his lordship to descend to earth.

I stared at him sitting there, and I felt cold inside. You've seen those old paintings of Jesus just before he's crucified? Well, Leo just looked like that. Same kind of hair, same kind of wispy tash and beard. Same expression.

My eyes went over him with about as much pleasure as ogling dog dirt in the middle of a lawn. He wore a T-shirt that had faded to grey it had been washed that many times. His jeans had holes in the knees where you could see hairy skin. He was barefoot.

I thought of his mother's bare feet with pretty, painted nails.

He had long thin toes. The kind that you could use to pick up a dropped hairbrush. God Almighty, why on earth had I bothered to trek out here to see bloody Leo Carter?

So, it was Faith's idea. She wanted to find out why Leo had sent me the letter. Remember? The one that claimed that Paul Robertson had been murdered. When everyone knew he'd lost control of the car and wound upside down in a field where he'd been throttled by his own seatbelt. Jesus. . . .

'Leo.' He didn't look up when I spoke. 'Leo. Hey.' I wasn't speaking gently. 'Leo? What's all this about sending me the letter?' He gazed at a blank wall. 'What the hell are you playing at?' Still nothing. 'Paul died because of an accident. No one murdered him.' I glared. 'You lunatic . . . you should be locked up.'

He didn't flinch.

So, what's so interesting about that wall? I found myself glance at it. I heard the sound of a truck passing by.

Ah . . . I've got it. You're watching the road . . . only you're watching it through a solid wall. Is there no end to a madman's talents?

I'd punched Leo in the mouth a couple of times before. The last time when we were fourteen. Paul had tripped on the stairs at school. He'd gone down half a dozen steps with a pile of exercise books in his hands.

Leo had stood looking down at him, both hands on the stair rail, chuckling away like an evil little devil. The sod had a mad stare even then. Girls said he'd got eyes like laser beams. They punched straight through you and out the other side.

Anyway, he stared down at Paul as he lay flat out on his stomach with the books scattered all around him. I went back up and smacked Leo one in the mouth. Bastard. . . .

Now, he was laser eyes again. Just like school.

It wouldn't have taken any effort on my part to punch him for old time's sake. In fact, seeing blood and saliva drooling down his T-shirt would have done me the power of good.

I took a step back to the door. Then I pointed at him. 'I don't know what you're playing at Leo, but leave it. If you send any more of those stupid letters you'll be in trouble. Do you hear? I'm going to come down on you like a ton of bricks.'

I shook my head. Daft sod's out of it. I turned and walked out of the room. Talk about a waste of time.

'Vic. It's true.'

'And what makes you think you know what's true or not?' I returned to the room with my fist clenched.

'Sit down.'

'Look, it's probably a game to you, but when you send those letters it hurts people.'

'Sit down. It's not easy to talk to you up there.'

'Leo. Watch my lips. Stop sending letters. No more. Got it?'

'Vic, I haven't spoken to you since I was eighteen.' He spoke in a light voice. Like it would easily break if he raised it. 'You went fishing.'

'Never mind what I did. You just stop the letters.'

'Sit down, Vic.'

'You know, I've a good mind to stick the things down your ruddy throat.'

'You've hit me before. I remember.'

'Good.'

'Tooth got broken.'

I saw him run his tongue under his lip. He was finding the chipped tooth.

'Years afterwards I'd lay awake at night and ask myself: why did Vic hit me?'

What he said cut deep enough into my anger to make me sit down.

'You should know,' I told him. 'Sometimes you asked for it.'

'Did I?' He looked puzzled.

'Not *asked* asked.'

'You still *hit* hit.'

'You know what I mean. It was your manner. How you *looked* at people.'

He nodded. 'It's wrong in this town to look at people in a certain kind of way.'

It's *how* he said it. He could have spoken in a sarcastic, or in a snob way, like he was looking down on North Suttoners as barbarians. But he seemed to speak as if he understood the truth of it.

When Leo spoke again it was still in that fragile sounding voice that had no emotion. 'I finished university early, you know?'

'I heard. Didn't you take to it?'

'It was during the second year that I got to understand that I'm different from everyone else.'

'How do you think you're different, Leo?'

'Don't know. Different . . . just different. Like a fish that's been forced to fly with the birds. You know?'

'So, what now? You looking for a job?' OK, OK, I was humouring the mad sod.

'A job?' He looked surprised by the question. 'No. No job. I'm different.'

'So you said.'

'No . . . it's like everyone's walking down the road in the same direction. Only I'm taking the backwards way. . . .' He thought for a moment. 'Like going in reverse.'

'Doesn't sound easy.'

'It's not. It's like this. I'm walking back up the road . . . checking all the things I've passed by earlier in my life. And I know that everyone else is moving in the opposite direction.'

'That's why you're different to anyone else?'

'Yes . . . I think so anyway. Do you catch many?'

'Catch many what?'

He nodded through the wall. 'When you're fishing.'

'Not bloody enough.'

'What are the fish?'

'Cod, skate, whiting; lobster if we're lucky.'

'They look like they should?'

'They've not turned into monsters, if that's what you mean?'

'I wondered, that's all.' He gave a tiny nod at the wall and cocked his head to one side. I heard the traffic on the road. A sound that rose and fell. It made the same sound as surf on the beach.

Leo lightly brushed the guitar strings then immediately damped them with his fingers.

'That's where Langthwaite Road goes,' he said. 'Out into the ocean.'

'So I heard.'

'A long, long time ago. Instead of making that left turn there it ran straight. No bend. It runs out to—'

'Langthwaite.'

We spoke the next words together.

'Langthwaite with a piddle in the middle and a square all around.'

It was the first time Leo had smiled tonight.

Again we both said the same thing at the same time. '*Old man, Swinburne.*'

This time I even cracked a smile. Old Man Swinburne was our history teacher; he had this poxy hearing-aid that would begin to whistle when he got excited, and he talked in a high voice. And seeing as he loved local history he'd constantly talk about Langthwaite in a high voice and the hearing-aid would obligingly whistle.

I said, 'He'd always go on about what it was like round here in Dick's days. Talk about a man obsessed.'

'I enjoyed it. When I walked home I could see what it was like. I could stand up here and imagine the road going straight out where the sea is now: to Langthwaite.'

'Of course, Old Man Swinny's dead now. Maybe they should have put it in on his gravestone.' I recited again. 'Langthwaite with a piddle in the middle and a square all around. If I had a tenner every time I'd heard him say that.' I shook my head.

'Can you remember what it meant, Vic?'

'No . . . hang on. Wasn't the river that ran through the town called The Piddle? And the square all around part were walls laid in a square shape to keep the pirates out?'

'Langthwaite's where you catch your fish now, Vic.'

'I know. More than two miles off shore.'

'I imagine fish swimming in and out of windows.'

I shook my head. 'There's nothing there but sand and weed. Not many fish either.'

'In my imagination, there are houses underwater.'

'In your imagination maybe. But there's nothing there.'

'Coastal erosion. Eating the land away.'

'You're not wrong, Leo. North Sutton'll go the same way if they're not careful.'

'And the road.'

'Might not be a bad thing if the road got swallowed up. Bloody thing.'

'I've been writing it down.'

'Huh?'

'I've been taking the backward way. I've written down everything I see.'

I noticed he was looking at files on a shelf. Tilting my head, I read what was written on the spines in curly felt tip: *Life Bites* by Leo.

'It's a kind of adventure story,' he explained. 'About what happens to a man going backwards when everyone else is going forwards.'

'Sounds too deep and meaningful for me, Leo.'

'You should read it.'

'I'm not much of a reader.'

'It describes what happened to Paul Robertson.'

'You're a bastard. You know that?'

I'd even started to warm to him when we were talking about Old Man Swinburne. Then back to this again. Dirty little shit. . . .

He never said anything. He just put down the guitar and walked out of the room. I looked across at the files. If *Life Bites* by Leo was his murder evidence then I didn't see any criminal investigation sprouting wings and flying. In another part of the house I heard Leo begin to sing. It was a flat, dirge of a sound. '*The man with the guitar's all right. The man with the guitar's all right, all right. . . .*'

Six

I didn't know where Leo had gone. I didn't much care come to that. Now I was alone in the room I wondered what had happened to Miss Carter and Faith.

Kettles take a long time to boil out on Langthwaite Road. That was the sour thought that kept repeating on me. Outside, the traffic sighed past. The curtains were open and I could see the headlights of the cars, shooting up the slick road. A glint of moonlight on the sea over a mile away. The lights of North Sutton. Nothing much else. The candles were bright enough for me to see the room. It's impossible, I know, but deep down you have this gut feeling that madness is contagious. So I looked, but didn't touch what Leo touched.

As well as Leo's paintings of heads with light bursting from them, there were also framed photos. These revealed scenes of Leo's past. One showed him aged about twelve with a guitar. Another, with his arm around a dog's neck. Yet another, looking into the camera lens through the strings of a tennis racket.

He was strange, even as a boy. His hair was longer than the other kids. There was this certain light in his eye. And something else: there were photographs with Paul and me, as well. I'd not expected to see them but there we were: the three of us aged around ten, all grinning into the camera like we were the best of friends. I didn't remember the photograph being taken. And I don't remember ever being friends with Loony Leo Carter, as some kids called him. He was always pain-in-the-neck boy whom everyone hated.

On shelves, there were Leo's toys from childhood (animals and clowns), school reports ('Leo is exceptionally intelligent but tends to lack focus and application'); a letter from a music producer dated three years ago ('Thank you for your demo disk. Your songs are perhaps the most unusual we've ever heard. However, they are too dark for our tastes. We wish you well in your career. . .'). A magazine called *Luddsmill.* (Its cover stated: *Corrosive poetry and incandescent short stories* by Leo.) If Leo was following the backward route, as he told me, maybe these old toys and photographs were his service stations on the way.

One object caught my attention. I held a candle to this to get a closer look. It was a little die-cast spaceship with red wings. *Put a rocket in your pocket!* ran the ad. I bought one with my birthday money when I was eight years old. I loved the thing to pieces. Carried it everywhere in my pocket. There was a plastic bubble canopy that contained two seats. In one was the pilot, the other was empty. The times I'd imagine myself into the vacant seat and how we'd go tearing across the universe.

I was so afraid I'd lose it I used a badge pin to scratch my initials in the paintwork on the underside of the wing. It did vanish one day when I left it in my coat pocket in the school cloakroom. More fool me, eh?

I broke my own look-don't-touch rule. To hell with contaminating madness. I picked up the spaceship and turned it over. In the candlelight I saw the letters: VB.

Thieving bastard. I gripped the spaceship in my balled fist.

Something about the toys being service stations on the road back into the past must have been right. I might not have been dragged kicking and screaming down memory lane, but down it I went. Reluctantly.

The first time my dad took me out fishing (as a job of work, rather than just a trip on his boat) I was eleven. His brother was laid up with a bad back so I guess Dad figured I should earn my keep.

'Keep in the middle of the boat,' he told me as we pulled away from the quay. 'She's going to bounce today.'

My old man wasn't wrong. The moment the boat left the harbour it lifted clean out of the water as a wave struck.

'The further out we get, the calmer it'll get,' he called over the sound of the motor. 'Just hang on tight . . . don't mess with anything.'

I watched green water surge like a million hills. Spray broke over the prow, wetting my face. Salt filled my mouth. I had to spit.

'That'll be a lesson to you, Vic.' My dad heaved the tiller. 'Never spit into the wind.'

I wiped my eye. 'It's not lobster weather, is it, Dad?' I hoped to impress him with my fishing knowledge.

'It's not that, Son. They'll stay home on a day like this.'

Again I tried to please him with what I knew about the fishing grounds. 'We going up to the scaurs?' These were broken fingers of rock that reached out to sea from under the cliffs.

He shook his head. 'With a sea like this? Don't be daft, Vic.'

So much for my fishing knowledge.

I guessed again. 'Tory Banks?'

'You'll get nothing much this time of year. Besides, the price you get for skate wouldn't pay for the diesel.' He nodded out to sea where water turned black. 'Old Langthwaite. We'll shoot for cod.'

I looked out across the swell that had grown nasty white heads.

'Looks rough out there, Dad.'

'Frightened?'

'No.'

'It'll calm down once we're over the steeple.'

I learned later that was a joke. Local fishermen talked about fishing over the steeple. Or shooting for crab in the graveyard. But the drowned church would be long gone.

Again I tried to sound interested but the bucking boat was making me nauseous. 'Dad?'

'What is it?'

'How'd you know where Langthwaite is?'

'You put your ear to the water. When you can hear children singing in the streets then you know you're there.' He shook his head, his eyes on the mud cliff. 'Just pulling your leg, Son.'

'How then?'

'See the cliffs? See how flat they are at the top?'

'Yeah.'

'Watch out for the little dip, like a V shaped cut. See it?'

'Over there?'

'No, to your left. Where the bushes are.'

'I can see it!' I shouted out, excited. Normally, I never could see anything he'd point out, which exasperated him no end. 'It's got bushes at both sides.'

'Good lad. That's where the Langthwaite road used to run.'

'Right over the cliff?'

'There was no cliff in those days.' He swung his arm like a pendulum, pointing with his finger. 'It ran straight out, due east.' He swung the tiller, turning the boat's prow out to sea. 'If I keep the cut in the cliff square at my back and run out straight for a couple of miles I'm following the line of the old road. When I've got Tracey Beacon directly off starboard then I know I'm right over Langthwaite.'

I crept to the gunwale and looked down into the water.

'You won't see anything, Vic. Langthwaite Road's long gone.' He pointed to a box. 'You can start laying out the lines in the bottom of the boat. And watch those hooks, they're fucking sharp.'

It was the first time I'd heard Dad say 'fuck' in a conversational way. He'd said it often enough stubbing his toe on a table leg. But then to him I wasn't a kid anymore when I worked the boat. I was another fisherman there to earn his keep. A few minutes later he seemed satisfied we'd arrived. He killed the motor, letting the boat coast.

'You can't hang around in this game, Vic,' he told me, as he clambered forward into the boat's middle. 'Come on, get those lines out . . . and for fuck's-sake don't tangle them.'

I handed him the buoy without being asked. I'd ridden along with him and my uncle enough as a passenger to know the routine. Now I was part of the team.

'Don't let the anchor foul the lines,' he said.

I picked up the small anchor and passed it to him. Taking the buoy and anchor from me he twisted the top half of his body and threw them overboard.

Next came the lines. Handling them came automatic to him after all these years.

'When you fish Langthwaite your lines have to be four hundred fathoms, it's bloody deep out here. You put your hook at every second fathom. See how they're baited? Mussels are best but fish guts'll do at a pinch. Push the bait right past the barb so the fish has to swallow the hook to get at it. Got that?'

I nodded. It was heavy work but my dad handled the line incredibly fast, and with a fine delicacy that made me think of how a surgeon works. He threw the line over the edge of the boat in such a way it unravelled in the air, so it sank through the water straight out, rather than in a tangle. Weights would carry the end of the line to the seabed, while the other end remained connected to the buoy. Such a line would be left to 'fish' by itself. We'd come the next morning to haul it in and find out what had hooked overnight.

I took the chance to kneel at the edge of the boat and look down into the water. Dad was right. The sea was calm here. I saw it was clear enough to be able to follow the pale lines stretching downward into the bones of old Langthwaite town. Of course, being a kid I imagined it would look like an underwater town with fish swimming along the streets and crabs scuttling in and out of doorways. There'd be skeletons too still sitting in chairs in drowned living rooms. I thought I heard the tolling of the church bell twenty fathoms down.

'Vic. You're here to work, not to daydream . . . pass me the first aid box . . . No, lad. It's there right under the seat.'

I passed him the box. He held up his finger. Blood painted it a juicy strawberry red.

He said, 'Told you those bloody hooks were sharp.'

We returned the next day to plenty of cod on the line. There was the corpse of a man, too. I remember shouting at my dad that we'd brought up one of the people from Langthwaite.

Dad snapped at me not to be silly and radioed the coastguard. That done, he told me to look away as he covered it with the tarpaulin. But you know what young kids are like. I couldn't take my eyes off it.

It didn't frighten me because it didn't look like a person. There were no arms or legs. The thing didn't even own a face. When I think back it looked more like a big, soggy lump of yellow foam rubber with shellfish and kelp clinging to it.

Not much more was said. Someone told me at school that the police thought it was the body of a tourist who'd disappeared when they went swimming from North Sutton beach more than a year before. The corpse must have become waterlogged and rolled about the sea bottom at Langthwaite fishing grounds for months.

Wait. It's just come back to me who told me about the corpse: Leo Carter.

Seven

Enough's enough. I can't stay here forever. Christ knows where Leo's buggered off to. And where's his mother and Faith? They must have been making that pot of tea for nearly half an hour.

Keeping the spaceship that Leo stole from me fifteen years ago, I went downstairs. For a moment I stood looking at the doors leading off from the hallway.

Well, which is the kitchen? Miss Carter had led Faith off down the passageway to the left. Left it is then, I told myself, and headed down the corridor with all that dark wood panelling hemming me in. Through the door at the end, I found the farmhouse kitchen but no Faith and no Miss Carter. The teapot was on the tray. The cups empty. I touched the kettle. It was hot but the gas ring had been switched off. Bloody cat and mouse this. Someone's making a fool of me. I shoved open another door. That led down to a basement. Another door led into an anteroom with a washing machine and butcher's slab. Knives hung down from the steel rail suspended above it. Switching off the light, I returned to the dingy hall at the foot of the stairs. There, I looked up, half expecting to see Leo come looming across the landing. But it was dark up there. I crossed the hall to another door. This was partly open. There were lights on inside the room.

I heard Miss Carter say in a soft voice, 'How does that feel?'

Then Faith's, 'All right. . . .' She was panting.

'I don't want to hurt you.'

'No . . . no . . . that's OK. As long as you don't press too hard.'

32

'How's that?'

Faith breathed in sharply. I though I heard her moan, too.

'Don't worry, Faith. I'll be as gentle as I can. Trust me.'

'There . . . that's better. Oh. Hold it there . . . yes, just there.' I heard my wife give a deep sigh.

What am I doing listening at the door? This is crazy. I pushed open the door and walked into the lounge. Miss Carter and Faith sat side by side on the couch. Faith was breathing deeply. I could see perspiration on her forehead.

Miss Carter looked up. 'I'm sorry about this, Vic. What must you think of me?'

'What are you doing?'

'I asked Faith to cut the cake. Like an idiot I didn't warn her about the knife. You see, I always keep them brutally sharp . . . there, hold that against your finger. And best keep your hand in the air.'

I crossed the room to Faith. 'How bad is it?'

'Not that bad.' She was trembling.

'It's a deep one, Faith,' Miss Carter told her. Then she turned to me. 'She'll need to get it looked at.'

Faith leaned back against the sofa. She looked faint. The bandage around her forefinger turned red.

'Wait here,' I said. 'I'll go home and get the car.'

'No.' Faith tried to sit up straight. 'I'll walk back with you.'

'I'm sorry, Faith. You aren't in a fit state to do that.' Miss Carter stood up. 'I'll get the car and run you to the hospital. It'll be quicker.'

'I'm sure I'll be all right.'

'Believe me, that's going to need a couple of stitches.'

I could see that Faith didn't want Miss Carter to drive her to the hospital.

'If you drove me home, Miss Carter. I could pick up—'

'No, Vic. I won't hear of it. This is my fault.' She smiled. 'And don't worry, I'll have her back to you in less than an hour.'

'I'll come with you. We can get a taxi home from the hospital.'

Miss Carter frowned. 'Ah, there's a bit of a problem. I don't leave Leo alone in the house when it's dark. Ever since he was ill . . . well, I don't leave him.'

'Leo can come with us.'

'He won't use the road at night. It upsets him. Sorry.'

'Upsets him?' I was ready to say I don't give a damn about Leo being upset by the road: I wanted to go with my wife to hospital and make sure she was all right.

Even as I opened my mouth to tell her this Faith spoke over me. 'Vic. It's all right. I'll go with Miss Carter.'

'But you might not—'

'Vic, Miss Carter will be with me. Don't worry.'

'I'll look after Faith, Vic. We'll be back before you know it.'

Uh. Guess I was beaten. 'I'll stay here with Leo, then.' I saw Faith recognize the sullen note in my voice. She gave me one of her *Behave yourself, Vic* glares.

'Help yourself to whatever you want to eat or drink. There's beer in the fridge and spirits in the cupboard over there.' Miss Carter smiled, her eyes giving me that twinkle. 'But stay away from the knives.'

I forced a smile. 'Don't worry, I will.'

I didn't like it. Faith was shaky on her feet. But there wasn't a lot I could do other than help Faith into the passenger seat of Miss Carter's crisp new BMW. The red tail-lights swept down the drive to Langthwaite Road, paused for a while as a pair of trucks thundered past, then with a squeal of tyres the car was away, heading in the direction of North Sutton.

It seemed odd to be standing there on the driveway of someone else's house as if it was my own. The breeze stiffened from the sea. The trees surrounding the house started to shiver and groan. Christ, I wouldn't live in this, I told myself, as I walked back across the drive to the front door. I remembered my cousins when they were little kids. They always called it the Witch House when we drove by.

Right then, I began to see their way of thinking. Miss Carter's house was miles from anywhere with no neighbours, and stood all on its lonesome on a hill. It always looked cold and empty as if its owner had just gone and died. All it needed to complete the bleak picture was a hearse standing outside the front door.

That, and a white face at the window.

I looked up at all that dark stone. There in the candlelit window was Leo. And, you've got it in one – white face, hair like Jesus; mad, staring eyes. He wasn't looking at me, he was watching Langthwaite bloody Road.

My hand tightened around the toy spaceship. I'd searched for it for weeks afterwards. Looked everywhere. With that recollection making me angry I went inside, closed the front door.

Eight

I waited in the living room for their return. The clock ticked loudly in the hallway. As I sat there it came back to me about Uncle Ray, Dad's brother, the same one who partnered him on the boat. He used to take long walks along Langthwaite Road, just like I've been doing (runs in the blood, eh?). He never cared for the sea and like plenty of sailors never learnt to swim. He'd always walk past the Carter house, as far as the bridge where the river flowed (years ago that would have been the River Piddle, which ran through Langthwaite; now it was known as The Calder). When he got back to town he'd have a couple of pints at the Duke of Danby then go home.

It must have been ten years ago when the Langthwaite Road did it again. My parents had gone out for their wedding anniversary; that means it must have been the end of October. I stayed in, watching a film that my Dad had rented for me. I'd nagged him into getting *The Evil Dead*. I was thirteen or so. Horror films wouldn't have any affect on me; that's what I told my mum and dad.

'Are you sure you'll be all right watching that thing?' my mother asked for the tenth time just as she was going out.

'It'll be a laugh,' I told her.

'Are you certain?'

'Horror films don't scare me.'

'We can drive down and get you another one. Your Dad won't mind.'

'Dad will mind.' He pulled on his shoes. 'I booked a table for eight. It's ten to now.'

So they left me to the horror film. After watching the first twenty minutes I thought it seemed darker than usual outside. Also, there were clicks and thumps coming from the bedrooms. I was alone in the house. And suddenly going upstairs to take a look round didn't seem such a good idea. I switched off the central heating. At least that changed it from a thumping sound to a tapping. Hot metal expands. Cold metal contracts.

The bit of science I knew still didn't give me the courage to go upstairs. What's more, even turning round to look back over the armchair now seemed dangerous. What if a face was there just inches from mine? I told myself everything would be OK if I kept looking forward at the screen: I reasoned that the face could only attack me if I didn't see it.

Not that there was a face there, of course. But then again, how could I be sure there wasn't a leering psycho face if I didn't check?

But if I looked back it would attack. This seemed to be a problem without a solution. Well, the best solution, I figured, was to keep watching the screen. Worse was to come. I'd been wrong about *The Evil Dead*. It was frightening. Blood terrifying might be a better description.

Then the telephone rang. My whole body lifted a foot out of the chair I was so startled. I stared at the telephone on the coffee table as it screamed at me.

Then I answered it. 'Hello.'

For some reason I knew that there would be something terrible about the call. My dad had been driving fast. They were late. Langthwaite Road was a real bitch. In winter it could turn from being wet to treacherous ice in minutes. Fogs rolled in from the sea killing visibility to near zero. Still cars would go to fast. They always went too fast.

'Hello?'

No reply. Maybe them not saying anything was the worst part. I listened harder. I could hear breathing, only it didn't sound right. Then a man began to speak. The voice was deep and whispery. He began to say something but then broke off as if he'd made a false start.

'Ber— ber. . . .'

'Hello.' By this time I felt sick. It was one of those zombie voices.

'Mur—' More laboured breathing like the caller had just climbed from the tomb. Next time the voice was clearer, 'There's something wrong.'

'Dad?'

'I've got a bad taste in my mouth.' After that, a click followed by the dialling tone.

I put the phone back quick, like it had turned into a dead animal in my hand. Who the hell was that? It sounded like Dad, but my dad didn't speak in such a slow, deliberate way. He didn't slur either. The best thing, I decided, was to watch the video. Just pretend it hadn't happened.

I fastened my eyes on *The Evil Dead* for another ten minutes, then the telephone rang again. I knew I had to pick it up, and I knew it would be the same slurred voice. I went cold inside.

I didn't speak. Just listened.

'Uhh.' A deep groan. 'I can't find a way out.'

'Dad, is that you?'

'It's just dark. . .'

'Dad?'

'I think something's gone wrong. . .'

'Is that you, Dad?'

'I've been thinking about it . . . I don't know what to do.'

'Where are you, Dad?'

'I was on Langthwaite Road. I know that.'

'Is Mum there?'

'But I don't know where I am now.' The voice was more than slurred. It sounded like someone falling asleep. 'You know . . . I can't find my way home.' The breathing came in long rasps into my ear. I was thinking about putting the phone down when he said. 'It's dark in here . . . it's dark . . . will you come and find me. . . ?'

'Dad—'

'Vic. Bring me home.'

Hearing my own name spoken by that voice did it for me. I slammed the phone down. Then I sat still without moving a finger. I went hot and cold. I felt sick. I wondered if I should phone someone. A relative? That seemed best, but who? Most were elderly; they might even be in bed by then. The obvious one seemed to be Uncle Ray. He lived just a couple of streets away. I dialled his number. Got ringing tones. No answer. I telephoned his mobile, ready to tell him something'd happened to mum and dad.

He answered. I heard a long, drawn-out breath in my ear then: 'Hmm-uh?'

'Uncle Ray?'

I heard him groan. 'Vic. I've got a bad taste in my mouth. . . .' Then he started murmuring, only I couldn't make out the words.

I got the credit for doing something right. I called Paul Robertson's dad who knew Uncle Ray's habits. He took a torch then went out to look for him on Langthwaite Road. He found him sitting on a grass bank with his feet in the gutter. Uncle Ray had gone for his walk as usual. A truck had run by too close. The nearside mirror high on the cab had clipped the back of his head. The blow had been hard enough to fracture his skull. That's why Uncle Ray slurred when he spoke on the phone. He couldn't walk and was too dazed to ask for help properly. All he could do was phone and mumble. Ten years on he's recovered enough to walk with a stick.

I sat in Miss Carter's lounge waiting for Faith to get back from the hospital. It's funny how you can think of different things when you're in a different environment. I'd forgotten about where Uncle Ray had the accident – out there on Langthwaite Road just a few minutes' walk from where I was sitting now. I suppose I must have blotted out the calls, too. I had nightmares about those for months afterwards I can tell you.

'Vic, I've got a bad taste in my mouth.'

My head snapped up. Leo stood in the doorway, staring at me. 'What the hell did you say?'

'There's blood in the kitchen, Vic. It's all over the chair. Well . . . the back of the chair.'

'You said something else.'

'No . . . I worried about the blood. Someone might have got hurt.'

'That's Faith.'

He looked right through me.

'Faith,' I snapped, 'I married Faith Escrow.'

'She was in the year below us.'

I nodded. I didn't want to get into an elaborate conversation with the idiot. Instead I said. 'She cut herself in the kitchen. Your mother's driven her to hospital.'

'Oh . . . there was all this blood. I began to get a little bit . . . worried.' That same fragile voice, like it was tricky for him to get the words through his lips without damaging them.

I got to my feet. 'I'd best clean it up.'

He stood back to let me through. I felt his breath on my face I passed that close. I held my own breath and entered the dark tunnel of a passage-way again.

His voice followed me. 'Do you want to know what happened to Paul Robertson?'

'No.' I opened the kitchen door 'Do you want to tell me why you stole my property?' Without turning, I held up the rocket so he could see it.

Nine

'Leo. I asked you why you stole it?' I nodded at the spaceship toy that I'd put on the kitchen table. By this time I was scrubbing Faith's blood with kitchen tissue.

Leo stood framed by the doorway. 'I wanted to talk to you in the lounge. I've poured you a glass of wine.'

'Bugger the wine. You knew that toy belonged to me.'

'I was going to bring you cake as well. There's a nice fire burning.'

I shook my head as I scrubbed the chair. 'I should have known better than to try and get any sense out of you.'

'I'm taking the backward way.'

'You can say that again, mate. Pass me that sponge . . . no, wet it first.'

'I wanted to talk to you, Vic. It's important.'

'You can see I'm busy, Leo. Why don't you go play or something.'

'I can play my guitar if you like?'

'Fine.'

'I've written lots of songs.'

'You're a bloody genius, Leo, did you know that?'

'Mainly about the old days. School and holidays.'

'Leo, make yourself useful. Pass me the detergent. There . . . that's it in the bottle by the sink.'

'This?'

'No. The green bottle . . . good grief.'

'This one?'

'Yes.'

'I'm sorry, Vic.'

'You must be a right little mother's helper, aren't you?'

'I play my guitar when she cooks.'

'Yeah, you're worth your weight in ruddy gold to her, aren't you?' I finished wiping the stains and pushed the chair back to the table. 'Bet you can't even tie your own shoelaces anymore.' I looked down at his bare feet. 'Or even put your own shoes on, come to that.'

'I guess lots of things became a hassle for me when I finished university.'

He still talked in that fragile way. As if he had to think about each word before he spoke it, in case he chose the wrong one. Muttonhead. His mother must be working her way into an early grave looking after an idiot son. But way back when she must have had a completely different idea about his future. Leo Carter had been one of the brightest hopes North Sutton High School had ever seen. To the other kids he was the weirdest, no doubting that. He was artistic, he played guitar, wrote songs, he painted weirdo portraits with light beams shooting out of heads. He also whipped up the Leo Crack Ups. This happened at least once a year. Boys at the school would, for mysterious reasons, gather in this huge gang. There might have been a fight the day before, or someone had been expelled; anyway something got their juices flowing then the pack instinct kicked in. You'd get a hundred or more third formers charging through the school with the girls running behind all excited and ready to see what happened next. I think it was Paul who called this the Leo Crack Up.

The pack of boys would tear round the place, shouting their heads off, their faces blazing. When they found Leo in the library or walking by himself they'd attack. They'd kick the living crap out of him. They'd be shouting and laughing and pushing each other out of the way so they could get their boot in his mouth. Once they snapped three of his ribs. Leo was in hospital for a week.

Something happening like that must contribute to the way you turn out.

For Paul Robertson and me we assumed our future was at sea, fishing with our uncles and fathers. Although to my surprise Paul sidestepped that one and went and joined the KOYLA – the King's Own Yorkshire Light Artillery. I left school at sixteen and went fishing. Leo headed off to university. I don't know what he studied there. Something arty, I expect. But halfway through the course he had a breakdown and walked all the way home. Paul worked out that the walk back to North Sutton from London would have taken at least four days. After that, Leo never left the house. Of course that was meat and gravy to the gossips. Drug addiction. Homosexuality. Agoraphobia. Schizophrenia. Leukaemia. AIDS. Debt. Homesickness. Pathological indolence. Gossips worked overtime on every kind of rumour.

Now we'd reached today. An evening in cold November. I was washing my hands after scrubbing my wife's bloodstains. Leo Carter watched me from the doorway; brains scrambled beyond the point of no return. While across town Paul Robertson's ashes were taking a well-earned rest in the garden of remembrance.

Leo had said nothing for a while. He just did the eyeball laser beam thing, staring at me. He watched me push the tissue into the swing bin.

'I took the rocket,' he said.

'I know you did, Leo.'

'I took it out of Paul Robertson's bag.'

'You're a bastard, you know that?' I looked in the fridge. I was ready for a beer. They had lager. I hate lager. Behind bags of lettuce I saw bottles of Old Peculiar ... heck, that seemed apt. I pulled one out, twisted the cap, took a long cold drink. Now, that's nice beer.

I glared at Leo. 'If you took the rocket from Paul, why didn't you give it back to me?'

'I wondered what to do for the best. I decided I could keep it safe for you. I knew how much you valued it.'

'Thieving little devil.' I wasn't angry; this was all matter of fact.

'The road takes so much from people.'

'You thought it would take my spaceship.' I picked up the toy. The red wings glinted. I loved doing that, just tilting it slightly from side to side, watching the wings shine. For a young boy this is true beauty. And the seat next to the pilot was still empty. One more for a trip around the Milky Way. Yeah, I'd grown too big for even my imagination to fit into that little seat anymore.

I took a swallow of beer. 'Well, thanks, Leo – for keeping it safe all these years.' Sarky as hell, I know, but I gave him a salute with the bottle. 'Cheers. I'll take it home now.'

For the first time he seemed concerned. 'No.'

'Oh, but I will, mate.'

'Look it's still not safe to take it away.'

'Oh, I think I can manage it now.'

'But the road's still out there.'

'Langthwaite Road?'

He stepped forward, nodding quickly. 'The police say it's a blackspot.'

'I know that, Leo.'

'I've lived here all my life. I've seen the road take people. It – it keeps things that don't belong to it.'

'Oh, for God's sake, Leo.'

'Th-that's why I should keep the spaceship for now.'

'No can do. Mine.' I trousered it. *Put a rocket in your pocket*. The jingle came back as I took another swallow of beer. 'Now, that's good ale. Nice and cold, too.'

'Listen, Vic. . . .' The man's hands trembled. 'I wanted to tell you something important.'

'OK, tell me, then.' I glanced at the clock. Miss Carter should be back with Faith soon. Good. Was I ready for home.

'It's not easy.'

'Well, don't tell me, then. Your call, mate.'

'It's complicated.'

'And it's about Langthwaite Road?'

'Yes.'

'That it steals people and possessions.'

'In a way . . . it's a blackspot.'

'You're getting it confused with a *black hole*.' The beer was giving me a buzz.

'No, Vic. It gets hold of people and it doesn't let go.'

'Look, it's a nasty stretch of road. That's all.'

'All those deaths . . . you should have seen what happened to the people. The way they looked after the road got them, you know?'

'You shouldn't go nosing at accidents. I'm going to have another of these.' I binned the empty Old Peculier bottle and pulled another from the back of the fridge. It's strong beer and I was drinking on an empty stomach. Hit the spot all right.

Leo talked. 'The road pulls people in. It keeps their possessions. Listen, I've been taking things back from the road. But I've made it angry, Vic. It's not my fault. But it's angry and it won't let me leave.'

'Wait a minute, Leo. Do you take medication?'

'It won't let you leave now, Vic, that's why we—'

'You've gone and missed a dose, haven't you, you daft bugger?'

Leo took a deep breath. 'I've made a machine, Vic. Tonight I'm going to use it.'

'Use it for what?'

'You and I are going to use my machine to save everyone the road's taken.' His eyes glittered. 'Listen to me, Vic. We're going to bring Paul back.'

Ten

'Bring Paul Robertson back? Now, how are you going to do that, Leo?' This stupid talk of his . . . I could have smacked him in the mouth.

'I've built this machine. It's taken me months. There's things I took from the road. . . .' Leo stood there in the middle of the kitchen venting delusions. 'I haven't been able to make it work yet. Now I know why. I needed help.'

'Never a truer word said, old son.' Still taking deep swallows of beer, I searched the kitchen cupboards.

'It has things from the road. My song's on the green tape.'

'Green tape's the best.' I wasn't humouring him. I was taking the piss. 'Go on.'

'And I've connected all the components, you know? Like a circuit. It's got what the road values. What it worked so hard to get all these years. But I've found some. I brought them back, but I had to be careful not to get too close to the road, then I laid them out in—'

'OK, Leo. Where does your mother keep the pills and stuff?'

'I don't need medicine any more. I'm all done with it.'

'Like hell you are.'

'You swallow it . . . you're like drowsy . . . tired all the time. Makes you put on weight.'

'How awful.' More piss-take.

'You bloat.'

'Well, well, what a dilemma. Fat and sane, or thin and mad?' I found a packet. 'What are these?'

'My mother's.'

'Are you sure?'

'There's her name on the label. They help her relax.'

'Wow . . . and she'll need them with you.' I drained the bottle. *Noinkkk.* Opened another. It tasted sweeter by the mouthful. Warms the inner man. I drained half a bottle in one go.

'Leo.'

'Yes?'

'Your doctors will have prescribed medication. Where is it?'

'Vic.' Still the softly fragile voice. He didn't raise it even when I turned nasty. 'Vic. I've done with it. They're making me ill. My hands shake; I can't play the—'

'Leo, Leo. You're not listening. You need that stuff to stop your brains from boiling. Do you understand?'

'They make me nauseous.'

'Ah. I get it. You've been *pretending* to take the pills for your mother's benefit. Then what? Spit them out the window? Hide them in your shoes?'

He touched his forehead. Maybe the idiot's head had started to ache. Well, hard bloody cheese, old pal.

'This isn't what I'd planned. You were going to come here and we were going to make the machine work together.'

'Are they in the bathroom?'

'We're friends . . . you'd help me.'

'When were we ever friends?' I gave up on the medication being in the kitchen. 'Where's the stuff you take, Leo? You need it.'

'Don't.'

'Remember? It'll keep the monsters away.'

I walked back into the passageway to look in the other rooms. Leo followed but instead of following me into the lounge he turned and walked out of the house.

'Fine,' I called after him. 'You get some fresh air. It'll do you good.'

I was all ready to sit and drink beer until Faith and Miss fancy pants Carter came back from the hospital. *Only you've promised to look after Leo. You're the baby-sitter.* Shit. She'd left me responsible for the lunatic. I'd have to bring him back. But this time I'd shake him until he squeaked before I locked him in his room. I was sick of him making an idiot out of me. Finishing the beer off in a couple of gulps, I followed him outside.

I closed the door behind me. The wind had picked up from the sea. It was bitingly cold. Clouds flew across the sky, sometimes blocking the moon. Leo stood in darkness. I could see his silhouette against the car lights on Langthwaite Road.

'Leo,' I said. 'It's not warm enough to go arsing about in the dark.'

'Vic?'

There was something about his voice.

'*Vic?*'

'What?'

'The road's closer tonight.'

'If you like.'

'It's closer to the house. We've got to make the machine work, or it's—'

'Leo. Get yourself back here.'

'Please . . . you've got to help me work the machine. If we don't do anything, the road's going to be up here at our throats—'

'God's teeth. Leo, you've got nothing on your feet.'

'*Come on, we've got to make it work tonight.*'

Now he did sound agitated. Do I give him a slap? Drag him inside? Or do I humour him until his mother came home?

'Vic, don't you see it? The road's getting closer all the time. We can't leave it any longer.'

'Come here.'

'Vic, help me please.'

'Come here, you little idiot.'

As I moved toward him, he ran back to the house. You could see his bare feet flicking in the dark. The soft skin on the soles would be crunching down on sharp stones. *Serves you right.* I followed, ready to slam the door behind us. Then I'd show him.

Only he went and did it again. He veered away from the house, running across the grass. Christ, all I needed was for him to leg it into the hills. I chased after him. He didn't run far. At the side of the house was a garage with an up-and-over door. Grabbing the handle, he swung it open and disappeared inside.

I paused in the doorway, trying to see into the darkness. Now it struck me he might have gone to find a weapon.

'OK, Leo. It's time to stop this now.' I listened. There was some kind of movement. But I could see nothing in the dark other than my white breath bursting out like something from a steam engine. 'Come back to the house,' I told him. 'I'll make us a hot drink.'

A bright light flickered on. I squinted into the garage. No wonder I couldn't see far. At arm's length from my face was a wall of amplifiers.

They nearly touched the garage roof. A white electric guitar leaned against the centre amp.

I squeezed between the amp stack and garage wall. Behind the amps there was a leather armchair, more guitars, one of those old reel-to-reel tape machines. I noticed the tape on the spool was green. Leo stood with his back to me. He moved his hands across a blackboard that hung on the end wall; the thing was big enough to pretty much fill it.

He didn't look back but he knew I was there. 'You sit in the chair. You'll have to work the tape machine.'

'Leo. . . .'

'We need to make it work now. We're running out of time.'

'Take it easy, mate. Come back indoors.'

He touched objects that were nailed to the blackboard. The way his hands moved reminded you of a technician operating a control panel. A touch there. A twist here, followed by presses with his thumb. I moved closer. He'd drawn white chalk lines so the objects were linked in such a way as to resemble a circuit board.

Leo called to me, 'When I say "go" switch on the tape. Then you have to keep switching between fast and slow play. You've got to do it quickly while I work this. That's why I need two people to operate it.'

'This is the machine?'

He glanced back over his shoulder. 'Sit by the tape player. You've got to be ready when I tell you. Fast-slow-fast-slow. Got that?'

'Jesus Christ, Leo. What on earth have you got there?'

'Sit down, Vic. We're nearly out of time. The road must be halfway up the hill.'

'Is that blood?'

'Can't you hear how close it is?'

I shoved him aside.

'Vic, the road's going to destroy us if we don't do it now.'

'Where did you find this stuff?' I couldn't believe my eyes.

'I told you. I took it from the road.'

I looked at the pieces nailed there. 'These are surgical dressings, aren't they?'

'They were at accident sites. I managed to get them away from the road.'

'You're sick, mate. Do you know that?'

'They are its power; it feeds—'

'First-aid dressings soaked with blood. Someone's watch. A wallet. A doll. Cigarette lighter. Maps . . . is that blood on them, too?' I shook my head, a bad taste rising. 'Plastic water bottle. CDs. Windscreen cloths. Rear view mirror. A hubcap. Registration plate. Mobile phone. You've been a busy boy, haven't you?'

'It took lots of work.'

'It must have.' I looked at him. 'So you've been down to where cars have crashed and stolen all this stuff.'

'But stolen from the road. So it couldn't keep it.'

'Bollocks.' Then the penny dropped. 'When you took this stuff, Leo, was it just after the accidents?'

'You've got to move fast.'

'So there were passengers still in the cars? People who were hurt? And you robbed them?'

'No, saving it for them, before the road took—'

'Jesus, man, you win the prize.' Now I did want to strike out. 'Before the police and ambulances arrived, you robbed injured people?'

'No.'

'Dead people?'

'You don't understand. It's not like—'

'You sick freak.' I looked back at the blackboard – the way the white lines ran out from bloody dressings and crumpled wallets. 'All these white chalk marks . . . where do they lead?' I followed the lines with my finger. They converged on one point in the centre. When I reached where the lines imploded into one chalked disk I pulled my finger back fast.

'You really should have swallowed those pills,' I hissed. 'They're going to put you away for this.'

Nailed in the centre of the board was a shred of brown material nearly the size of my hand. It was wrinkled; the edges were raw. Uneven. From one corner bulged a rounded lump.

'I take it that's an earlobe,' I told him. 'So all this brown skin must be someone's cheek.'

I stepped back from it. Written in green chalk on the wall above the blackboard were the words: *ROAD TREASURE MACHINE*.

'I'll work it here, Vic. You sit by the tape recorder.'

He started to walk forward. I shoved him in the chest.

'Don't go anywhere near it,' I said.

'Vic, we've got to activate it now.'

'You're not touching it.' I shoved him again so hard he went back against the amplifiers. 'And your mother's going to have to explain all this to the police.'

'Vic, we're going to be too late. The road's up to—'

'Yeah, yeah, the road's going to come and eat us all up.'

'Please, Vic . . . please let me use the machine. It will bring back Paul and the others.'

'Get back to the house. Now.'

'It won't take long. You'll see Paul.'

I shook my head.

Turning, he reached out to a power point on the wall. He flicked the switch. The amps behind him began to hum.

'I'm not playing along with you any more,' I told him.

'I really believed you'd help me.' His eyes had that martyred look.

'You're ill, Leo. Stealing from injured people isn't right.'

'I had to. It's the only way to stop the road.'

'You're not well in the head. But you don't know that, do you? You think all this is normal.' I nodded at the blackboard with its bloody trophy display. 'All this is going to get you—'

Without any fuss he stepped forward and moved a lever on the tape machine. The moment the spools turned a sound like thunder rocked the garage.

'*Damn it!*' I pushed my hands against my ears as hard as I could. '*Turn the bloody thing off!*'

It was so loud it hurt the inside of my head. I lunged forward, tried to find the lever, twisted one. It changed the tape speed, that's all. The sound groaned downward, deep bass notes punched into my stomach. Giving up on finding the off switch, I grabbed the spools and ripped the tape from the machine. Those sounds, amplified to God knows what, were painful enough, but they only lasted a second. Once the tape was out the sound stopped.

My nose began to run. When I wiped the back of my hand across it I was surprised to see blood smearing the skin. Good grief, it had been so loud it made my nose bleed.

I know someone else who's going to get a nosebleed faster than you can say, Jumping Jack Flash. Squeezing through the gap between the amps and the brick wall, I ran out on to the driveway. Halfway down the drive, and walking toward Langthwaite Road, was Leo. The moonlight was bright enough to show his bare feet moving quickly. Hanging by the strap from one shoulder was the white guitar. He wore it like a soldier would carry a rifle. When I followed him this time my fists were clenched.

'Leo?' I called after him. '*Leo!*'

Eleven

Leo touched his cheek where my open hand had cracked against his face.

'Next time it's this.' I showed him my balled fist.

'Why are you hitting me? I'm trying to stop you from being harmed.'

'Look, before I get really nasty, just go back up to the house.'

Leo stood at the edge of the driveway. The moon shone down on him and he was giving me the martyred Christ look again. We were only a few yards from the road now. The sound of the trucks was loud enough to nag the headache that had started since Leo's audio-work had all but sliced my brain in half.

Instead of looking miserable Leo suddenly opened his eyes wide. 'You know, we can still do it.'

'Leo.'

'We can do it right here.'

He slipped the guitar strap from his shoulder and held the instrument in its playing position.

By this time I was half-resigned to his madness. 'You can't play your guitar here. It won't work.'

He showed me the body of the electric guitar. A wire hung down almost as far as his knees.

'It's got a radio pick-up. The receiver's plugged into the amps.'

'So you want to stand out here in the dark, in a freezing cold wind, and play your guitar? God help me.'

Even so, I'd had a bellyful of being the idiot's keeper. I was half-inclined to let him play barefoot in the dark if it kept him occupied until his mother – his soft as butter, over-indulgent mother – returned home to tuck darling genius into bed. Yeah, why not. I'm wearing sea-boots and a jacket. Let him freeze his nuts off out here. His funeral.

He turned the volume control. Then he picked a string with the nail of his forefinger. From up in the garage the guitar note came buzzing back at us. A real missile of a sound. It whistled over our heads, over the road, over the fields and out to sea.

'If I can hit the right sequence of notes. . .'

Hell, if he talked about warring with the road again and resurrecting Paul I knew my fist would find a place in his mouth. But instead of talking he worked the strings. He picked out a sequence of notes at something like funeral pace. The transmitter plugged into the guitar jack channelled radio signals through the stack of amps in the garage a hundred yards away. Every touch of the steel strings sent a barrage of sound down the hillside.

It was weird music. There was an alien kind of rhythm but not a lot in the way of melody. The guitar's voice ranged from buzzing thumps to a howling roar. You heard that sound and it made you think of dinosaurs calling to each other across a swamp. When his left hand moved up the frets the notes rose to a jet engine screech before mutating into a human-sounding scream.

Leo's face in the moonlight altered – an expression of ecstasy, as if beautiful things were happening inside of him. His eyes blazed. In his mind he was a Messiah. A Messiah working miracles that were bigger, brighter and more beautiful than all the rest. He rolled his eyes from the road upwards. The sky fascinated him. Maybe he saw angels blazing overhead. I glanced up. What I saw were fists of wind-blasted cloud punching the moon.

In an excited voice he called to me, 'It's working . . . *it's working.*'

Come on, Miss Carter. Now it's going to be a toss-up who ends up a basket case first. Me or Leo? I couldn't believe I was standing there on a November night listening to a madman play guitar solos to a bloody road. Jesus wept.

Leo began to walk toward the road. 'It's moving back!'

His hand went at the strings in a rapid stabbing movement. The thing now sounded like a machine gun, driving away invaders.

'It's working, Vic. We're doing it.'

By this time he was twenty paces from the road. A bus rumbled by. I saw passengers' faces looking at us.

What the hell's with those two lunatics? That's what they were thinking, sure as eggs are eggs. I remember wondering if anyone on the bus recognized me. I'd be a laughing stock in town. Dueting with Leo Loony Carter? Christ, I wouldn't be able to show my face. . . .

A car went by, sounding its horn. The driver and passenger were pointing and laughing. Leo was playing like lives depended on it, shaking his head, long hair flying out, mouth chomping air-pie the way idiots do.

'Leo, it's worked,' I told him. 'Time to go home now. Show's over.'

He didn't answer; he was busy making the guitar howl.

A couple of cars slowed down. People shouted abuse through the windows. They were laughing, pulling faces. I'm sure one was Luke Reed. I'd get hell in the pub come Friday night. All thanks to Leo Carter. Another car pulled up. A kid of around seventeen lobbed a beer can in Leo's direction. It struck him in the face. Leo never noticed. He played like he was trying to set the air alight. Guitar sounds roared down from the garage.

The kid in the car shouted, 'You mad tosser. . .' He did the mime with his hand.

The driver was enjoying the scene, too. He pulled slowly away, jabbing forked fingers in the air, shouting some abuse at Leo that I couldn't hear above the sound of the guitar. A truck tried to pass as the car driver accelerated away without checking the way was clear. The trucker braked hard. I saw brake lights blaze in a mass of red, then the rig jack-knifed.

'Christ Almighty!' I shouted the words as I ran along the side of the road. The truck skidded sideways, the whole rear end swinging round to straddle the road. I saw the car with the shouting kids miss being crushed by a hair's-breadth; they tore off like they'd a better place to be.

The truck skidded on, the trailer whipped out, its back wheels dropping into the ditch at the side of the road. Then the whole rig stopped dead with a terrific bang. Smoke that stank of rubber filled the air. The back doors of the trailer had been flung open, dumping the load out on to the road. Broken boxes lay scattered a hundred yards or more.

And Leo played on.

From the boxes objects began to creep. Little dwarf men with dirty yellow legs and bulbous bodies. One ran toward me. The thing seemed to have springs for legs the way it jerked up and down as it ran.

'Nice one, Leo,' I grunted. 'Battery hens . . . hundreds of them.'

51

The battery hens had sick looking dwarf bodies with the feathers all pecked out. They swarmed over the road. They ran through the fence into the fields. Some fell into the ditch where they flapped their skinny wings in the water. What a mess. What a bloody mess.

'I'll check the driver.' I might as well have talked to the hens rather than to Leo. Blind bit of notice he was taking. He played faster now, the notes running into one.

I jogged down the road toward the truck. Great. All it needs now is a car to come tearing down here. The driver'll never see the truck in time.

The runty-looking battery hens swarmed over the road. Some were injured. I found myself stepping on them. More than once I slipped on gory poultry. Then, swearing, I'd have to pull myself up and run again. The truck had stopped part way off the highway, the rear end over-hanging the ditch, but the cab had jacked to the right, blocking the road. I reached the cab; the door had opened part way. I pulled it full open and looked in.

'Are you OK?'

The driver turned his head from left to right as if trying to focus his eyes.

'Can you get out of the cab by yourself?'

He gazed down at me, then the eyes focused. 'You stupid bastard.' He raised his foot then stamped down into my face. I fell back. I heard the sound my skull made as it cracked against the asphalt. As I rolled over on to my stomach, struggling to get on all fours I heard him swearing. 'What the fuck were you doing with the guitar . . . you must have known you'd cause an accident?'

'It wasn't me. I was—'

He kicked me in the back. Red lightning tore the inside of my head.

'You cretins. Look what you've done. You'll never get all those chick-ens back in a month of fucking Sundays!'

I knelt up, raising my arm just in case he kicked again. But the trucker had made it as far as the grass verge. He was holding his own arm at the elbow. It swung the wrong way when he moved. Groaning, he sat down.

'Thanks to you I've gone and busted it.' He cradled the arm in his lap. 'That's my ruddy over-time gone for Christmas.'

He was going to rant but he wasn't going to do any more kicking. To hell with the trucker, to hell with Leo, to hell with the sound of the guitar shrieking like crazy. I knew one salient fact. It was down to me to stop cars ploughing into the jack-knifed truck.

Twelve

That fall hit me harder than I realized. As I walked through those God awful battery hens (they cry like babies, you know, not cluck), my head was spinning, blood streamed down from a gash in my scalp, my legs were soft as mush. Half a dozen times I fell flat on my face. When I stumbled the squealing hens swarmed all over me – alien things with eyes that stared right into you. They pecked at my hair and eyes. And all the time, Leo played the guitar. It was shrieking and howling. The road vibrated under me the thing was that loud. I wiped my eyes over and over. They watered so much I could hardly see.

If a car was to come now, or another truck. . . . Hell. There'd be carnage.

'Leo. Switch that thing off!'

It was stupid to even make the effort to say it. Leo was in his own world, playing his mad little heart out. I wiped my eyes, then strained to focus. The truck blocked the road. I made my way round it. There were lights ahead, bearing down on me. I waved both hands shouting for them to stop. The car pulled up short of the truck. Then he backed away, hazard lights flashing orange. The driver had sense. They'd warn traffic heading along the road toward North Sutton. Now for traffic coming in the other direction.

Hell's bells. Walking toward me, following the white lines in the middle of the road, came Leo. He held the guitar high in front of him like some cock-eyed pilgrim holding up a cross. The neck gripped in one hand while he still played with the other. The notes went rocketing over the fields like the sounds of bloody warfare. And he had this holy expression on his face, his eyes fixed forward and slightly raised like God himself loomed over the horizon.

I slipped on a carcass. Went down to chin the pavement, heard a tooth break. When I stood up again the world was starting to turn around me. I swayed. Then staggered forward. Sometimes the moon was at my feet as if I dribbled a football. The music bored right through my head. *Get off the road, you idiot.* I thought someone else had spoken then I realized it was me. I stumbled off the road, fell to my knees, let my face sink into cold grass. There were other things, too. Bunches of flowers. Cards fluttered in the breeze. *To Paul, we can't believe you're gone. Dave and Marion. . . . To our mate Robbo. Rest in Peace. From everyone at the Marquis. . . . To a much loved son. . . .* The sea gale blew harder, stripping petals from the flowers.

Jobs to do, Vic. Got to stop cars . . . Langthwaite Road's a mincing machine. You know that . . . only needs one jack-knifed truck. . .

I pushed myself up into a kneeling position. Out there in the field is where my friend Paul Robertson had flown his car . . . garrotted himself with his own seatbelt. The times I've walked out here to imagine him hanging there upside down in the car. The black strap's crushing into his throat and he's making this sound . . . like a deep moan that comes out through his throat because it can't escape his mouth. He's conscious, his eyes are open. They're huge and terrified because he knows what's happening. but the seatbelt lock's jammed.

I wiped my eyes. There, in the middle of the ploughed field, was a car. It lay upside down. One wheel still turned, steam whistled from the engine. I'd not even heard it come off the road.

Who would? Not with the guitar screaming like a bag of ghosts. I pushed myself forward to surf down the grass bank on my stomach. Then I was on my feet, rolling over the fence. When my feet touched the ground at the other side I started to run. Soft muck sucked at my boots. The harder I ran the slower I got. My legs ached like damnation. Someone was at the car first. They'd pulled open the door. Now they were trying to help the driver. I saw the figure in the moonlight, pulling at the driver by the arm. Only they weren't helping.

'Hey!' I shouted.

They were pulling a watch off the man's wrist.

My God. So that's what Leo had been doing. He'd got down here before me. The bastard was robbing the injured man in the car. I lunged at the figure but he dodged away, running easily across the mud. The figure was dark. I had an impression of short hair. So it wasn't Leo after all. Not that it mattered. What mattered was—

I froze as I crouched beside the car. Hanging upside down. Face swollen; purple. The mouth open in a frozen yawn. I stared. Paul

Robertson. There'd been a mistake. He wasn't really dead . . . but now he'd had an accident in the same place that. . . .

I shook my head; the world was revolving at a speed that turned me sick to the stomach. How was that? How could anyone mistake identifying a body?

'Don't worry, mate.' I told him. 'I'll soon have you out.' I lunged into the upside-down car. Paul's arms hung down like a pair of thick vines. I snaked through them, reaching out for the seatbelt lock. When I had my thumb on the button I pressed. Nothing happened. I kept pressing. I felt Paul's body twitch. Then it convulsed against mine.

'Stay with me, Paul! I'll get you out!'

I pushed hard with my thumb. This time the seatbelt buckle snapped from the lock. Suddenly Paul came down on me, his weight crushing me against the car roof. His face pressed against mine. His eyes were now open. They stared into mine from just inches away.

'Paul. Don't worry . . . I'm going to get you out . . . you'll be OK. . . .'

I wormed my way from under him. He tracked me with his eyes. The shock of the accident had dazed him. He didn't recognize me.

Then he opened his mouth and slammed his face against mine. I felt his teeth crunch into the skin of my cheek. I screamed at him to stop. He didn't. He didn't move. He just lay on top of me, biting. When I wrenched back something gave way on my face. It hurt like hell but I'd got away from his mouth. This time I kept backing out. I didn't stop until the car's roof had vanished from under me and I was on all fours on the mud. I backed away further. The car lay there in the field; a dark mound; a steel tumulus.

A pale arm flopped through the window. Paul's head followed it. Slowly, without fuss or effort, he squirmed from the car. He rolled over on to his stomach. Then like some over-sized maggot he began to worm on his belly toward me, leaving a furrow in the soil.

I glanced back at the road. Lit by moonlight, Leo still stood there, playing a sequence of cascading notes. I stood up only to fall flat again. Dizziness came at me in waves. The moon rolled. Sometimes it was above me. Sometimes below. With a deep breath I pushed myself to my feet again. Once I had my balance I plodded through the mud toward the road. My skull felt it was in pieces. There was a deep hole in my cheek that poured blood. *I've got a bad taste in my mouth.* . . . That was the only thought that was clear in my head at that moment. *I've got a bad taste in my mouth*. I only looked back once. Paul still followed. He dragged himself along using his arms. His dead legs trailed behind him.

At the fence I started to climb over, then realized my legs were going. I slumped forward with my arms over the top rail. Everything blanked for a few seconds. The sound of the guitar receded. For a spell I felt nothing. Heard nothing. I can't tell how long it lasted. No more than a minute, I guess. When the sound of the guitar came rolling back and my head began to ache again I realized someone was pulling my jacket open. I opened my eyes. A boy of around ten stood in front of me. He'd unzipped my jacket. Now he had his hand inside it, groping at my breast pocket.

Boy?

I thought: boy. Only his face was shrivelled. Lines radiated from the mouth, etching deep gullies that reached his hairline. The nose bulged oddly from the centre of the face. The eyes were black hollows.

That boy's dead, I thought dizzily. He's been dead a long time. The boy drew my wallet from my jacket. Still only half conscious, I looked at my left arm as it hung over the fence. A little girl with blonde hair was tugging my wristwatch over my knuckles. Her entire face had been torn off. It hung inside-out from her throat.

Pretty mask, I told myself, then threw up. When I looked up again the pair were climbing the grass bank to the road. They ran past Leo. He noticed them. Played harder, sending howling guitar sounds higher and higher. A hand closed over my ankle. I looked down. Paul stared up at me; his mouth hung open; his jaw must have been broken. I kicked free of the hand, climbed over the fence. Then, panting, heart labouring, I made it up the bank to the road. Leo jerked the neck of the guitar. Now the instrument emulated falling bombs . . . feedback plunging down into an explosions of sound. Shrapnel echoes. Screams of feedback. Murdered orphan notes that decayed in the night air.

The moon burned hard now. I could see the full stretch of Langthwaite Road from the crossroads to where it kinked a sharp left at Annie Tyndall Wood. It was littered with broken cars.

Leo's face blazed. 'They're back. I've brought them back!'

He didn't stop playing. At the side of the road I saw a pair of pulpy grey hands appear on the grass verge. Paul was making his comeback, too. I ran in the direction of the truck. Battery hens cleared a path for me. They revealed a motorbike on the road, a 1950s' BSA. A man in leathers with flying goggles lay on the ground. He sat up when I got close. His forehead had caved in to expose brain.

I saw that the cars belonged to every decade. From open-topped things that resembled carts with wooden wheels and open-top engines, to a '20s' Bentley, to a WWII Jeep, to a '60s' holiday coach. There were trucks, bikes, vans, cars. They lay on their sides, or on their backs. Some were blackened shells. Some torn to pieces by the collision, leaving scrap metal and individual seats scattered across road-tar.

This was the battlefield between road and humanity. All the war's casualties were there. The schoolboy walking home who'd been hit by a car. The farmer whose tractor had turned over in the ditch. The party girl who'd had too much champagne before running her Mini into a tree.

Leo's guitar called them all back. They crawled from wrecked vehicles. They emerged from the ditch. Climbed over fences. Came down from where they'd been flung into trees. Leo Pied Pipered them. They were coming this way.

I heard a scream. The girl and boy who'd stolen my watch and wallet were feeding on the truck driver with the broken arm. He tried to scramble free but his face was already gone. They worked on his throat. The screams faded.

With so many figures blocking my way I turned and ran. Ahead was Leo. But beyond Leo more of the things were closing in. Above me, the moon had become a monstrous yellow eye, peering down to see what happened next.

Thirteen

This is what happened next: a ball of light roared out of the darkness from the direction of town. Leo played the guitar in the centre of the road. He gazed into the sky, the image of one those paintings of Christ on the Cross gazing up toward Heaven. Guitar notes swooped down across the fields, weaving power chords with sweeter notes that rose then fell to die over the ocean. By this time I was around thirty paces from Leo. The things that walked still came forward slowly. I stared at the ball of light. These were powerful headlights on a big executive car. It raced toward us. Eighty? Ninety? The driver was going for broke. He was stopping for nothing.

Leo didn't move. I saw the car glide from the side of the road until it followed the centre line. I glanced at Leo's bare feet. One foot was to the right of the painted line, the other to the left. That was a time for mad thoughts. Maybe Leo's insanity was contagious, after all. Because the thought that hit me was: *The road's fighting back.*

'Leo . . . Leo! Get off the road!'

I shouted the words, but it was too late. The car was only yards from him now, its lights blinding. The motor screamed.

'*Leo!*'

He turned to face the car just as it closed in. It went for him like a panther. I froze ready for the impact, already seeing in my mind's eye Leo being smashed apart. But the car bucked, just as if some invisible force had struck it in right flank. How it missed Leo, I don't know: the door mirror brushed his T-shirt, ripping a vent in the side, his hair fluttered in the slipstream.

Then it was past him. It veered and I put my hand up, expecting it to slam into me. Only it kept going. I turned as it screamed by inches from me. I saw the passengers in the old Mercedes. They were all dead. Long dead. Rotting.

The car ripped into the grass verge in an explosion of soil then it somersaulted end-over-end into the field, throwing up plumes of rust and mud before coming to rest. There, in the moonlight, it became nothing more than a mound of dead metal.

Leo still played. And as he played, the walking things approached. But eventually they stopped in a line thirty paces from him. They weren't coming any closer.

I walked up to him. He lowered his eyes from the sky to look at me. Those laser-beam eyes shooting eerie lights.

I asked him straight: 'How'd you do it, Leo?'

He smiled at me, a faint one, but a smile.

'Do what, Vic?'

'How are you making me see all this stuff?'

He didn't reply.

'You've made me hallucinate. I want to know how you did it.' I looked back at the road-kill lured by the guitar music. 'Zombies goofing on rock music is old fashioned, Leo. That's ancient pop video stuff.'

He shrugged one shoulder as he continued playing. They were discordant sounds now – random chords, squealing sustains that made my head ache.

'I didn't eat anything, Leo. I only drank out of sealed bottles. But you managed to slip me something, didn't you? One of your pills . . . something that makes you hallucinate.'

He shook his head.

'It's time to stop this, Leo.'

He shook his head again.

'Stop playing.'

'Can't.'

'I said—' I grabbed hold of the guitar, wrenched it out of his hand, then swung the wooden body into his mouth. His head snapped back. Blood formed a near-black outline around his lips.

'Give me the guitar.' He sprayed blood when he spoke. 'Give it back, Vic. I've got to keep playing, or—'

'Or the road's going to eat us. Yeah.' I threw the guitar aside. It bounced on the asphalt where it settled on its back. The strings still rang a metallic jangle from the speaker stack in the garage. 'It's time to stop this now, Leo.'

'You have stopped it, Vic.' His eyes focused on mine. 'You should be very proud. You got what you wanted.' Unsteadily, he walked across the road to the grass verge. There he sat down with one knee raised so he could rest his head forward on his arm. Blood dripped from the gash in his mouth. He was beaten now. Exhaustion dragged at him like a dead weight.

I glanced back along the road. In the moonlight I saw the black strip of tar run out across the fields. The truck blocked the road. A few battery hens still bobbed their heads on the grass verge. The driver sat cradling his arm. Nothing had bitten him after all; even so, he only looked half-conscious. Leo's walking road-dead had gone. There were no corpse boys and girls to steal watches and wallets and mobile phones.

I went across to Leo. He didn't raise his head fully but I saw his eyes roll up so he could see me through his fringe. As much as hurt there was disgust. As if I'd stolen his most treasured possession. Payback time, eh?

I patted my pocket, feeling the hard winged shape of the spaceship.

'I nearly did it.' Leo's voice was tired. 'I nearly stopped the road for good. . . .'

'Shut up.'

'The road couldn't have harmed anyone else, if you'd let me—'

'*Leo, shut up.*'

I walked back to where the guitar lay in the road with the intention of moving the instrument, or maybe lobbing it into the ditch if the mood took me. Then telephone the police from the house. The wind blew hard as I walked. It caught the guitar strings. The amp stack picked up the signal and the instrument moaned like a ghost. How did Leo slip me the pill that triggered the hallucination? Come to think of it, did the bottled beer have a screw top? What better way to hide your illegal stash then dissolve the substance in beer and stick it at the back of the fridge. The beer did seem to affect me faster than usual . . . it was all simpler than I thought. I'd gulped down the madman's drug of choice. *Ho, ho, ho. . . . He's fooled you every step of the way, Vic. He made a monkey out of you. Well, I'll make a jailbird of him for what he's done.*

The cold winds were biting. Langthwaite Road was deserted now. Along with the zombies, the usual traffic had gone . . . maybe it was getting late. I'd lost track of time. I might even have been lying unconscious as the drug fooled around with my brain cells. Pulling up my jacket sleeve, I checked my watch. Well, that wasn't the case exactly. I eye-balled the back of my wrist where the watch should have been. The strap must have broken when I was tussling with Leo. Send the bill for a replacement to Miss Carter. She can afford it.

Meanwhile, the guitar lay like a lump of white bone on the black road. I bent down, gripped it by the neck. Pulled.

Hell . . . do roads melt in winter? The tar stuck the instrument tighter than glue. I examined the road surface. It was black. Glossy. More like glass than asphalt. Maybe that's why this was a black-spot? The road-surface had worn smooth. Tyres slipped off like the stuff was Teflon. I put both hands round the guitar neck, then bracing my foot against the road, I pulled harder. Damn it, if it wasn't stuck solid. Must be something spilt on the road. I found myself trying to see if a resin or chemical had been splashed there, something to cement the instrument down. The asphalt was certainly slick enough to give it a wet look. I could see my reflection.

Only it wasn't my reflection. It was the face of the dead boy who'd stolen my wallet. With puckered dimples where the eyes should be. And creases in the skin radiating out from the lump of a nose. There were more faces swimming there. Paul Robertson with his jaw open wide; eyes staring. The little blonde girl *without* a face. A jostling crowd of heads calling up at me like they were on the far side of a glass screen. I heard muffled voices. *Calling for help, Vic. No, they are* begging *for help. . . .* And the stuff in the beer's kicking in again . . . the drug's not left my blood yet . . . I raised my head. The world tilted as the moon ballooned hugely above me. Leo watched from the roadside.

What do you see, Leo? Do you see light beams shooting from my head? Just like the portraits in your room?

I stood up. Dark shapes flitted along the road. They seemed like shadows . . . the kind formed by clouds. There was no real shape to them but they were large, very dark, and moved quickly. They flowed by me, heading toward town. Dazed, I thought of migrating birds, or of shoals of fish. But wait . . . what they reminded me of most were sharks. Big, evil sharks swimming just beneath the surface of the road.

Then, at last, I understood: these were the road demons. They'd prowled this river of tar for a century or more. They'd tracked cars, trucks, even pedestrians. Then, when the time was right, closed in for the kill. When I closed my eyes, I imagined them keeping pace with Paul's car that night five weeks ago. All it takes is for them to reach up through the highway and give the front wheels a nudge. The car spins out of control. In less then ten seconds Paul is hanging upside down, choking his life out on the seatbelt. Then scavengers follow the predators. Hungrily picking what they need from the dead and dying and . . .

. . . and it's the drug, Vic. That's what's making you see these things shooting through the blackness of the road. That's what's making you believe this stuff.

I looked at Leo. He had lights shining from his head. A sunburst of purple, red, amber – ghost lights. And the light in the road is black. A river of black light through which the things that are dead – *and things that make innocent travellers dead* – swim. This is black light; this is the colour of death.

The white BMW sped by me. Without slowing it rammed into the side of the jack-knifed lorry. The massive trailer tyres took the force of the car's impact. They burst, allowing the car to impale itself on the axles. I ran to the car to find the bodies of Faith and Leo's mother. Something vicious had chewed mouthfuls of skin from their faces.

'Leo . . . Leo!' I scrambled across the grass to where he sat. 'Why didn't you warn me! I never even saw them!'

Dazed he tried to look at me. Failed. His head slumped down.

He spoke in a murmur. 'Saw who?'

'Faith and your mother. They've hit the truck.'

'There's nothing there, Vic.'

I twisted back. There was the truck. A few battery hens. But nothing else.

'Leo, I saw the car go right into the side.'

'It's not happened yet.'

Hell . . . I'd imagined it. The bloody drug. . . .

Then Leo spoke again. 'It will happen though . . . soon . . . next few minutes.'

'Liar.'

He shook his head, defeated. 'Wait and see. . . .' He tilted his head. 'Can't you hear it now?'

I listened. I could hear the sound of a car heading this way out of town.

But Leo's mother would slow down before making a left turn on to the driveway to the house. Only the car was accelerating. I could hear the note of the engine rising.

Cold winds blew into my face, taking the sound away from me. Then it was back louder than ever. I saw headlights a quarter of a mile away; the car surging faster and faster. Once more I saw the road demons in my mind's eye. Black shapes pouring out through the asphalt. They'd slide up the tyres. Infiltrate the engine. There they'd run their senses across the cable linkages, brakes, clutch, accelerator. Dark tentacles would coil round the carb, exerting pressure. Soon the pedal would depress all by itself. The engine would race hard. The car accelerates. Nothing the driver could do would slow the car. The driver loses control at the bend. Or they'd slam into the first obstacle they reached.

I remembered the hulking mass of the truck blocking the road. In my mind's eye. I saw Leo's mother pumping at the pedals. But no response. Now she'd be watching the needle rise. Leaving seventy, crossing the eighty line, nudging ninety.

Faith shouting, 'What's wrong?'

'I don't know. It's the car. I can't—'

'For God's sake. Slow down!'

But the only thing going to stop the car is the side of the truck. The impact would rip their beautiful bodies to pieces.

Leo had succeeded until I prevented him . . . he was stopping the road . . . I lunged at the guitar where it lay. Reached down, knocked the strings. The barrage of notes roared down the hillside. Immediately, the guitar came free in my hand. I lifted it. Feedback rose into a howl that called to the moon. I could see the car now. It hadn't merely slowed . . . it stopped. As simple as that.

Leo was barely conscious, but he lifted his face to look at me. Then his head sagged down again. He rolled on his back, arms out by his sides. I couldn't play the guitar. But I knew how to make the sounds. I held the guitar by the neck; with my free hand I slashed the strings. One snapped with a crack like thunder. The others carried the note, sheer volume sustaining it. The car, I saw, was still at a standstill. When I dampened the strings into silence the car's motor roared. It became a pulsating ball of light that hurtled toward me. I hit the strings again. Once more the car was still.

Bloody drugs, eh? See what they've done to you, mate? See what they're doing to your mind. . . ?

I could put the guitar down, couldn't I? Surely Miss Carter and Faith wouldn't come to any harm. Only there was a stronger voice saying, Don't you believe it. So I kept the sound of the guitar rolling – discordant thrashing noises that shattered the night air. From the car came the shadows. They swam back along the road surface. The road was dark. Only they were darker. They sped toward me. The road demons knew what had spoilt their plan. They were coming back for me now.

Were they attacking? Or had I Pied Pipered them? I knew one way to find out.

My eyes flicked across to Leo. He watched me steadily. There was no expression on his face. Reaching into my pocket, I pulled out the toy spaceship. I threw it underarm to where it landed beside him on the grass.

'Keep that safe for me, Leo. Until I get back, OK?'

He blinked. Then reaching out, grasped the toy that I'd treasured so much as a child.

Black shadows swarmed along the road, joining with one another, splitting away, pooling again . . . liquid darkness running through road-tar. The guitar sang in my hands as I turned and ran. The jolting of my body shook the strings, making them vibrate. The radio pick-up transmitted the signal to the amp stack in the garage. The amps gave it voice. And what a voice! A cosmic voice that filled the night sky. I ran along Langthwaite Road.

I've Pied Pipered them. They're following. They'll go where I go.

Fourteen

The road makes a sharp left at Annie Tyndall Wood. I continued straight on, running down through a gap in the fence where yet another car had plunged through a few weeks ago. I kept moving, sticking to the narrow dirt track flanked by trees. I was following the old route of Langthwaite Road from the days when it ran out to Langthwaite village. The way was almost overgrown now. But I could see enough in the moonlight not to lose it. I ran with the guitar. I could still hear its beautiful sounds calling to the shadows. They followed me in a pulsating mass. Black light. The colour of death. They were closer now. I saw fingers of darkness reaching out to me. They could trip me just like they tripped the young boy as he crossed the road last July. Just as they could reach out to nudge a steering wheel, or probe and pick at a weak tyre wall.

Grass snagged my ankles. Brambles tried to stop me running but I was pushing hard. I'd got the adrenalin flowing. I was giving it all I'd got. I wasn't stopping yet. When the wood ended I raced over grass, heading for the V shaped dent in the ground ahead. A moment later I was over the rim of soil to lope down the steep incline in a cascading mass of dirt and pebbles. When I reached the bottom I glanced back to see the flood of shadow pour over the top then come sliding down the cliff after me.

As I jogged down the beach I remembered what my father told me. About keeping the cleft that marked the position of the old Langthwaite Road directly at my back. I crossed the sands to the sea. The tide had turned to expose moonlit pools and glistening fronds of kelp.

The shadows followed. Getting closer and closer.

I never even noticed how cold it was. I plunged into the surf with the guitar held high over my head to keep it dry. The waves pushed me back. Well, they did their best but I drove forward through the flow. When I couldn't wade any more I swam, using my free arm, and still holding the guitar free of the waves.

Behind me, shadows moved across the water, a blade-shaped stain that followed.

Ahead, were the fishing grounds where the lost village of old Langthwaite lay on the ocean bed. Moonbeams danced on the water. Far away, the voice of the guitar was calling. Distorted by distance now, it sounded like the gigantic bells of a submerged cathedral.

My arm ached. I knew I was tiring. But I wasn't going to give up swimming. Not for a long time yet.

Fifteen

Miss Carter never did know why her car ran out of control on that November evening. Mechanics could find nothing wrong. It's just one of those apparently random peculiarities of life. The throttle stuck wide open for a dozen seconds, then as quickly the accelerator pedal freed itself. She stopped six feet short of the jack-knifed poultry truck. It didn't stop her and Faith Blake, however, from having the shakes when they climbed out of the car. And one thing's for sure, the scare didn't do Faith any lasting harm. She's expecting a baby now. And if the timing's right young Miss or Master Blake might be putting in their first public appearance round about midsummer's day.

After that night of pandemonium on Langthwaite's bloody road I returned to my life as a fisherman. Neither Faith nor I discuss what happened exactly. I stick with the version of events that runs something like this: Leo Carter suffered a relapse; in the throes of his mental disturbance he caused the accident in which the truck driver broke his arm, and the battery hens scuttled to freedom; local kids say some of the birds still survive in a feral state in Annie Tyndall Wood, though their feathers have grown back now; and, no, I never told anyone that Leo might have slipped drugs into my beer. Regarding the nightmares I had later, and there were plenty of them, I explained to Faith that the reason I woke yelling blue murder at night was because I'd experienced hallucinations after I'd fallen and struck my head on the road. It's getting better though. I'm becoming the old Vic Blake again. You'd hardly describe me as 'lovable' or 'laugh-a-minute Vic Blake' but I'm not so grumpy these days, and have been known to crack a joke or two. And when I paint the room that will be our baby's nursery I find myself singing along to the radio with something not unlike a smile on my face.

Now I can use Langthwaite Road without shivers crawling up my spine. Leo Carter is still there; you can pass his house and see him staring out of his bedroom window at that stretch of highway, waiting for it to misbehave again.

So as always in this state of affairs we call 'the real world' life goes on. I continue working the coast here at North Sutton, always in search of the best lobster. But I've never gone back to the fishing grounds that were once a swathe of dry land called Langthwaite. Not bloody likely. Because fishermen who go there find their lines being fouled by underwater obstructions, lately their nets have begun to haul up parts of cars from bygone eras – old headlamps, spoked wheels, crumpled bonnets, mangled exhaust pipes.

And, of course, there are those recurring dreams that cling to the inside of my skull with the tenacity of limpets sticking to a rock. Often I dream that instead of driving the car along Langthwaite Road I sail my fishing boat over that strip of tarmac running through the fields. There, the road demons swim alongside, waiting for me to make a mistake so they can tip over the boat. Then they'll carry me away in the river of darkness that somehow flows beneath the road all the way out to the submerged village of Langthwaite, where in the dream there are houses and streets occupied by fish not people, and a church bell that tolls for lost souls at the turn of the tide.

2

ASCENT

*AD 835. The Church embraced the Celtic festival of Samhain, which was celebrated on the first day of November. However, ecclesiastical authorities disingenuously rededicated it as All Saints' Day. The pagan roots for All Saints' Eve run deeper; it didn't merely serve as an arena for ghosts and demons – for this is the night when natural laws are suspended, reversed, perverted. **Beware** . . .*

The Touch of Velvet *by Professor Ruth Porteous, Director of Contemporary Myth, Flyyte University, Illinois.*

All my research, of late, is concerned with levitation. The mysterious power to hoist a body, animate or inanimate, into the air. One of its supreme exponents was Joseph of Cupertino (1603-1663). Eye-witnesses say that before he floated skyward the saint gave 'a little shriek.'

H.P. Lovecraft to Alfred Galpin, 4 September 1918

I didn't give a 'little shriek', I gave a big one. A bloody great roar that rattled the bedside lamp and set the dogs barking next door. One moment I lay on my bed, while wondering if I should take another look at the dressing on my appendectomy wound; a wound that itched as its raw lips knit themselves together; the next moment I hurtled from the mattress to the ceiling.

Pain hit me with such brutal force I howled. If a battle tank is capable of sensations then, surely, this is what it feels like when a missile punctures its armour plate. I clutched at my side, clamped my teeth together, screwed shut my eyes, howled louder then I'd ever done before. All that intense pain swamped rational thought; it hurt too much to bother about listening or seeing; there was only that fiery stab in my side as if torturers poured molten iron into the void, which had once played host to my appendix. Even though the pain eventually eased my concerns centred on the surgery. Had the wound ripped open? Is that stinging symptomatic of abscess rupture? Were the sutures still intact?

Cold air blasted into my face, yet my torso burned like a furnace. Then:

Scents. The Halloween barbecue at the tennis club near my home: intense savoury aromas of sausage, hamburger, kebabs, a rich marinade of herbs and red wine. That distinct sharp smell of the night air as autumn transmutes to winter; a blend of woodsmoke, ripe berries, mushrooms pushing their white fingertips through the turf.

Sounds. Cars purring along the road; TV laughter from an open bedroom window. At number 54 Doyle's rock band rehearsed in the garage. Drums thundered in unholy union with a screaming electric guitar.

Sensation. Rising, rising, rising. . . .

Sights.

But why did **sight** take so long to kick in? It can only be because the sights were so impossible that they failed to register inside my head for a minute or more. Yet when sight returned I saw the following with perfect clarity: I floated in the cold October air above the roof of my house. Below me: brown roof tiles, TV aerials, chimney pots, lawns, bushes, paths, driveway, the car by the front door. All lit by streetlights.

And streetlights? I saw hundreds of them, forming a fiery orange ocean beneath me. More lights at the tennis club revealed the grey oblongs of its courts, each one marked out with precise white lines. Along Castle Road danced the Rappour children; they swung sweet-filled pails in one hand and devil pitchforks in the other. I saw the flutter of black plastic capes. They must have been wearing masks but I was too high to tell.

'Catch hold of my hand!'

All I could make out in the darkness as I rose 500 feet above the ground was a pale shape.

The voice came again. 'Please, catch hold of me. I'm going to fall!'

The pale shape that swam out of the dark sky resolved itself into a woman of around thirty, her blonde hair rippling in the breeze. My skin crawled as I recognized the extent of her fear. It transformed her eyes into something like a pair of blue marbles that bulged from their sockets. In the whites of her eyes veins had swollen into thick red filaments as emotion ratcheted up blood pressure.

She reached out to me, fingers grasping. 'Please hold me. I'm going to fall . . . *I'm going to fall. . . .*'

'Get my hand,' I panted. 'Hold on.'

It's a fundamental response. A fellow human in danger. If you can reach them you can save them. This wasn't time for rational thought: all we understood at that moment as we drifted high above the rooftops was that to hold hands would bring mutual protection.

Her fingertips brushed mine. 'Nearly. . . .'

'I can't reach . . .' she cried.

'Try again.' The only experience of weightlessness I'd known was in water. So, as if I swam through the night air, I kicked my legs in an attempt to drive myself forward. Questions of why she floated there in her white nightdress didn't occur. Nor how I'd levitated through the solid, bedroom ceiling. Or why had only certain individuals been 'elevated'? After all, some people beneath me were still happily attached to the earth. This turbulent swirl of events happened so quickly. All I could do was act on instinct. So: once more I tried to reach the woman as air currents pushed her away. Her hair fluttered while those huge blue eyes locked on to mine as she desperately tried to reach me.

'Listen.' Her voice quivered with tension. 'We've got to get away from here. They're in the clouds.' Her eyes rolled up toward the under-belly of cumulus that was dimly illuminated by light pollution from below.

'But what's—'

'Shh! Can't you hear them? That sound . . . if you listen, you can make out the sound of flapping wings.' As if she'd hit an air pocket she dropped ten feet. '*Oh! Get my hand! You must get hold of my hand!*' Panic shot through her voice. '*Please! I'm slipping!*'

This time I had to reach downward as if the woman stood in a hole at my feet. Only the bottom of the 'hole' was transparent. Beneath her billowing nightdress from where her bare legs kicked I could see the geometric roof shapes of houses on my road, a bus rumbled around the corner. In the tennis-club gardens I could see the tops of heads as people ate their hamburgers. One of the trick-or-treat kids spilled their pail. A cascade of foil-wrapped sweets twinkled on the pavement.

'Oh, God!' The woman's voice became a scream. 'It's leaving me. I can feel it. I'm slipping! Get my hand. FOR GOD'S SAKE, CATCH ME!'

I thrust my hand downward to meet her up-stretched arms. Our fingers brushed again; my eyes met hers as hope gave way to nothing less than a sense of doom that seemed to explode those blue irises.

Then she left me. Gravity had her once again in its grip. No, more than that. Gravity seemed to take her back with a vengeance. *She's mine; you can't have her; I'm keeping her down here.* The nightdress fluttered against a backdrop of rooftops. All I could do for her was witness what happened next. She plunged 500 feet into a floodlit tennis court. The force of the impact didn't just break bones; it disintegrated her. The brilliant lamps revealed a mass of fragments break away from the body to roll across the surface of the court. Then her white cotton nightdress turned all red.

Now: rewind back a few days. Work had gone well on the script. The company secured funding from a major commercial investor. The producer finalized contractual terms with the animators. Production would begin 7 January and finish 31 April. Mistress Fate, however, abhors a straight line from A to B. Instead of neatly following that straight route from project initiation to completion the production snapped away on a weird tangent.

But I'm getting ahead of myself. My initial idea for the film had been clear-cut. Over the Christmas of 1929 the cult writer of the weird, the wonderful and the awe-inspiring, H.P. Lovecraft, penned thirty-six sonnets. All these streamed from his pen in a glorious outburst of activity in a matter of seven days, and formed something with the mouthwatering title *Fungi from Yuggoth*. These sonnets, which I genuinely love, told of cosmic voyages, demonic apparitions, explorers uncovering stuff that should stay hidden, all leavened with lighter touches that reveal Lovecraft yearning for his lost homeland of yore. OK, the plan: I write the script. The producer locks down funding. We make *Fungi from*

Yuggoth. But it's the straight line thing again, and Mistress Fate's hatred of anything straightforward.

First problem. A student searches the former home of Alfred Galpin, one of Lovecraft's friends. She finds a letter from Lovecraft to Galpin that contains the *thirty-seventh* sonnet in the *Fungi from Yuggoth* cycle. Scholars had hitherto agreed that there had always been thirty-six, the last one being *Continuity*. So I began work on incorporating the newly found poem into the movie script; the final scene is now *Ascent*. For anyone with an interest in Lovecraft there is debate whether the sonnet is indisputably his work. But here are the first two lines:

The Earth cast me into that Moon-drawn grave
Where ghosting comets through the ether crawl . . .

Second problem. On meeting the production team to fine-tune the budget my appendix became dangerously inflamed. Medics say that an appendectomy is one of the simplest surgical procedures. They don't even gut you like a fish anymore; instead they conduct something called a laparoscopic intervention. That means they make two small incisions in the side of your stomach – one for camera, one for snipping tool to remove the festering appendix. It's fast; the patient recovers quickly with hardly any pain.

'Hardly any pain' meant two sleepless nights after returning home from the hospital. Janine is a stoic wife. However, after my recital of pained grunts she tended to shy away from our bedroom. So there I lay in the centre of the bed, a beached writer. I divided my time between watching television and making tentative prods at the dressing on the right hand side of my belly. The white sticking plaster boasted Van Gogh style brush strokes in reds and browns. This pigment, the nurse explained, is normal seepage. Now 'seepage' is a word I don't like at the best of times. There's no such thing as a 'nice seepage'. You don't visit a restaurant and hear the waiter boast, 'You'll enjoy Chef's special today. The fillet of beef has the most delicious seepage.'

So I repeatedly studied the Appendectomy FAQ sheet issued by the surgical department. The paragraph under the heading 'Post Operative Dangers' formed its own gravitational pull and drew my attention time and again to: **Seepage of prurient exudates.** There was so much I didn't like about that line: the grave, black type. That word 'seepage' again. And 'prurient' and 'exudates' triggered warning klaxons inside my head.

Being ill sets you apart from the normal world. The usual rules don't apply. You can't move properly, especially after an appendectomy. A five-second stroll to the bathroom is now a ten minute shuffle as you try not to move any muscles in the stomach, nor cause the surgical wound (wounds in my case) to perform anything that resembles a grin in your side. Every step uploads mental pictures of gut sutures breaking open, cascading intestine, blood and more blood.

Although Janine cheerfully brought me meals, eating was dire. Even when I chewed gingerly as a kitten it felt as if storm-troopers were driving bayonets into my stomach. Sleep evaded me. Lying in one position is torture. This litany I can maintain for hours. I've not even mentioned the horror of knowing you're going to sneeze after you wake from the operation. And as for the prospect of intimacy. . . .

31 October: I decided to stop being an invalid. I managed to dress in sweatshirt and loosely elasticized jogging bottoms, and took pleasure in accomplishing the garment donning contortions without harming my surgical gashes. By early evening I managed to walk out on to the drive-way for a taste of fresh air. My first trip to the outside world in four days. The first wave of trick-or-treaters had begun to scurry from house to house – these were the youngest ones, accompanied by parents or big brothers and sisters. Costumes were cute rather than scary. With Janine patiently standing beside me, holding the box of novelty horror sweets, I managed to hand out edible teeth and monster eyeballs to the children.

Then my side started to hurt again and all I could think about were those grim words: **seepage of prurient exudates**, so I climbed the stairs back to the bedroom. Fortunately, I found only the same old tawny smears on my dressing. Nothing freshly seeping, nor prurient.

I promised myself I wouldn't lie there like some anomalous blob found in a tomb, so I half-lay, propped on pillows, to work on the script. What I needed to do now was to insinuate sonnet thirty-seven, *Ascent*, into the climax of the story. I had Lovecraft's words of course; my job was to match compelling visual images to those stanzas. As I worked I could hear excited calls as children scared treats out of local residents. My thoughts were a commingling of Lovecraft, that archetypal weirdmonger from Providence, USA, his eerie verse, and memories of my own Halloween adventures as a child. Although when I was a kid Halloween had to vie for importance with Guy Fawkes night, when we burnt the effigy of the would-be bomber of Parliament in 1605. Come to think of it, during that season we had a concentration of festivals with pagan roots. As well as Guy Fawkes Night these swathes of Northern England enjoyed 'Mischief Night'. Whereas Halloween had Celtic roots, Mischief Night must have been a pagan relic from Viking invaders. Mischief Night meant children weren't restrained by normal rules of behaviour; what's more, it was customary to commit acts of mischief – usually knocking on doors and running away, or throwing eggs at neighbours' windows. All this drifted inside my head as I gazed out through the bedroom window over the nighttime grounds of the tennis club. And once more I was drawn back to the conclusion that when you're ill you find yourself in another world – one where normal rules don't apply. A moment after that trenchant observation I found myself falling *up* toward the bedroom ceiling.

Beneath me, the ruin of the fallen woman formed a dark splash mark against the tennis court. *She fell*, I told myself; *the same could happen to me. I've got to get down.* Once more the only action that made any sense was to try and swim through the air like you'd swim to the bottom of a swimming pool. Yet the moment I struck out, that upward force caught hold of me again. A scream erupted from my mouth as it hoisted me skywards. The streetlights blurred into a sea of orange fire as a brutal tug upwards threatened to tear open the appendectomy wounds. A pain so intense that I didn't have time to ponder on the mechanics of how I flew vertically from the earth's surface, as if the world was so sick of my presence it had spit me out. At best, all I could understand of my situation was that I rushed upward with the speed of a rocket. And whereas I'd been looking down on dozens of houses together with a couple of roads I now saw hundreds of buildings – not only houses, but schools, factories, warehouses, pubs, supermarkets, while five miles away pale fingers of apartment blocks pointed into the cloud's underbelly.

Gulping for air in the icy slipstream, I guessed, when my senses returned to some approximation of order, that I must be close to 5,000 feet from the planet's surface. A fall of 500 feet had literally detonated the body of the woman. At *5,000 feet* a plunge to earth would mean I hit the ground with the force of a high explosive bomb. The mental image of such a descent, the acceleration, the screaming as I knew what end lay in wait for me, provoked a wave of vertigo that made me retch. Bizarrely, it was the flare up of pain induced by the muscle spasm that kept my mind in balance. That hurt, burning away just above my hip, became the safety line to cling to.

'Halloo there . . . halloo. . . .' From beneath me a man in a raincoat fluttered upward with a huge grin on his face. 'Halloo!' When his eyes locked on mine I saw they were quite mad. The inexplicable act of levitation had cracked his sanity. Once more he sang out, 'Halloo, there, yourself. It's quite lovely, isn't it? All those lights, the big factories, and all. Quite lovely. Look, sir, I can see my house from here.' Laughter bubbled from his lips in a spray of saliva. The grin became a grimace of panic. 'Won't you take hold of my hand, sir? I need your hand like I need the embrace of the Virgin Mary right now.' As he lunged at me I punched him away. Although my fist smashed his nose it all seemed absurdly hilarious to him. The last I saw of the madman was him rising above me toward the red belly of the cloud, laughing all the way as if this was the funniest day of his life. Remorse filled me. Why had I struck the man? It wasn't his fault shock had tipped him over the edge, was it? Instinct, however, whispered that if he'd gripped hold of me, he wouldn't have let go until we'd both gone crashing downward.

The lunatic had risen faster than me. In moments I'd lost sight of him against the clouds that hung in a threatening mass of bloody reds. Streetlights lent them a kind of hell-fire glow that stoked the fear. They seemed to loom with ominous possibilities. As this sense of danger filled me I heard the madman again. Even though I couldn't see him, I could make out his distant laughing, 'Halloo, there. Halloo, yourself. Good evening, sir, good evening.' The laughter returned only briefly before it morphed into a scream of agony. 'No, no, no. . . .'

He's falling, I told myself. If he hits you he'll take you with him. My muscles tensed as I prepared to contort my body anyway I could to avoid his chubby form if it tumbled down out of the clouds toward me. But when I heard his screams again they weren't approaching – they were receding. He howled as some force bore him even higher.

Shudders ran through me. Not just the blast of the north wind but fear, and not solely the fear of falling, but a fear instilled by an insight that danger loomed above me, up there in the red clouds.

Once more came the pull, as if gravity had flipped into reverse, repelling me from the ground. The wounds in my side stung. Cold currents zithered through my hair as that uncanny levitating force accelerated me higher. Now, when I glanced back, I couldn't even see individual houses. Roads were arterial lines of light along which silvery beads of vehicle headlights flowed. How much higher? If I didn't fall to my death, the cold, together with the thinness of the atmosphere, would finish me.

Because I'd been staring either up or down I hadn't been checking horizontally. When I did, I saw more figures floating there. What's more, they converged into my airspace. For a moment I anticipated a dozen or more bodies would clash together as we rode the invisible escalator. A hundred yards away, fifty, forty, thirty . . . I saw approaching human shapes resolve into individuals. Adult men and women. I even recognized one of them. A white-bearded man of around seventy. He'd been my old mathematics teacher at school; now, clad only in blue pyjama bottoms, his plump body flew through the air toward me. Most of the people were shouting (or sobbing or screaming), and as such I couldn't make out any individual words. One man, however, of around twenty, dressed in a business suit, with his green tie flapping in the breeze screamed, 'Judgement Day!' and, 'Rapture!'

A woman aged forty, I guess, clad in a silk kimono with a gold dragon embroidered on the back drifted closest to me. Surreally, she clasped a bottle of red wine to her chest, while her pepper and salt hair was swept upward by the slipstream, until it resembled the monster-woman's hair in *Bride of Frankenstein*; a mass of horizontal black and silver streaks. She didn't shout. Her expression had a stone-like quality to it; nevertheless, her bulging eyes rolled in her head as if taking in her surroundings, and yet not so much in shock: no . . . she'd expected this.

My old teacher of mathematics locked his eyes on mine. His tongue bulged from his mouth; even though he tried he couldn't shape any words.

Then – whoosh! He dropped; this was no gentle descent; it was a violent plunge downward from the group. To him it must have felt like his entire stomach tried to exit his mouth. For an instant I saw his eyes blazing up at me, an expression of horror deforming his face. Both hands clutched his ribs over a heart pounding against the chest wall. How long does it take to reach the earth falling from 5,000 feet? Twenty seconds? Fifteen? The impact must turn bones, flesh, brain and skin into jelly.

The woman in the dragon kimono floated within six feet of me as we ascended. She gripped the wine bottle as if it was the only thing keeping her aloft. When her eyes rolled to meet mine I identified awe as much as fear.

'I knew . . .' she gasped. 'I knew right from when I was five years old. They said I'd imagined it . . . we lived on the top floor of the apartment block . . . one night I watched my father go out on to the balcony to smoke a cigarette. Something came down . . . it was black and shiny . . . it took hold of him and carried him away. . .' Then, what she said next, turned my blood even colder. 'Listen,' she whispered, 'don't you hear them? Wings . . . you can hear wings . . . thousands of them. . . .'

I followed her stare to that reddish cloud. The underbelly of the cumulus might be no more than a few hundred feet away, yet just inches above my head I could make out a mist – an impossible mist in that hard breeze. Eerily motionless, it was a pale yellow colour; faint, indeed so faint it appeared gauzy . . . a blond vapour from another realm.

What I saw above and below crowded my thoughts but, good God, yes, it was what I heard that dominated now. Above me . . . faintly . . . I heard a clattering sound. I recalled watching birds in an aviary, hundreds of them, disturbed by a noise, all flapping their wings at once.

'I know what they are,' the woman breathed. 'When I grew up I searched for an image that matched what carried my father away from the balcony.' She poured wine into her mouth from the bottle. Red liquid streamed down her chin; moments hereafter, it would fall as crimson rain on the earth. 'Night-gaunt. That's what it was. A Night-gaunt stole my father away.' A sad, booze-sodden smile tightened her lips. 'That Night-gaunt robbed me of my sobriety, too.'

The dozen people I ascended with entered the yellow mist. A second or two later we were above it. A horizontal plane of misty yellow stretched from horizon to horizon. Instantly, the sound of flapping grew louder. With it came clicks as if hard surfaces snapped together. Then came the swish – no doubt about it, a solid object had suddenly darted through the air.

'They're coming,' howled the woman, as much in triumph as terror. 'They are coming! I told my family. Nobody believed me . . . but you'll believe. You'll see them for yourselves!'

We no longer ascended. More to the point, we seemed to bob up and down now. One moment we were above the yellowy layer. Then beneath it. To me, it appeared to form a membrane. One just a few inches deep. And one which we rose through before quickly dropping again. Many of the people who fell screamed as if they expected to plunge to earth but the invisible force that levitated them caught their bodies the moment they pierced the yellow mist on the downward movement then thrust them up above the thin layer again to repeat the bobbing action.

Meanwhile . . . *meanwhile* . . . the deadly beat of wings grew louder. A cracking sound almost; the way pigeons sometimes flap their wings so hard they beat against their own bodies to make that machine gun snapping.

The intoxicated woman sang out, 'They're here. Can't you see them? They're coming!' Her face assumed an expression of such joy it became more shocking than one of terror. 'One will be my father. They took him away so he could become one of them. He's coming to save me.' Then her voice rose higher into a girlish, *'Dad . . . Daddy . . . Daddy.'*

Her lost father swept down from the clouds to her. His dark body was long and slender. Projecting from the crown of his head were two pointed horns that must have been a full two feet in length. Supporting the lithe body, a pair of black wings that were as glossy as patent leather. Behind the flying man whipped a long tail armed with a V-shaped barb.

'Daddy, it's me. Gloria! Do you remember me, Daddy?'

Long muscular arms caught hold of the woman. A second later he bore her aloft through the clouds into his heavenly kingdom.

All too clearly I heard her screams of agony. Shortly after that the wine bottle plunged by me. Then scraps of her hair. Then half her face, trailing a stream of blood.

That was no father – transformed or otherwise. When my fellow riders on the night air rose above the membrane of vapour the Night-gaunts swept out of the clouds to snatch them with their talons. Once more I saw the barbed tail, the vast bat-like wings, the bodies that were as shiny as black plastic. But there were no faces on those creatures' heads. Only mouths that opened wide.

One of things darted at me, its limbs stretching out, a shadowy shape that was the epitome of predatory menace. When I anticipated I'd be carried into the clouds like the others to be torn apart, the force supporting me weakened and I dropped beneath the layer of yellow mist. The Night-gaunt didn't follow. Instead it recoiled from the yellow barrier as if it would have blasted the skin from its body. The faceless head fixed on me in a way that suggested rage but, nevertheless, it darted back up into the cloud as if defeated.

Yet, it wasn't over. Once more I bobbed back up through the yellow layer. So did my surviving companions. One by one they were seized then eagerly carried aloft into the boiling mass of red cumulus. Seconds later shreds of clothing dropped past me. Then came other objects – wet, red things, hunks of raw meat, pink bone stripped of flesh.

Then it came. From the north I saw a dark shadow gliding toward me. It swam through the clear air between the cloud's underbelly and the yellow mist that formed the membrane through which the Night-gaunts couldn't penetrate. It had no shape, as such, but I sensed this leviathan had a monstrous bulk, bigger than a blue whale – bigger than a cruise liner. Without any hurry or fuss it approached. Even though there were no features or limbs I sensed its shadowy form grow; it became strangely puffed as if that once streamlined body grew tumescent.

My attention had been distracted by the vast intruder. I hadn't realized I'd risen above the yellow mist again. A Night-gaunt seized hold of me. Its talons clutched my wrists, while it wrapped its long, black legs around my waist. The horned skull was level with my own, just inches away. I gazed into the leathery front of an eyeless head where a face should have been. Its mouth opened to reveal needle-sharp teeth. Its legs tightened around me, the thighs pressing harder against my waist. The surgical wounds should have hurt beyond belief, but the sensation at that moment was a strangely provocative tingle. It squeezed harder bringing a sense inside of me of melting abandonment. My heart pounded.

Then the huge shadow arrived; a torpedo shape surging through the night air; a vastness then filled my field of vision.

It passed by in a second and was gone. The Night-gaunt's taloned hands still gripped my wrists. But that's all. Blood poured from severed arteries. Then the talons relaxed allowing the remains of the limbs to fall away.

And at that moment I knew this fact: *we human beings aren't the prey. We are merely bait.*

3

THE EXTRAORDINARY LIMITS
OF DARKNESS

Mistah Kurtz – he dead.

The offing was barred by a black bank of clouds, and the tranquil waterway leading to the uttermost ends of the earth flowed sombre under an overcast sky – seemed to lead into the heart of an immense darkness.

Heart of Darkness by Joseph Conrad

'The horror! The horror!'

I can't say why exactly I furnish his utterance with marks of exclamation. Marlow, the seaman and confirmed wanderer, merely whispered the words as he woke from the throes of a dream in the cabin of the *Rosa* as she rode at anchor in the maw of Zebrugge. But it was a whisper such as I've never heard before. Not so much those words 'The horror! The horror!' but the aura surrounding the words, the dark charisma that brought me out of my bunk so sharply I banged my head on the ceiling beam.

'Marlow?' I cried. 'What's wrong?'

'Wrong?' He sighed like a man might who's just received his last-minute reprieve from a death sentence. 'Nothing's wrong. Just a little dream.'

When I lit a candle I saw he was staring at the shadowed corners of the cabin as if he expected to find something not to his liking.

'Sir,' he began, 'we're quite alone in here, aren't we?'

'Yes.'

'You didn't see another standing there by the wash basin?'

'No, of course not.'

He nodded. 'That's what I thought. It's just that. . .' He blinked as if the action would wipe away whatever dream image might have lingered on his retina. There was an expression on his face, however, that appeared to be the soul-twin of his waking words, 'The horror! The horror!' The whisper of which appeared to defy acoustics and still linger in the cabin, then again, was my imagination becoming a plaything of the waves washing against the hull? I admit I found myself staring at Marlow, as he sat there in his bunk, his back straight, his legs crossed beneath the blanket. Marlow the yellow-faced Buddha. The first moment I clapped eyes on him in Harwich, that's the description that delivered itself on me, unbidden. Granted, the description is rude, unflattering, but the force with which it struck is undeniable. Marlow is a seaman and wanderer, yet he so often poses there Buddha-like; sunken cheeks, yellow complexion, a gift of absolute stillness as he contemplates the inner landscape of his mind. There he was now, lit by the light of my candle, sitting in the cabin of the cross-channel ferry . . . yet not in the cabin, not in the ferry, not in the light of the candle, not with me at all. No . . . at that moment he roamed some place faraway, lit not by an exotic sun, but by those resonant, deadly words: THE HORROR . . . THE HORROR. . . .

In order to prevent myself from slipping under the macabre spell that seemed to hold Marlow in its thrall I looked out of the porthole. After the Zeppelin raid on Zebrugge last week the entire town lay in darkness. Yet the stars can't be quenched by Man. I saw entire constellations reflected in the ocean that bulged and deflated in the cold night air. Moored in darkness all around us were the transport ships that carried our army to Flanders and the Somme.

'I don't think I believed it until now,' I told him, 'but after witnessing this armada with my own eyes I'm sure it will be over by Christmas.'

He gazed at me. When I met the gaze it was like peering into the depths of an ancient grave.

'The war,' I repeated. 'It will be over by Christmas.'

The Buddha, cross-legged on his P&O bunk, blinked his slowest of blinks again. Then all of a sudden, as if the words had been marching relentlessly through him for days eager to liberate truth, he began to tell me this tale as we lay at anchor amid the British Naval Fleet off mainland Europe, those dogs of war in fitful sleep.

MARLOW'S ACCOUNT

Remember that afternoon on the beach when I told you about my expedition to Africa. Did I say expedition? If you wish, substitute 'expedition' for the word 'folly' or 'frolic'. Having lived so many years as a seaman, I found my home town such a drab place that even when my brother sailors were retreating to their townhouses to trim their rose gardens and cultivate their families, I felt this need for adventure. It was like a dull ache in a bad tooth. I didn't relish the adventure for adventure's sake. I simply knew that it was my lot in life to embark on yet another exploration, because even though I'd encounter hardship and loneliness, the alternative was worse. The wilds of the Congo are hell. The ivy-clad villas of Essex are a deeper hell. You remember my yarn of the journey up-river by steam-paddle boat to find Kurtz, and bring him back to civilization with his mountain of ivory? We found him and his ivory after a gruelling voyage. The ivory was poor quality. Kurtz had become a murderous tyrant who fed the darkest of his appetites in ways I can't even begin to put into words. I daresay even the Emperor Caligula, who had hacked off his nephew's head because of an irritating cough, would have paled at the sight of what Kurtz inflicted on the natives. On the return journey Kurtz died. We left his body in a muddy grave by the river. But we brought his diaries back with us. And it was in one of those diaries that a seed of what was to come began to grow. As so often with these things there is a long, involved sequence of events that ferment away in their own dark world before we become aware of them. But the grist of it is, that on New Year's Day, 1913, I found myself disembarking at the African port of Dakar. I was as disappointed with the place as I was with my companions on my new expedition. Some men quaff their whisky in anticipation of the riotous laughter-filled evening ahead of them. Some drink the spirit in the joyless certainty of the crushing headache and dry throat of the hangover that waits for them come morning. I – I'm sorry to say – am attached to the latter. Dakar is a miserable town: cheaply built houses and ware-houses in the modern French-style. The land is flat; there are palms; there is dust. The climate manages to inflict a burning sun combined with a cold, northerly wind. My companions in adventure hadn't been to Africa before. In fact, they hadn't been further south than their wintering quarters in Monte Carlo. They insisted on dressing in a bizarre confec-tion of white suits with feathered hats, imagining that it is the necessity of every civilized gentleman to promenade in such a way so as to impress on the African the European's godlike stature. The French crew of the ship were so richly amused by my companions strutting down the gang-plank at Dakar that many of them lapsed into helpless laughter.

There were three days of wrangling with customs officers over the fourteen cases of gin my expedition had brought with them (those and the rifles, pistols, blasting powder and magnesium torches) – after that we were delivered to the train station for the five-day journey to where Kurtz had so considerately buried his riches for us to find.

And what of me? Why had I agreed to accompany these men on the expedition? I didn't know them. The offer of three per cent of the net wealth of the treasure didn't really appeal. No, curse the devil on my back, it was the adventure! It was the promise of travel to Africa; it was a suggestion of sleeping in snake-infested huts in malarial swamps where hippos roared one awake in the middle of the night. That was the devil that brought me so meekly to heel in the company's British office – the one and the same company that employed me to navigate a moribund boat into the heart of the Congo to find the despicable Kurtz. What was the alternative? Yes, yes, the alternative would be a winter at leisure in my English sitting room, with tea and buttered scones, and gleaming cutlery and spotless bedding and . . . oh, the crushing hand of boredom. Always boredom. Eternal boredom. Forever and ever without end. . . .

So that is how I found myself in the company office with one of its esteemed directors who exhibited himself behind his vast and stately galleon of a desk. There, he folded his arms so he could stroke his own elbows as he dropped the wonderful phrases into my ear. His long, grey hair fell across the rich velvet collar of his coat as he uttered those phrases . . . those honey-dipped phrases. 'A journey to where few white men have been . . . hardships will be great but the rewards greater. Three per cent of Kurtz's treasures will be yours – once the value has been assessed, of course. Sail from Portsmouth on Christmas Eve. Africa by New Year's Day. You will be in the company of three gallant gentlemen, three fellow adventurers – Doctor Lyman, Sir Anthony Winterflood, and Henry Sanders. Sanders is a solicitor, a good solid man, dependable as the Bank of England.'

On the voyage my companions hadn't talked about the treasure we'd find. They spoke incessantly of the sport. The sport was the thing. In England there was sport of course, but not the sport they favoured. They talked of a 'grand sport' to be had in Africa. A great and wonderful sport that would enrich their lives and their memories for many a year to come. They rarely spoke to me, even though I was supposedly an equal member of the team. And they rarely mentioned the rigours of the journey to come. But sport? Yes, indeed, the talk was of the fine sport to be had on the Dark Continent.

Toward the end of that first week of the new year, with 1912 flung on the scrap heap of time, and with 1913 rearing up in front of us like an untrod mountain we boarded the train for our journey into Africa's secret heart. The company had chartered the train specially for us. They had no doubt we would return it to the coast laden with Kurtz's fabulous treasure. Our transport consisted of one derelict-looking locomotive – the plaque on its side advertised that it had been built in Doncaster, England in 1859. Behind the loco that was merrily spitting boiling water all over the platform was the tender heaped with more coal – although a poor, muddy coal I noted with some misgivings. Next in line after the tender were two goods vans that would carry our treasure, then the carriage containing a cook's galley and half a dozen cabins that offered our private quarters; then at the very end of the train an elegant structure of carved timbers combined with an extravagant amount of glass. This final carriage of our treasure train was a communal lounge. Apart from the train's crew we four would be the only passengers carried by that astonishing luxury-liner of dry land.

By the time I'd unpacked my case, washed and shaved the train had shrieked its way out of the station. As you would imagine from the nature of the iron beast our progress was stately to say the least. At no time did we accelerate faster than twelve miles per hour. The terrain immediately outside Dakar is flat, open land; however, within thirty minutes thorn trees began rising from the dry earth like skeletons frozen in time. Leaves? Yes, they must have borne leaves but all I recall of the skeletal branches were immense, dagger-like thorns, and the way the trees multiplied quite discretely until whereas I'd been watching a few dozen trees sliding by on an open plain I now saw a dense thicket of thorn trees that closed in on the track until we had no more of a view than if we'd been travelling through a tunnel of woven thorn trees. I had hoped to sit on my cabin bunk and watch elephants wander across a savannah, or be entertained by monkeys leaping through their arboreal kingdom. Yet there was nothing but thorn trees. Damned thorn trees through which we moved at our twelve miles per hour. Thorn trees that appeared to be home to nothing – not even birds.

With the view being nothing I busied myself with my papers regarding the next leg of the expedition. In three days' time the train would reach the end of its track; from there we would cross country on foot until we reached a lake. Waiting there would be a sailing barque which I would skipper to an island where Kurtz had concealed his glittering hoard. There were matters concerning the transportation of provisions that I needed to discuss with my travelling companions, so I took my map to the salon in the hope of finding them there. Of the three, however, only Doctor Lyman had ventured from his cabin.

The heat in our tunnel of thorns had become formidable. Doctor Lyman was sitting on a sofa of plush velvet in his black frockcoat, perhaps in readiness of attracting the awe-struck glances of any native who happened to be peeping from the thorn forest. He was a plump man with a round face and round hands that protruded from beneath starched shirt cuffs. His hair was neatly parted down the centre; the scalp revealed itself as a bright pink strip of overheated skin. His black boots were polished, as were the buttons on that frock-coat. He was astonishing, and wore a pink carnation in his lapel. On the little table beside him a glass, containing gin and peppermint cordial, trembled from the vibrations induced by the twelve mile an hour rush through the spiky jungle. That same vibration made the rifle propped up against the sofa slide sideways, so he had to steady it to prevent it falling. An action he repeated frequently during the following.

I cleared my throat. 'Doctor Lyman, good morning.'

He nodded then sipped his gin and pep – he and his companions always drank gin and pep, chilled by a veritable rock of ice, so the contents of their glasses were never a mystery for me. I knew drinking liquor in a hot climate wasn't helpful to one's constitution so avoided it. The doctor's nod seemed to be the extent of his conversation with me. After adjusting his carnation and wiping a speck of dust from the black sleeve of his frockcoat he returned to his silent, dignified pose, while the train chack-chacked at precisely twelve miles an hour. His face became very red. Yet by an effort of will-power he checked the escape of perspiration from his skin. Doctor Lyman was a man of formidable will-power. Maybe the power of his mind retarded the speed of the train. He blinked to the rhythm of the chack . . . chack . . . chack. . . .

'Doctor Lyman. . .' I wasn't going to be cheated of this vital discussion on logistics. 'Doctor Lyman, I've been checking our travel itinerary against the map. . . .'

'Excellent! You have everything on the nail. The company told me that you were just the man for the job. Their words to me were: he'd have everything on the nail – right on the very nail! Good work, sir.'

'Thank you, but I thought we should talk about how many native bearers we'll require for—'

'Oh, as many as you need. The company told me that you'd plan everything with aplomb. They speak very highly of you. After all, you brought the papers that belonged to Kurtz back to London.' He sipped his gin and pep; the little iceberg clunked against the glass. 'This time they'll reward you amply, so I'm given to understand.' He nodded, satisfied that he'd granted me precious moments of his time. There you have it, this wasn't so much as an expeditionary team, rather than myself playing Cook's tour representative to three of my social betters who wished to see something of savage lands from the comfort of the carriage.

And what a carriage. The windows were vast. The carpet underfoot deep. The carved furniture boasted an abundance of delicate scrollwork and soft upholstery. From the roof hung crystal chandeliers. This was the salon of a duchess that somehow had been gifted wheels and set rolling – rolling at twelve miles per hour, mind – through a thorn forest in Africa. As I witnessed later, a mere pull on a velvet bell rope would cause a French waiter dressed in a pristine white jacket to manifest himself into the carriage where he would ask with the gravest of respect what meal or drink we required. Gin and pep – always gin and pep for my companions. And ice – plenty of ice! Meanwhile the train maintained its stately twelve miles per hour on a track that didn't seem to possess even a whisper of a bend. Nor did it venture upon a single break in our thorn tree tunnel. I decided, in the meantime, to await my other travelling companions before broaching the subject of the bearers again. Although I suspected they'd quickly congratulate me on my energy and organizational skill before returning to their debate about the sport. This was 'the sport' they'd discussed so avidly on the ship. Oh, the rapture that blazed in their eyes 'the sport in Africa is extraordinary' they'd murmur, with a disquieting intimacy to each other. 'It is quite worth the trip for that alone.' Their talk always made me weary and irritable. Hang their sport, I'd tell myself. I glanced across the swaying carriage with its chinking chandeliers to the round-faced, red-faced man. The rapture filled his eyes again. He was thinking about his sport. Sport filled him from his polished boots to the pink stripe of scalp that ran across the top of his head. Blast his sport. Blast his indolence. All this and a miserly twelve miles an hour.

The monotonous rhythm of the chack ... chack ... chack of iron wheels on an iron track suddenly vanished with the arrival of the other two adventurers. One, Sir Anthony was dressed in green silk pyjamas in a style best described as Chinese, his companion, the solicitor, wore an immaculate white suit. They carried repeating rifles, while their faces wore such expressions of joy. When they spoke it proved this was too special a time to waste on coherent speech. 'Fine animals! Ten of them.' Then to me. 'Open the window man ... no! no! The one on the left.' Then to the Doctor. 'Your rifle! Quick! Quick! Before they run into the forest! Have you opened that window yet, man! There! Stand back!'

The doctor couldn't believe their good fortune. 'Sport,' he insisted on repeating, in a daze of pure happiness. 'Is there sport? So soon? Are you sure?'

'We have our sport, gentlemen, praise be. Ready with the rifle, Doctor!' The man in the pyjamas cocked his rifle and poked the muzzle through the window I'd slid back to create a cavernous aperture in the side of the carriage. I smelt hot dust and the sun-scorched branches of the thorn trees. 'Do you see them?' Sir Anthony's voice rose into high piping. 'Ah! There they are!'

Walking along the dusty borderland between the rail track and the start of the thorn trees fifty paces away was a line. A loose, undulating line of ten figures. Five men, five women – husbands and wives. It seemed they carried bundles of everything they possessed on their heads. One woman carried a dozing child in a papoose on her back. The natives were an ebony black that glistened in the sunlight. All ten were very thin, their knees appeared as bulbous oddities compared to the narrowness of their thighs and shins. They were barefoot. All were naked. Naked, that is, apart from a belt of some red material worn around their waists.

My three companions discharged their weapons with so much fervour it was as if those long-awaited gunshots had been held in pent-up frustration all their adult lives. The powder discharged the bullets at speed. But the will-power of the three men sped the lead shot to velocities that seemed to melt the air around them. They fired again and again. The men and women fell without murmur. Maybe in some unknown way they knew this was their fate. Perhaps they'd seen it in their dreams. Maybe a witchdoctor told them to be at this place at this time to meet their destiny. They didn't cry out; they didn't flinch; they didn't react with any expression of pain or unhappiness at reaching the end of their lives on that dirt track. As the rifles discharged the tiny but swift cargos the natives simply knelt down in the dirt, their burdens falling from their heads, their eyes were suddenly tired looking, that's all. And there they died.

'Aim for the faces,' the doctor called out with a blend of urgency and delight. The last round in his magazine enlarged upon his short statement as it demonstrated most clearly the effect of such a shot to the front of a human head. The rifle bullet popped through the face – in the centre of the flared nostrils to be more precise – before bursting out through the back of the skull, resulting in the entire head deflating to perhaps half its former volume. The African toppled sideways into a cluster of weeds.

The train driver continued his majestic twelve miles per hour. The thorn trees were unbroken, from the engine a rain of soot fell on the still bodies that lay on the hot earth.

The doctor permitted himself to perspire a little from his beetroot face now as he tugged on the bell rope. 'Gin and peppermint,' he ordered as the white-jacketed waiter appeared. 'Three.' He held up three fingers. 'With ice – plenty of ice.'

*

The sport . . . oh, this *sport*. The three athletes devoted soul, mind and fibre to their sport. And as the train *chacked* along the iron rails deeper into the heart of the eternal forest they played their hardest. By the time the sun descended into a red blaze somewhere in that empire of thorns I sat at the dining-table. There I was served my hors d'oeuvre of salad with grilled sole and lemon. The cutlery shone, the white cotton tablecloth was perfection, and the golden honeysuckle display in the centre was amazing.

The three athletes stood at the very end of the carriage. Sustained by gin and pep they fired their rifles for hour after hour. Mere shards of conversation reached me.

'A full six feet he was. Took two shots to—'

'The face, I say, aim for the face.'

'. . . their nakedness. What comes out of 'em isn't the colour of blood at all.'

'Now, gentlemen. Here's another.' *Bang!* 'See! The face!'

'A difficult shot.'

'Tricky, very tricky.'

'But admirably effective. Admirable!'

'Strikes the nail right on the head it does!'

'By Jove! Good musketry, sir!'

Men, women, old, young, lame, simple, and one with a face as fair as the Christ who takes us aloft when our toil is done. They all fell to the gentlemen's rifle-work. Mothers, bambinos, sliver-haired patriarchs. Oh, I can see the Africans lying on the hot soil even now. The train chacked at twelve miles an hour. The red sunset was glorious. I picked at my fish to avoid having a bone stick in my throat; meanwhile, the doctor's bullet was a golden star that, to me, appeared to glide gracefully toward a grandma who carried a bundle of sticks on her head, and led a child by his hand. The grandma's skin was as dark as the bark of the thorn trees, her bare feet were broad from tramping over baked earth for seventy years. The golden star that was the doctor's bullet settled on the bridge of her nose, then ever so slowly melted through the skin, to continue its mysterious journey into the dreams and visions and wonders contained in her brain.

'See!' the doctor exclaimed. 'Always aim for the face.'

'You'll have to be quick, Sir Anthony, the child is running into the bushes!'

'Ah, got it!'

'Bad luck, Sir Anthony, you've only winged it.'

Chack . . . chack . . . chack . . . twelve miles an hour . . . never more than twelve miles an hour. . . .

Going into the forest was like journeying into the underworld. The thorn trees became thicker, more gnarled, more ancient looking. And they looked less like wood than stone. It was as if the trees were formed from dark rock that had been extruded from the ground. There must have been leaves, yet for the life of me, I don't recall any leaves. Only spikes that would pierce the flesh if you attempted to walk through that deadly copse. All this and twelve miles an hour. And interminable sport.

Why didn't the natives retreat into the forest when their countrymen were being noisily despatched by the three adventurers with their repeating rifles? The fact is that those Africans walking alongside the track formed a sparse traffic indeed. Our three in their moving hide only had the opportunity to enjoy their sport every thirty minutes or so. Even though the train rumbled at a miserable twelve miles an hour it encountered natives at intervals of at least six miles apart. So, those that were going to give their lives in order to entertain the gentlemen wouldn't have heard the earlier gunshots, least of all witnessed the stately hunt.

Twelve miles an hour. The waiter in his white jacket poured a claret for my approval.

'Very nice. Thank you.'

'Merci, monsieur.'

A youth with no longer a head to call his own fell into some thistles.

Next, on my fine china plate, a row of delicately roasted lamb chops, served with saffron rice, and a casserole of courgette, tomato, spring onion, and blue-black slivers of egg-plant. Twelve miles an hour. The train driver sounded the whistle to spare the life of a rabbit sitting on the track. I saw it safely decamp into the forest. The athletes fired on a family padding along the path in the relative cool of the evening. For the first time a reaction. A woman with pink strips tied in her hair ran after the train. She shouted in a fabulous tongue. Shouts of rage, or grief, or gratitude at the hunters returning her loved ones to the laps of the gods. I don't know. Just that it was very noisy.

I found a piece of eggshell in the vegetable casserole. That annoyed me immensely. To me, discovering eggshell in food is worse than finding a fly.

The solicitor felled the shouting woman with his revolver. She'd almost reached the train as it rumbled into our heart of darkness.

'Face.' The doctor's approval was heartfelt. 'Dead centre of the face.'

My cabin at midnight. The air was so hot it was as if you inhaled it over a lighted stove. Still the train rumbled along at its mandatory twelve miles per hour. I lay on the bunk with the window open. There were no stars; only darkness; a colossal overwhelming darkness. My companions must have retired to bed. Apart from the chack of iron wheels on iron track there was no other sound. From time to time I moved around my compact room with its expensive wood panelling. Many times I washed my face in my bathroom. I always avoided looking in the mirror. I didn't like what I saw there. Then I'd return to the bunk, where I lay staring up into the darkness. At last the train began to slow. Fantastically, or so it seemed to me, our unassailable – our sacred! – twelve miles per hour dropped to ten, then was nine. Soon we crawled. Then stopped. After eighteen hours of sullen, yet indefatigable process the train was still. All of a sudden the iron beast that was our locomotive seemed to hold its breath. Silence! And such a silence . . . it was an invasive force. Ye gods, I remember that silence to this day. I put my hands over my ears and groaned. After eighteen hours of *chack, chack, chack* the sudden absence of mechanical noise hurt my eardrums. Why had we stopped? For water to slake the thirst of the iron beast perhaps. Then the change was wrought. . . .

Our journey on the train had rendered Africa a seemingly distant place. Until then I couldn't hear the sounds of the forest because of our locomotive grunting and chacking. This wilderness could hitherto have been a savage island glimpsed only indistinctly from the bridge of a ship. Now we were at rest the presence – the living, breathing, palpitating, aromatic presence of this primeval land sidled into the train. The thorn tree forest began at its regulation fifty paces from the track, that I knew, but what I sensed was entirely different. The forest crept closer. I could feel its prickling presence. Now I divined unseen forms of prodigious size lurking in the darkness beneath its branches. Even though I didn't so much as glance out of the window I was as certain as I am of my own name that a thousand malevolent eyes had fixed on the stationary train. When we moved nothing could destroy us. Now I had no doubt that we could be blasted to atoms by the merest flick of a lizard's tail. The window – that widely open window drew my gaze. Now a panther could leap through it. That twelve miles an hour was our magical protection. I realized that now. Without motion we were vulnerable as ants beneath a boy's stamping foot.

'*Marlow!*'

My cabin door bashed open. The doctor stood there in his silk dressing-gown, his chest heaving, his face red in the light of the lamp he held. In the other plump fist he clutched his rifle by its barrel.

'Marlow! Quick man! You must catch him before he gets away!'

Before I could ask what was happening, the lamp had been thrust into my hand and the doctor bundled me out through the carriage door on to Africa's baked mud.

'There he is,' hissed the doctor. 'Bring him to us!'

The train journey had seemed, to me, like a dream. When I found myself standing on the crisp soil, with the carriages at a standstill behind me and the light of the lamp revealing something of the tangle of thorn branches, that was when I re-entered the world of reality.

'Hurry man,' hissed the doctor. He pointed at an abandoned rail carriage that lay on its side in that naked borderland between track and forest. 'He'll get away.'

'*What?*' The irritation in my voice was plain to hear.

Sir Anthony leaned out of the carriage window in his pyjamas. 'There's a native dressed in gold. *Flush him out.*'

The three gentlemen, the bloodthirsty beggars, were armed with rifles. With utmost indignation I approached the wreck of the carriage. In the light of the lamp I saw it was a twin of the opulent vessel that bore us in luxury through the wilderness. Although it had suffered here. Broken windows. Insects had devoured the plush upholstery. Chandeliers lay shattered in the remains of a great deal of crockery. A stink of rot. I noticed also, growing there in the centre of the wreck, a young thorn tree.

'Hurry up, Marlow.'

'Don't take all night about it.'

'Flush him out. The devil's covered from head to foot in gold.'

I moved around to the far side of the carriage to find our victim. Indeed there he was. A native boy of around thirteen. His dusty body was black as onyx. One foot, I noticed, was abnormally large. And he shone with gold. Gold amulets, a gold collar; he wore a cotton shirt that was decorated by oblong panels of gold. I'd never seen anyone as extraordinary. His large, round eyes regarded mine. He didn't appear afraid. He merely waited for an outcome.

'Marlow. Flush him out. Then stand back so we can get a clear shot.' Rifles cocked with a loud clicking. 'And for heaven's sake give us light!'

I raised the lamp to illuminate the child of gold. Then I advanced on him waving my arms like a man might wave his arms to shoo chickens back into their coop. Still facing me, the boy moved slowly backward. The large foot, with unusually broad toes, caused him to limp. I shooed. He still retreated. As soon as he was clear of the carriage wreck my countrymen would have their sport. I moved more to the right.

I was a little closer now. I glanced away from the brown eyes that fixed on mine to the boy's golden adornments. They caught the lamplight with yellow flashes. Oh, they were splendid all right. They were also cut from the gold sheets of foil that are used to wrap chocolate. Bless me, the youth had decorated himself with confectioners' tinfoil. I maintained a distance of perhaps ten paces from him as I shooed, slowly flapping my arms as I did so.

From behind me came annoyed shouts. 'Out of the way, Marlow!'

'We can't get a clean shot.'

'I can't fire until you step aside.'

'Marlow . . . you fool.'

I maintained my flapping gesture until the boy in his gold tinfoil had backed into the forest where the night vanished him. Just for a few paces I entered the fringes of that wall of thorn. Although I no longer saw the boy in my lamplight I beheld a man. He'd stood there silently watching what had transpired. He must have been a great age. His white eyebrows and hair were a marked contrast to the ebony skin. His arms were thin as twigs and his bare shoulders were as wrinkled as brown paper. Only there was something about his eyes . . . something shockingly wrong. What should have been the whites of the eyes were a bright yellow in colour. Almost a luminous yellow, like a candle flame placed behind amber glass. His face was expressionless. Then he stepped forward. He gripped my forearm in his right hand and my elbow in his left. For a moment he leaned forward a shade to look into my eyes with that pair of yellow orbs. I fancy now that he muttered some words in a sing-song voice, but at the time I'd swear he'd said nothing. But memory is no fossil. It continues to evolve. After that he melted back into the forest.

I returned to the train and the sportsmen's jeers.

'Marlow, what the devil were you playing at?'

'You ruined a perfectly good shot.'

'The face . . . had it clear as day until you stood in the way.'

'And what about our gold?'

'Didn't you see how he draped himself in the stuff?'

'Where will we find gold like that again for the picking?'

In a temper I barked at them. 'There is no gold!'

The train driver sounded his whistle; steam gushed through the wheels of the locomotive as the carriage shuddered. By the time I climbed back on board we were moving once more, gradually accelerating toward our magical twelve miles per hour.

With the dawn came searing brightness. The air in my cabin grew stifling; perspiration broke through my skin if I did so much as sit upright. So all that day I lay on my bunk. Beyond the window the unbroken thorn forest slid by. Chack, chack, chack . . . The three gentlemen irked me so much I decided to keep myself absent from the salon carriage. The waiter brought meals to me along with jugs of boiled water, that being my preferred drink in a hot climate. All through that long, hot day I heard the snap of rifle shots. However, I refrained from viewing the messy results of their sport.

By the time the sun had begun to set once more my anger at the men had increased. I found myself wrenching back the door of my cabin before dashing down into that duchess's parlour on wheels; oh, the chandeliers were tinkling merrily as the train swayed along. The flowers were fresh in their vases. Only this time the solicitor and Sir Anthony weren't there. Instead, there was only the doctor. He sat on a plush sofa as he stared at his gin, pep and melting pearls of ice dance in the glass on a little walnut table.

His eyes were almost closed, but he peeped through the fleshy splits.

'You've found it!' I shouted at him. 'There's no need to go any further!'

The doctor took his time to speak. 'Go rest. The journey is more arduous than I could have believed.'

'Didn't you hear me?' I wanted to hit him. 'You already have it. You've found Kurtz's treasure.'

'Have I, by Jove.' The doctor's voice was a ghost of a sound. No more than a breath. It was a miracle I heard it at all. Not for a moment did he remove his gaze from the glass of liquor.

'Do you know what Kurtz's treasure is? It's not ivory, it's not pearls, not diamonds. What Kurtz valued most – his prized possession – was his ability to commit the most savage acts without guilt. Kurtz was the consummate torturer and violator. It invigorated him. Every death he caused had the same virtue of a conscientious man saving another penny for his future prosperity. That talent for slaughter is Kurtz's gold. You've proved you have it. So, there is no need to go further. Take your wretched treasure home with you. See if you can invest it! See what kind of reward murder brings to you!'

'I'm going to lie down in my cabin,' he whispered. Then he looked at me. The whites of his eyes had turned quite yellow. It was as if someone shone a candle through amber.

Within the hour the sun had set. In turn I visited each of the sportsmen in their cabin, those athletes who gave so much to indulge their sport.

Sir Anthony sat on his bathroom floor with his back to the wall. When I spoke his name he managed only by dint of great effort to look at me. His eyes – a bright yellow. It reminded me of the gold foil stitched to the boy's clothing.

In the solicitor's cabin he lay beneath the blankets as if cold to his bones. I, however, found the heat stifling. He didn't say a word; instead his tongue constantly marched back and forth across his lips. When I looked more closely into his face his part open eyes formed slits of an uncannily brilliant yellow.

The doctor. He sat on his bunk, his back jammed tight against the wall.

He regarded the corner of cabin with absolute terror. He was shaking violently. The fever had ransacked his body of all physical strength. When he saw me he beckoned – such relief at being no longer alone.

'Marlow,' he gasped. 'Do you see who's standing there?'

I looked at his frock coat swaying on its peg.

He clutched at my shirt sleeve. 'You know who that is, don't you?'

I said nothing.

'It's Kurtz, isn't it?'

'Kurtz is dead.'

'Yes, he is, isn't he?' With horror the doctor stared into the cabin wall. 'And there's something extraordinary about his eyes.'

They called out as I packed my bag.

'Please help me!'

'Marlow . . . water . . .'

'Marlow! Kurtz is here. He's staring at me. Those eyes! Marlow, in the name of God. . . .'

The bacillus that felled the three sportsmen could, I suppose, have been in the very air. I suspect, however, it emerged from tainted water that had been used to make the ice that chilled their drinks. To make good its escape from the frigid prison all the germ required was a little warmth.

Twelve miles an hour. That's how fast that haunted, nightmare world travelled on its track. Not fast enough to break my neck when I jumped free of it. Moments later, with both feet firmly planted on African soil, I had my long walk in front of me. Behind me, the train continued its even longer journey along that track through an entire universe of thorn trees, and I watched it dwindle into the distance – into the heart of an even greater darkness.

And that, my friends, is the end of Marlow's story. The ferry Rosa rode at anchor off the coast of Belgium. As dawn broke over the grey sea I watched Marlow as he sat there, a Buddha pose of now silent introspection.

'Marlow,' I began, 'when you awoke you asked me if we were alone in the cabin.'

He said nothing, merely stared into space with brooding eyes.

I continued, 'Did you see a figure there?' When there was no response I added, 'And was there something extraordinary about its eyes?'

With that grey dawn the troops began to disembark from the ships for the final stage of their journey toward the killing fields of Europe.

4

THE PASS

They came as they always did.

From the west, when the evening mist spilled down from the mountains into the pass.

Perhaps their pig brains told them they could not be seen. But we saw them all right. We saw their humped, monstrous forms; we heard the thud of trotters across rock; we saw the outline of their hairless porcine heads; we heard their swinish grunts as they moved toward us with all the loathsome horror of a disease spreading across a human face.

'Every night,' the boy whispered, marvelling. 'They come every night. Don't they ever learn?'

'No.' The man drew back the bolt of his rifle.

'But there are so many of them. Where do they come from?'

'Out of the mountains.'

'But you'd think they'd realize. They must see what happens to the others when they try and get through the pass.'

'They've got no brains. At least not like you or I.'

'I can't smell them. I thought you said they reeked like a sty?'

'When they get close enough you'll get a nose full.'

'And they've done this every night for the last five years?'

'You've got a lot of questions, lad.'

'But there are—'

'Best check that rifle, lad. If we can't stop them they'll be all over us. Then what's going to prevent them tearing our village to pieces? Our folk with it as well.'

'They've never got through?'

'No, thank God. But they've managed to get into other villages.'

'What happened?'

'What do you think happened, soft lad?'

'Oh.'

A girl, feeding a belt of ammunition into a machine-gun, spat, 'What you'd do is, take a pen to the map; then you scratch out the name of the village. Once those monsters have finished there's nothing left. I heard they even rooted bodies out of their graves and ate them, too. They'll eat anything. I heard how they fought each other over a baby's arm. Their tusks can rip open your belly like—'

'That's enough,' said the man. 'The lad knows as well as anyone what they're like.'

'We've told him often enough,' I said.

'What's that supposed to mean?' The man gave me a cold look as if he could read some secret meaning in my words.

I shrugged. 'Like I say, we've told him often enough. He should know by now.'

'Enough to stop asking silly questions.' The girl cocked the machine-gun.

'Exactly,' I said, hoping I'd diverted the man's suspicion from my remark. But then these were tough days. A disbelieving look, or even a badly timed sneeze could seem like treachery. People were frightened. That's a fact. We'd hardly enough to feed ourselves. The crops were poor nowadays. Even if those things now shuffling down from the mountain paths were to tear up even a single field of potatoes we'd be hungry by January.

The man called out to a bunch of men hunkered down over a coffee pot, taking turns to warm their hands on it. 'OK. Get to your positions and mark your targets.' He coughed and spat. 'But don't shoot until you get the signal. Bullets are worth their weight in gold, remember.'

Coughing, stretching, muttering, they climbed to their feet. One man farted. No one commented.

The truth is, at times like this my own bowels got hot and began to churn over and over. I'd taken my place on the barricade for the past eighteen months or more but it still got me every time. Belly rumbles. Cramps. A supper that felt like a balled fist in my guts. I wouldn't begin to digest that lump of bread until this was over for the night.

The new boy, the one with all the questions, must have knots for guts by this time.

He even asked to go relieve himself.

'You should have thought of that earlier.'

'But—'

'But nothing, lad. It takes every single one of us to stop those things breaking through. It might be your bullet that makes the difference between us going to our beds tonight or us running for our lives.'

The boy began to sweat. He stared with wide frightened eyes at the humped shapes coming through the mist. I heard swinish grunts echo from the rock. If you craned your head a bit higher you would see the bones of all the creatures we'd shot in the last five years on the chasm floor. But still they flooded through the pass.

'They're coming from the west . . .' I heard the boy's puzzled mutter. 'Where from in the west?'

'Take your time,' called the man. 'Choose your targets . . . and carefully. Head shots preferred.'

All along the wall I heard the sound of rifles being cocked. Then we leaned forward resting the barrels on top of the coping stones. Every shot had to count.

The girl brought the muzzle of the heavy machine-gun to bear on the pig-like creatures swarming through what remained of the border crossing and into the main body of the pass itself. She'd fire in short bursts. That heavy machine-gun had a gluttonous appetite for ammunition.

Night after night we'd poured a torrent of ammo into the beasts. If we ever ran out of bullets we'd be hog-meat in a twinkling. And that's the truth.

'Steady . . .' sang out the man. 'Aim for heads. Aim for a beast at your side of the pass. No cross shooting. If you wound your target move on to the next. Don't waste shots . . . that's what the axes are for.'

And so on. I'd heard this chapter and verse month in, month out.

Through the mist the shapes came. Blurred humped things at first with massive skulls. But as they emerged from the grey murk, I saw the glint of their tusks that could rip your belly wide open, and there were the massive jaws, all dripping and slobbering with hell-born hunger. I've heard it said those mouths could take a child's head whole.

I thought of my two sleeping in their cots and I knew I'd make every bullet hit its target good and square tonight.

The creatures moved like a tide along the pass. Soon I couldn't see an inch of the track, only a mass of bodies. As they emerged from the mist I chose my first target. Its torso was as thick as a sow's. The skin of its face made me think of a rubber mask. Here and there a reddish hair bristled. While the pig-like eyes burned with equal measures of hunger and hatred.

'Steady . . . steady,' the man called out to us. 'Take your time. Choose your target . . . don't pull the trigger. Squeeze.'

I allowed the monster to move into the cross-hairs of the telescopic sight. Now the head was a great bloated ball of muscle and bone. The mouth dripped. The tongue, a pink writhing tentacle as thick as a baby's arm.

Easy does it . . . another five seconds then squeeze the trigger as—

'Stop!'

It was the boy's voice. He'd moved back from the wall as if it had suddenly burnt him. 'Stop!' he shouted again. 'Don't anyone shoot. There's been a mistake!'

'No mistake, boy,' boomed the man. 'Pick your target.'

'Wait . . . just wait. Can't you see?'

'Cut the larking, boy. Everyone else, keep your sights on your target.'

'No!' The boy had dropped the rifle and was shaking his head as if he couldn't believe his own eyes. 'What's wrong with you all?'

'Come back and take your position at the wall, boy.' The man spoke calmly. 'Don't make a fool of yourself.' To everyone else he called. 'Right, they're pretty thick on the ground tonight. Fire on my command.'

The boy was still shaking his head. 'What are you all doing?' he cried. 'Those aren't monsters: they're PEOPLE!'

'Shut up now, boy. Everyone got a target?'

'Don't! They're people like us.'

The girl at the machine-gun spat, 'Shut your stupid mouth.'

Others joined in, snapping viciously at the boy.

'You blind or something?'

'Your mother'll be ashamed when she finds out how you carried on.'

'They're monsters . . .'

'Filthy monsters.'

'Monster lover.'

'He must be short sighted.'

'Or stupid.'

'He's better left down in the village shovelling horse shit.'

'Moron.'

'It's you who are morons!' The boy's face flared red. 'Can't you see? They're not monsters. They don't look anything like pigs. They haven't got snouts! They haven't got tusks. Look! They're people just like us!'

'Pay no attention to the boy,' called the man. 'Keep your eye on your target. OK . . . on the count of three. One . . .'

The boy screeched, 'They're *people*! They're men and women. Look, they've got children. For God's sake, just look at them. . . .'

'Two.'

'There's a little girl wrapped in a blanket!'

I looked through my telescopic sight.

Girl in a blanket.

No.

I see pig eyes.

I see a wet snout. Silvery with mucus. . . .

'Don't shoot!' The boy tugged at my arm. 'It's a woman. She's holding up her baby to show you. It's just a little baby . . . those are starving people . . . not monsters. Listen to me! She's holding up her baby!'

I fixed my eye on the target.

I see tusks.

I see a monster . . .

I do . . . believe me. I see a monster.

Through the rifle's sight I saw the hog-like creature raise a boulder high above its head, ready to hurl it at me.

'Three . . .' The man's voice bellowed. 'FIRE!'

'No!' the boy screamed. 'It's a mother and baby!'

I fired at the monster. They boy must have jolted my arm.

Because the bullet smacked into the boulder.

Fragments of it splashed down on to the ground.

And I saw the fragments were red.

5

BLAST FROM THE PAST

ONE

'Watch out, Matthew, a German vehicle will hurt just as much as a British one.'

More than once that evening I'd blundered out into the fog-choked streets of Frankfurt. Dettlef tugged me back to safety as a truck lumbered by in the fog.

'Idiot should have his lights on,' I grunted. 'Now . . . where's that other bar?'

'Ah, the one by the station.' Dettlef's German accent was thicker now that the multitude of beers started to take hold. 'You know, my friend, we should really be seeking a place where we could eat. Perhaps McDonald's. Big Mac. Big, BIG fries.'

I shook my head. 'Frankfurter.'

'Yes,' he chuckled. 'I'll find you a nice restaurant that serves nice frankfurter, or, as we say more correctly, bratwurst. With it, we shall have nice French fries and nice beer – nothing nicer!'

We did our best to hold each other up as we walked. 'Did I tell you?' I began. 'Did I . . . my God, this fog is thick. I've walked all around this city all flipping day and I've not seen a flipping building. All is murk, all is murk. . . .'

'But we've seen inside a lot of blue-day bars.'

We laughed again. 'Blue-day bars.' We couldn't remember how the joke was born, or what it actually meant, but it got funnier every time someone mentioned it. By the time we hit the schnapps it would be blue-day hilarious.

'Now, where was I?' I peered into the cotton-wool wall of fog.

'Before Frankfurt? Hounslow, Middlesex, you said.'

'No, figuratively speaking. I was telling you something. Can I hellers remember what it was I – ah, that's it!'

'Ack! *That's it!*' he echoed and we ran into a fit of giggles again.

'I was saying, I've eaten hamburgers in Hamburg, drunk Newcastle Brown Ale in Newcastle, hell of a job finding the stuff though; ah, Yorkshire pudding in Yorkshire . . . drank port in Portugal.'

'And I've eaten a pomegranate in Wales.'

'Pomegranate in Wales?' Again this seemed hilarious in our beer sodden state. '*Pomegranate . . . Wales!*'

We collapsed into mirth.

Then our laughter was drowned by a terrific rumbling sound.

'*Mein Gott . . .*'

'What the hell . . . Jesus. What a monster – look at the size of it.'

The leviathan lumbered out of the fog; an enormous grey box of a shape that shivered the paving slabs beneath our feet. Seconds later it had vanished back into the fog, accompanied by a great thundering that echoed from the deserted buildings.

'*Gott.* You know what that was, Matthew?'

I supported myself by holding on to a lamppost as I shook my head.

'A Tiger.'

'*A Tiger?* It looked more like some kind of tank to me.'

'Yes. A German Tiger Tank. You know? World War Two.'

'He'll have no trouble parking it, then. But hell of a thing to bring into town at night.'

'Strange.' Dettlef became thoughtful. 'Perhaps there is some kind of military hardware show, yes?'

'Yes, indeedy. Now, point me in the direction of those frankfurters.'

Yesterday, I'd flown from Heathrow, the biggest airport in Europe to Frankfurt, the second biggest in Europe. I was writing a piece on the Frankfurt Book Fair, which is staged in what appears to be the biggest building on earth, the Messe. I'd planned a two day visit to the fair, talking to attending publishers' representatives, literary agents and raw paper merchants. But after tramping round hundreds of stands manned by publishers from Albania to Croatia, from Rumania to Zaire – all proudly showing their own language versions of Stephen King's *The Shining* – so help me, I'd had more than enough. Anyway, with twenty pages of notes in my reporters' pad there was ample material for the article. In the taxi rank I bumped into a fellow hack from Berlin who was writing a near-identical piece for his magazine. We decided to do the logical thing: embark on a God almighty bar crawl around Frankfurt on the company expense account. Dettlef Voss was a good boozing companion. I seemed to meet up with him at least three times a year, either at the Frankfurt Book Fair, the Munich Beer Festival or Cannes. He was a towering blond-haired man of thirty-four with Charles Hawtrey spectacles, and a passion I shared for good beer and smoke-filled bars that played live blues. Our idea of heaven would be a basement bar so hot it made the walls themselves sweat. In that sweet vision of afterlife Robert Johnson, B.B. King, and the Electric god himself, James Marshall Hendrix, would play blistering Blues guitar until Kingdom Come.

On his left cheek Dettlef Voss bore a scar that would have been the perfect duelling scar for a Prussian cavalry officer; only he had acquired it as a child, when he left a china plate on a gas hob. It exploded with the force of a small, but potent hand grenade. The shrapnel beheaded his mother's cherished potted orchid as well as slashing that T-shaped scar into his cheek.

Anyhow. There I was. Leaning against the lamppost in October, in some deserted area of downtown Frankfurt. Fog thick enough to cut with a cake knife. Pretty much squiffed, with a squiffed German journalist . . . and along came that sixty-ton Nazi tank salvaged from the Battle of the Bulge, its motor thundering away, loud enough to wake the dead. Not only wake them but shake their bones right down into their funeral boots.

'Right,' I declared, as I took a breath deep enough to hopefully keep my booze-induced wobbly legs supporting me until I ingested sobering-food. 'Take me to frankfurter heaven.'

'Frankfurter heaven it is.'

We both walked in that over-precise, look-at-me-occifer-I'm not-*hic!*-not-drunk way, that only the profoundly inebriated can manage. We'd managed about a hundred paces when we saw the Tiger Tank again. It had stopped just short of a junction. We chuckled and joked how absurd it was that a sixty-ton battle tank would halt for a red light.

'Just show me a police car that can stop that blighter,' Dettlef exclaimed, as he pointed a finger at me so closely it was in danger of stabbing me in the eye.

We continued our strangely upright walk toward the tank. Its engine idled; thick blue smoke rolled into the fog.

'The dirty blighter,' Dettlef gasped his quirky Britishism in outrage. 'He's not running on unleaded. Just look at that filthy exhaust fumes . . . dirty, dirty blighter.'

'My God. There's another one. You know, Dettlef, that's it with bloody World War Two tanks, you don't see one all day, then a whole bunch of 'em come at once.'

'Eh?'

'Don't worry. Old English joke. Will explain later. Once I've gorged on your nation's finest sausages.'

We walked on into the fog. The German tank gave a throaty roar. The sound was so loud it vibrated the bones in my head. Probably loosened a filling or two into the bargain as well.

Thirty metres further on, just a little more than a silhouette in the fog, the second tank ambled across the junction. Its turret cranked to the right, swinging the gun to the left in a way reminiscent of some great iron Dalek.

'What do you think—' Dettlef began. But he never finished what he was going to say.

For myself, I don't think I even heard it. Yet I felt a tremendous punch in the left side of my head.

The Tiger Tank had fired its massive gun. The flash from the muzzle turned the fog a brilliant white that damn well nearly blinded me. Then I'd swear the shell actually tore a hole in the fog before it slammed into the side of the second tank. The thing erupted like a volcano, ripping away the turret and gun in one piece to crash down on to parked cars twenty metres away from us. The decapitated tank belched black smoke from the newly revealed orifice where the turret had once sat.

'Jee-sus!' Dettlef clamped his hands to his ears. 'There are people in there,' he cried out while staring at the exploded tank. '*There are people!*'

The fog closed in again. But I could still see. . . . Christ. Not that I wanted to see what was happening to the poor devils.

From the now burning tank the figure of a man appeared; he was blazing from head to foot. Grotesquely, as if playing a comic drunk, he rolled out of the vehicle and went walking away down the street, spinning round and round, arms swinging out. Another man made it from the wreck, but fell straight down on to the pavement, and lay there in a big pool of fire that burned a greasy orange.

The big Tiger Tank lumbered on. Like some implacable beast that had just made its kill, it rumbled slowly away from us, its turret turning smoothly left and right. It avoided the still blazing tank that it had destroyed so brutally a moment ago. Without pause it rolled straight over the burning man, lying flat in the road. Pieces of burning flesh stuck to the Tiger's caterpillar tracks to perform a grisly merry-go-round as that killing machine prowled away into the night-time fog.

I made it to the shop doorway. Then every drop of beer I'd drunk in the last three hours cascaded on to the ground.

TWO

'What's happening?' I asked Dettlef five minutes later. 'I mean, did you see . . . did you see what happened?'

Of course he'd seen. He started to speak but suddenly aircraft tore low across the rooftops. They were sinister-looking machines with swept back wings that resembled shark fins. Even the nose of the aircraft was pointed like that of a shark. I'd never seen anything like it before. But Dettlef nodded, as if he was witnessing an event that, deep down, he'd always known would be inevitable.

'Messerschmitt 262s,' he told me. 'Nazi jet fighters.'

'They didn't have jets in the war, did they?'

'Oh, yes they did, my friend. Late in the conflict the Luftwaffe boasted of several kind, including the Arado bomber and the People's Fighter that was to be flown by the Hitler Youth. The Messerschmitt 262 was the most successful. Hundreds were made. They could out-fly any allied prop-engined fighter.'

'OK, OK, I accept that.' I was stone cold sober now. 'But what I can't accept is what they are doing here. Now! That . . . that Tiger Tank just blew the other tank – and those men – to Kingdom Come. For God's sake, what is happening?'

'We are seeing the fruition of an evil plan. This is—'

He was cut short by a series of furious explosions that shattered windows all along the street. Dettlef pulled me under a shop-front canopy as glass fell into the street in a glittering avalanche. Suddenly there was the sound of explosions everywhere as some distant artillery position rained shells into the city.

More Nazi jet fighters screeched overhead. Weird airborne sharks, slicing through the night and fog.

'You said,' I began, panting with fear, 'you thought you knew what was happening?'

'Later . . . later, Matthew. Please . . . let us hide ourselves away.'

'Hide?'

'Yes. Please hide . . . in this alleyway.'

'Why?'

'Because here come my countrymen.'

We backed into the alleyway as half-a-dozen Panzer tanks rumbled down the street, engines coughing blue smoke, caterpillar tracks crushing broken glass to powder on the tarmac. A little way along the street stood a McDonald's; its lights blazed through the fog.

The leading tank paused. The turret turned. Then it loosed a shell at point-blank range through the plate glass window. Instantly the lights went out as every fluorescent tube in the restaurant shattered. The tanks moved on, turrets slowly revolving left to right then back again in that weird Dalek kind of way. Then came half-track vehicles. I could see the silhouettes of men standing in the back, their rifles at the ready. Next, the sound of feet crunching on glass shards as hundreds upon hundreds of men in grey uniforms marched by.

'German infantry,' Dettlef whispered. The men in characteristic steel helmets carried rifles, sub-machine guns, 'potato masher' hand grenades, anti-tank weapons. Even though the shelling continued they didn't crouch low as I would have expected. They marched as if they were a conquering army.

More Messerschmitt jets whined low overhead. They must have been hunting enemy planes because I could hear a *puk-puk-puk!* – the sound of their cannon fire. Immediately after that came a thunderous explosion; a glow bloomed in the fog above me as the plane in the jet's sights disintegrated in a ball of flame.

Another 10,000 Nazi soldiers marched by. They began to sing a marching song. The song was upbeat, the men were exultant. Their voices reverberated from the buildings. And they sang so loud it made the ground vibrate beneath my feet. I noticed there was something else about the marching men.

Dettlef saw it, too. He touched my arm. 'Do you see the men's faces?'

I nodded. 'All those soldiers . . . they're all dead, aren't they?'

THREE

When the army had marched by, and their jubilant singing had faded into the distance, we left the safety of the alleyway, and ran along the street. The explosions had destroyed the street lighting. McDonald's lay in darkness, its windows smashed, plastic seating torn to shreds like so much waste paper. I could still smell the burgers and fries, while above it all, a cardboard cut-out of Ronald McDonald, grinning his wide clown grin, spun round from its string in the centre of the ceiling. My eyes searched for bodies in the debris of plastic plants and children's Happy Meal cartons. I held my breath, expecting to see dozens of young people lying there, skin diced by shrapnel, blood pumping crimson from torn arteries.

'What happened to them?' I asked in a daze. 'Where did they all go? The place was packed with teenagers.'

Dettlef shook his head. 'I'm afraid I have answers for your questions. But we must find somewhere more . . . congenial?'

I couldn't move. 'Those soldiers. They really were all dead, weren't they?' Images of those men had burned themselves into the fabric of my brain. The faces were bloodless; decomposition had set in causing patches of black on foreheads, cheeks and jaws. Their lips were white. Their eyes were . . . I shivered, feeling whatever was left in my stomach hit the back of my throat again. I puked a steaming jet on to broken glass. Because, Christ yes, I remembered their eyes. They were big and bright and stood proud of their sockets as if their own eyeballs had been removed and replaced with hard-boiled eggs. I just could not get the image out of my head. White eyes, bulging grotesquely. Worse, was the expression it gave the rotting faces. Those men were exultant. They gloried in their victory.

109

'Matthew . . . Matthew. Can you hear me?'

'Yes. Sorry, I think the shock's starting to kick in.'

'Please. We walk just a few more metres. There is a bar. We sit down there.'

We made it to the bar. The place lay in darkness but appeared relatively unscathed apart from a broken window.

'No, not there. Too close to the door, Matthew. Sit at the back.'

More shells exploded in the distance. Bottles rattled their own *danse macabre* on the shelves.

'Where are the people? This bar was full, too. What has happened to everyone?'

'I think the explanation is what we see with our own eyes,' Dettlef began. 'Sometime this evening an Event occurred. Some supernatural mechanism was activated. Now we find ourselves in a modern German city. Yet its people have gone into, ah . . . ah. . .' He struggled to find the appropriate word. 'Its modern people have vanished. They have been supernaturally transported. . .' Again he laboured to trace the apt phrase. 'Transported to another place, an unearthly place – yes? And now they have been replaced by that corpse army.'

'But they are fighting a war out there. We saw the tank explode. Men were burning to death . . . or at least men that appeared to move like living men were burning. This can't be happening . . . I must . . . I must be asleep. This is a nightmare.'

'A nightmare, yes. But you are not sleeping.'

'But how could this happen? Come on, Dettlef! You're not saying we've been transported back to 1945?'

'Clearly not, Matthew. Buildings and cars are modern. That newspaper on the table bears today's date. No, I repeat, my friend: I believe a supernatural mechanism has been triggered. Do you recall Hitler's V1 and V2 flying bombs?'

'Yes, thousands hit London in World War Two.'

'Well, in the closing weeks of the war there were rumours circulating amongst frantic German people that there were other *Vergeltungswaffe* weapons. Ones that would make the V1 and V2 missiles look like toys. Huge, terrible weapons that would prevent the Soviet army marching into Berlin.'

'You mean that this . . . what we saw outside?'

'That's exactly what I mean, Matthew. We are seeing Hitler's last strike at the Allies. Even though it be from the heart of Hell itself.' He nodded, grim-faced. 'We are witnessing the effect of the V3.'

'Only it's no mechanical weapon?'

'Precisely. It's one with a supernatural origin. You must remember that the Nazi party did not begin life as a political group. Originally, the Nazis had their roots in an occult society, similar to the United Kingdom's Order of the Golden Dawn to which your Arthur Machen and the evil Allister Crowley were members.'

'And the Nazi swastika is originally a Buddhist solar symbol. Only it was reversed to harness the powers of darkness. I remember that, but surely it's only mumbo jumbo.'

Dettlef shook his head. 'My father wrote books on this subject. He researched the occult connection to the Nazi party. Himmler himself ordered his SS to search the world for magic talismans, spells, voodoo rites, anything that might help in the fight against the Allies. Himmler even brought back holy men from Tibet to instruct Hitler on the use of secret forces.'

'You mean Hitler and his cronies somehow managed to raise their own dead to carry on fighting? But why now? Why more than sixty years after the end of the war?'

Dettlef shrugged. 'Magic isn't a science. It is unpredictable. Perhaps the supernatural mechanism lay dormant – like an unexploded bomb, yes? Then tick-tock-tick-tock. Maybe some accident triggers it. Or an old Nazi living out his days in the Spanish sunshine finally perfects the means of activating what we see now.'

Artillery shells droned overhead, the note becoming a rising whistle as the ordnance accelerated earthward to hit a building across the street. Bottles jumped from the shelves. The smell of schnapps fumes filled the air.

'Where are you going?' I asked, as Dettlef stood up and dusted down his coat.

'Why . . . naturally, I'm going to join the fight, of course.'

I stared at him. Just an hour ago we had been drinking together. Now was this the same man who was going to war for a long dead maniac? Should I try to stop him? A bottle lay on the floor, its bottom knocked out by the fall to the ground. Could I snatch it up and stab the jagged end into his face? Maybe the throat? I reached for the bottle.

'Matthew . . . what are you doing with that bottle? It's sharp; you'll cut yourself.'

'You can't fight.'

'Of course I will – and shall.'

'You were never a Nazi.'

'Ach so.' His smile was a grim one. 'I never was a Nazi. And I'm not now. I will fight on the side of the Allies.'

With a relieved sigh I allowed the bottle to slip from my fingers where it fell with a clink to the floor.

He looked me in the eye. 'You were going to attack me with that, weren't you?'

I nodded.

'Good for you!' He smiled. 'Then you will make a good fighter also. Come.'

'But what will happen? I mean, if what we have here is a battle between two ghost armies, let them slog it out. It can't affect us.'

'It can and it will. Many times in history, in many cultures there are legends just like this. Where magicians raised armies of the dead to fight for the living. One of the most recent occurrences was in The First World War, when, by good fortune an English officer invoked the long dead bowmen of Agincourt to prevent the German infantry overrunning the outnumbered English.'

'You mean, whichever ghost army wins tonight will change history?'

'If the Nazi triumphs then perhaps when you next look at a coin in your pocket you will see stamped there the head of Adolf Hitler.'

I took a deep breath. 'It looks as if we've no time to lose.'

Then started the longest night of my life. As we walked along the street we came across an American Jeep. It had crashed into a parked Volvo. The GI driver of the Jeep lay dead in the road.

'Bazookas. Carbine rifles. Ammunition. Grenades. Good.' Dettlef nodded with satisfaction. 'Now we fight the Nazi bastard, yes?'

'Yes,' I agreed. 'Now we fight the Nazi bastard.'

'We'll have to try as hard as we can to carry as many weapons as possible. I will be able to show you how to shoot them.'

'Why carry them? The Jeep's not badly damaged. And the keys are in the ignition.'

Within ten minutes we were in the thick of the fighting. I drove the open-topped Jeep with Dettlef standing in the back, bracing himself against the steel roll bar. I hadn't thought through any special tactics. This wasn't the time to devise elegant strategies. I simply steered alongside a German Tiger Tank as Dettlef fired the bazooka. With a tremendous clang the armour-piercing missile punched a hole in the side of the turret. Smoke billowed out of the hole. Up came the turret hatch and out tumbled the crew, burning from head to foot.

'To your left,' Dettlef warned.

I picked up my tommygun and fired the whole drum of ammunition into advancing infantrymen. The bullets tore them to shreds. They went down shrieking. The undead bodies seemed to be pumped hard with a fluid that certainly wasn't blood. One bullet hole was enough to unleash a jet of black liquid the colour of old engine oil. Instantly, bodies crumpled like deflated balloons, their faces wrinkling into slack bags of dead flesh.

I picked up another tommygun. I blasted away at the troops with a whole blizzard of red-hot lead; they went down by the dozen. Behind me, Dettlef fired the bazooka again; a halftrack went up in flames.

'Best make ourselves scarce, Matthew,' he shouted. 'There are too many here.'

I reversed the Jeep, its tyres buzzing in a wild frenzy of smoke. Then hit first gear . . . second . . . then third . . . and we were powering along the roadway. At junctions I turned at random. Every moment or so I'd bring the vehicle to a screeching stop so Dettlef could fire the bazooka at another Panzer tank. It would burst into flame, and it looked for all the world that a monster rose bloomed there in the street, uncurling beautiful pink and gold petals of living fire.

More troops ran toward us. Now, black-uniformed SS. I stood up in the seat and fired the machine-gun at them. All the time I was howling; a demented opera of exultation, terror and fury.

It wasn't all one-sided. Even though their reactions appeared dulled, their movements sluggish, the enemy still fired back at us. Bullets shattered the Jeep's windscreen, or slammed into its steel bodywork. Dettlef took a grenade fragment in one arm which bled in a great wash of crimson until he could tie his handkerchief around this arm, nipping the torn skin shut to staunch the blood's flow.

So this time I found myself wielding the bazooka to take out a Nazi armoured car in a blaze of glory. Moments later, I was driving again through the night and fog, with explosions crashing all around. On the corner of Berlinerstrasse and Domstrasse I recognized the distinctive fanlike outline of Frankfurt's Museum of Modern Art. Hours earlier it had been intact. Now shell holes pocked the walls. Artworks lay strewn in the street, and the Jeep's wheels crunched over priceless paintings by the likes of Joseph Beuys, Jackson Pollock, Andy Warhol.

An SS officer tried to flag us down. I waited until I saw his zombie face with its bluish-black skin, the lips pulled tight into an unearthly grimace. I fired my pistol into his face. A jet of oily liquid hissed out to spatter the side of the jeep and the SS zombie simply folded up like a suit of empty clothes. The next turn brought us out near the Messe, the massive exhibition centre, which hosted the world-famous Frankfurt Book Fair. I saw the iron man sculpture there, still hammering his anvil. As we approached I heard the drone of aircraft engines. Flying low over us was a United States B17 bomber. Its two starboard engines blazed, sending out showers of sparks. It glided with eerie slowness, following the line of the street. Then it hit the ten-storey high sculpture, turning it and the plane into a huge fireball that surreally transformed the fog into a brilliant orange.

I turned into a side street. A line of Nazi infantry stood in front of us. This time I didn't bother with the gun. I drove at them, popping their bloated bodies like so many balloons.

A moment later, when the road was clear, Dettlef tapped me on the shoulder. 'Pause here, Matthew. We can reload.'

As I picked up the handgun from the floor of the Jeep I saw a newspaper. It was British. The date, 1 October, 1945. The headline:

CHURCHILL SPEAKS:
'THE TIDE OF WAR HAS TURNED IN OUR FAVOUR.'

I glanced at other column headings. LUFTWAFFE BLITZ MOSCOW . . . JAPS LOSE LAST CARRIER . . . WAR IN THE PACIFIC OVER SOON, PROCLAIMS PATTON . . . ARTHUR ASKEY IN DOODLEBUG CATASTROPHE . . . LAUREL AND HARDY TOP WAR BONDS DRIVE . . . THE WHITE HOUSE SLIGHTLY DAMAGED BY INCENDIARIES.

'It's started, hasn't it?'

I held out the newspaper to Dettlef. He glanced at it then looked up at me, his face grim.

He nodded. 'Already history is altering. For us, the war ended in May 1945. According to this the world was still at war in the October of that year.'

More Nazi jets screeched overhead. Their menacing shark snouts nosed out fresh victims from the bomber formations.

I clipped another drum of ammo into the tommygun. 'Perhaps we can still tip the balance in our favour.'

'God knows, we must try.'

So it started again. Firing machine-guns into hordes of SS troops. Ribbons of fluid squirted from their bodies as they slumped. Then we fired bazookas, sending tank crews soaring into eternity on wings of Pentecostal fire. We slogged along city roads in the battle-scarred Jeep. A rear tyre now flat, steam rolled from a bullet-punctured radiator. But still we fought on, killing tanks, annihilating yet more zombie storm troopers. We passed burning Sherman tanks and more American jeeps and trucks.

I found I was making promises to myself. With the next tank destroyed it will be over. Maybe we could tip the balance. I glanced at the newspaper in my fist, willing the headlines to magically alter. An October newspaper of 1945 should contain peacetime news. Sure, there would be gripes about rationing, fuel shortages and conscription; Frank Sinatra would be sending Bobby-soxers wild in New York City. But it would show the world in a state of relative peace. And, more importantly, Hitler dead.

I turned a corner. Buildings blazed there. A couple of Tiger Tanks were firing their 88mm guns through what remained of office windows.

'Stop!' Dettlef shouted. 'I'm going to give these two devils their wings.' He fired the bazooka. The first tank burst open in imitation of a volcano. The turret flew through the air to crash down beside us with an almighty clang, the dead gunner still wedged inside. But then he had been dead these last sixty years or so. I couldn't feel remorse for destroying the already long-term deceased.

Dettlef triggered the bazooka again. I saw the beer bottle-sized missile zip through the night air to hit the front of the second tank. Then bounce off.

115

Dettlef groaned. 'My God. Move, Matthew. *Move, move!*'

I gunned the engine. It rattled noisily then released a whoosh of steam from the ruptured radiator. A moment later the motor died on us. Meanwhile, the surviving Tiger Tank slowly approached us; its turret rotated as the gunner took aim.

'Run!' I yelled. We both leapt from the Jeep as the tank fired. The shell cut the Jeep into two clean halves. Armed with nothing but the tommy-guns we'd been able to snatch from the vehicle's seats we ran into an alleyway.

And straight into a patrol of foot soldiers.

I gaped. I was shaking too much to bring the machine-gun to bear on the zombie faces. Then I saw a death-bloated hand come up to remove a match from the corner of a lip.

'Well, what the hell we got here, boys?' came a Midwest drawl. 'A couple of civvies with tommyguns and blood on their shoes. Lootenant, hey, Loo-tenant!' He hollered back down the line. 'What d' ya make of these two love birds?'

FOUR

As quickly as we got into the fighting we were out of it. Laughing, joking, back-slapping, calling me Limey, the American GIs hoisted us on to a truck, and we were taken out of the front line to an impromptu camp in a Toyota showroom where we were plied with hot coffee and chocolate cake. I told Dettlef to pretend he'd lost his voice. Being in a room of battle-hardened zombie GI Joes wasn't the healthiest place in the world for a German, even a German born long after World War II had ended.

A lieutenant brought more cake and coffee to where we were sitting to a table still covered with glossy leaflets for the latest Toyota 4x4.

'We're from the 9th Infantry Division. United States Army. Which outfit are you from?'

I did the answering. 'We're civilian. Volunteers. We found ourselves caught up in the middle of the fighting. We came across some abandoned weapons and just did our bit.'

'You've been fighting the swine?'

I nodded. 'We managed to knock out a few tanks. I think we got lucky.'

'You sure did get lucky. The Lord knows you were. You'll get a medal or two for this. But if the enemy had picked you up first, they'd have shot you there and then for not wearing a uniform.'

We sat there and talked over coffee. The shelling had become distant now. Perhaps the battle for Frankfurt had been won. The GI Joes were in good spirits. Still, it was weird to chat to a man who must have been dead sixty years. His face was a bluish-grey; black lumps looking something like dried walnuts poked through the skin covering his forehead. More of them formed a crisp line along the side of one jaw. His right eye seemed near enough normal; the other looked as if a black pool ball had been wedged into the socket. When he opened his mouth to push in more cake I noticed no skin covered the gums. There was just bare bone from where yellow teeth jutted.

He drained the last of his coffee. 'We best get you two bussed out of here. There's still rogue enemy patrols out there; we haven't flushed all the swine out yet.'

As he stood up to go the door swung open. There, in the foggy street beyond, were a hundred black uniformed figures. Even from here I could make out the glint of the silver death's head insignia on the collars.

Dettlef snapped to his feet, his eyes wide with shock. 'Oh, God,' he hissed at me. 'SS.'

Wildly I looked round for a gun.

Too late. They marched in, sub-machine-guns gripped tight in their dead hands.

I spun round, expecting to see the GI's snatch up their carbines. But something strange happened. This wasn't what I expected at all. The GIs lazed around chatting, smoking cigarettes. When they saw the SS troops walk into the building all they did was give them a cheerful wave and a few easy-going, 'Hi, Krauts.'

'Hello, Yanks,' responded the SS men. Then they went straight to the table where they started helping themselves to coffee and chocolate cake. Soon some of the GIs were chatting to the Nazi soldiers. They handed out cigarettes. An American corporal showed an SS sergeant a photograph in a movie magazine and both men laughed . . . that full-blooded laugh of two friends sharing a joke.

'Dettlef,' I whispered, 'what the hell's happening? Why aren't they fighting?'

'I don't know. Maybe they are. . . .'

His voice trailed away. A cruel-faced man in an ankle-length leather coat and civilian suit beneath had walked in. He stared at us in a way that made our blood run cold. Then he spoke to the commanding SS officer, then both walked across to the American lieutenant who'd spoken to me earlier. The next moment they moved purposefully toward us. Both the SS officer and the GI pulled their handguns from the holsters.

The lieutenant turned to the two Nazis. 'Are you sure these are the two?'

'Positive,' the man in the leather coat spat the word. 'These two have been killing our men and destroying our tanks all over Frankfurt.'

'Just a moment.' The lieutenant turned to a fellow soldier. 'Sergeant, take two men and keep a close on these two civilians.'

'The Limey?'

'Yes. They are not to move from this room.'

We watched as the SS officer and the man in the leather coat moved away into the corner of the room where there was a field telephone.

Sarge, matchstick gripped in the corner of his purple lips, ambled up with a pair of GIs. Both had their carbines slung casually under their arms.

'What you two fellers been up to?' Sarge asked, a wide grin on his dead-as-nails face. 'AWOL? Or been selling unlicensed hooch to us Dough Boys?'

'Look,' I said desperately, 'there's something I don't understand here. You're American?'

'Sure as Buffalo Bill I am.'

'And these men in black. The SS. These are German, right?'

'You sure are some brainiac, aren't you, feller? 'Course they're Kraut.'

'Then why aren't you fighting them?'

The blue-black face broke into a scowl, turning the bloated eyes into slits. 'Say, which side of the damn moon have you been on for the last six months?'

'The war in Europe didn't end in May?'

'No. Jeez – really: *where have you two been?* Kowalski . . . hey,

Kowalski!' He pulled the match from the corner of his mouth and expertly flicked it into a Styrofoam cup bearing the words TOYOTA: LIVE LIFE TO THE FULL. 'Kowalski. Come here and tell these two love birds what's been happening for the last six months.'

A gangling figure ambled up. You couldn't even begin to guess his age because his face was a mass of radiating scars that looked like crimson daisy petals. Two bright yellow eyes bugged out in that pool ball way that we were starting to grow accustomed to by now.

'Kowalski,' Sarge ordered. 'Educate these two.'

Kowalski had the polished tones of a college boy. 'For the last six months? Ah, Sarge, do you want me to go back to—'

'Just tell them from March 2.'

'March 2 was the day when Adolf Hitler died in the plane crash. America and Great Britain were negotiating the armistice with Goering when the, ahm, Soviet Red Army launched a surprise attack on American held lines near the Rhine. The Russian purpose being to capture all of, ahm, Europe. On March 4, German High Command ordered all German military forces to side with American, Canadian and British troops to repulse the communist attack.'

'You mean Germany, Britain, America and the whole Western Allied Forces are now on the same side, and are at war with Russia?'

'Catch on quick, don't he?' Sarge wedged another matchstick between his teeth. 'Say, you two love birds, what exactly did you do to get the Germans so riled?'

My gaze shifted across to where the American lieutenant spoke on the telephone. He was nodding while shooting cold glances in our direction.

Dettlef asked, 'Who rules Germany now?'

Sarge ruminated for a moment. 'It's a – a tet-rookie. . . .'

'Tetrarchy, Sarge,' the college boy corrected.

'That's what I said, son. Basically means the Krauts have four bosses. They are Admiral Dönitz, Rudolph Hess, the rocket guy, Von Braun. And some doctor. Eh, Menke.'

'Mengele,' the college boy corrected again. 'Doctor Mengele.'

'That's the feller, Doctor Mengele. You can always trust a doctor, can't you?'

FIVE

The American lieutenant said, 'I've been ordered to hand you over to the German authorities. I've no qualms about that. Personally, I think you are scum. You might have set the war effort back weeks with your barbarous attacks on these brave fighting men.' He waved a hand toward the zombie SS troops.

As we were led away, a GI spat into my face. 'Commie bastards. Hope you got your fifteen pieces of silver.'

The lieutenant said, 'As from now you are officially in the hands of Herr Vossenack of the Gestapo.'

Outside, searchlights sliced brilliant rods of light through the thinning fog. Combined squadrons of B17s and Dorniers rumbled overhead, heading east to blitz the Russian lines. Walking side-by-side along the street were two platoons, one American, the other German. A truck that had been hit by a shell lay on its side, pouring ammunition on to the tarmac. The bullets shone a brassy yellow in the reflected glare of searchlights. For all the world it seemed as if some mechanical beast lay there, spilling its metallic guts at our feet.

'We were too late,' I told Dettlef, as we marched in the direction of an open-backed truck. 'They've succeeded. History has changed.'

'Pray you are not correct. What will become of a new powerful Nazi Germany, allied to the Americans, with Doctor Mengele as leader?'

'Perhaps the Nazis have created a thousand-year Reich after all. Perhaps when we return to the Frankfurt we knew, we'll find swastika banners hanging from every lamppost.'

Dettlef spoke with a heavy voice. 'Don't count on us returning to present day Frankfurt, my friend.'

We'd stopped in front of a wall bearing posters advertising new albums from REM, Oasis and Robbie Williams. Standing fifteen paces from us, a dozen soldiers armed with rifles.

'Firing squad party . . .' The voice of the SS officer rang down the street. 'Firing squad take aim.'

I held my breath . . . screwed my eyes tight shut.

'*FIRE!*'

I fell back, the bullets knocked the breath from my body. As I collapsed I saw Dettlef twisting round. It was as if someone had thrown a handful of strawberry jam into his face.

I lie flat. My heart is still beating. It is a huge drum, pounding with all the fury of Armageddon in my chest. It is so powerful it seems as if it will never ever stop.

Then, with a lurch, it does just that.

SIX

And now my heart beats to another rhythm. And I march to the sound of a different drum. My blood, these days, runs so cold and so dark in my veins.

Buildings burn; looted DVD discs cover the city pavement; they're as plentiful as seashells glittering on a beach. In the gutter lies a corpse with a mobile phone clutched in its hand.

Dettlef is at my side as we crouch in the doorway of the pizza restaurant, waiting for the signal. My old friend's dead face is blue; his lips are white and bloodless. He turns to gaze at me with eyes that are as black as coal. He is in uniform. The armband he wears is now drenched with the blood of people he has killed.

And I know I look the same as him.

Our commanding officer blows a whistle; the signal to attack. I draw the bolt on my rifle and begin the advance on the enemy's final stronghold. There is a sign at the corner of the street; it is pocked with bullet holes; the words on the plaque hold no meaning for me when I read:

Pennsylvania Avenue

Nor do I recognize the white house where the leader of our enemy has taken shelter.

An old memory still resonates faintly inside my head. I recall myself asking Dettlef these words one fog-bound night long ago, *'You mean, whichever ghost army wins tonight will change history?'*

And Detleff's response: *'If the Nazi triumphs then perhaps when you next look at a coin in your pocket you will see stamped there the head of Adolf Hitler.'*

121

I know I have coins in my pocket . . . but I haven't examined them since that fateful day we embarked on our bar crawl of Frankfurt. When this final battle is done I'll reach into my pocket and pull out that handful of coins. What head will be stamped there? Will it be Adolf Hitler? Will it be Stalin? Only time will tell. Because here it comes: the attack whistle's final blast.

6

A BRIDGE TO EVERYWHERE

Oh life as futile, then, as frail!
Oh for thy voice to soothe and bless!
   What hope of answer, or redress?
Behind the Veil, behind the Veil.

In Memoriam – Tennyson

After it was over he came to talk to me. He's softly spoken. And tends to think about the words he will use before giving voice to them. This might make my friend seem hesitant to some, but for him it's important to know that he's clearly understood. This is his account of what happened to him. On the day he believed would be the worst day of his life:

I walked away from the courthouse knowing that I owned nothing. They'd taken the car last week, so I'd had to travel by bus into town. Afterwards, I didn't even have the bus fare home . . . well, I'm using the word 'home' loosely. That should be 'I didn't have the fare back to the room where I spent many a sleepless night. And many a miserable day, too.'

A man with a dog tied to a piece of string asked me for spare change. When I said I didn't have any that's when it hit me. I *really* didn't have any change.

The beggar spat on my jacket and sneered. 'You mean bastard. I hope you rot in Hell.'

Right then, I wanted to grab this guy with his hard little eyes and weasel face and yell, 'Do you know what's just happened to me? *Do you?*'

And the thing is *he* had change. He carried it in a plastic bag in one hand, a weighty, bulging pouch of coins, swinging it like I don't know what. He had enough change for a ticket to get me back to my room. Of course, I said nothing. Why waste my breath? I walked away while hunting through my empty . . . *so* empty . . . pockets for a tissue to wipe the guy's filthy spit from my clothes.

They say: It never rains but it pours.

So, so true. You always know when it's spring because that's when the hail hits. And it came blasting down the street. An idiot on a motorbike sat on it revving its motor so violently that it felt like my head was going to split. The pain in my ears from the racket was incredible, and all the time I had to keep my head down because the hail was blinding. Following me were a bunch of kids who were laughing like maniacs. For a while I was convinced they were laughing at me. That they'd been in the court; that they knew everything I'd ever worked for had been torn from me in the space of twenty minutes. The streets were littered with wrappers, hamburger clams, paper cups, dog crap, junked food. I'd never seen the place look so disgusting. And the kids laughed louder while making a stupid hooting sound. On the corner, the biker raced the motor like he was competing to see who could make the most godawful noise. Hailstones came down harder. By accident I tore the top button off of my jacket. If I took my hand out of my pocket to hold the jacket closed my hand froze. If I warmed my hand in my pocket the collar of the jacket flapped open, admitting a blast of cold, mean air that funnelled down inside my clothes, making my teeth chatter.

The streets were awash with grinning people. There were more smirking men and women in brightly lit shops, handing bundles of cash over counters. Window signs mocked me: AT HALF PRICE, HOW CAN YOU NOT afford to buy? Or TWO STEAKS FOR THE PRICE OF ONE. Yeah, how much does a walletful of nothing but cold northerly air buy you?

Closing my eyes to slits to try and keep out the stinging hail, I walked out of town. But I could do nothing to close my ears against the scream of traffic, or shelter exposed skin from the blast of cold winds. When I tried to move faster I slammed into a guardrail at the side of the road, which sent a gust of pain through my hip. The pain was so sickening I had to pause for a moment. I must have looked like a madman there, trying to hold shut my flapping jacket with one hand, while clutching my throbbing hip with the other, and all the time my mouth opened and shut like a goldfish as I gulped down bitterly cold air in reaction to the shock of the blow.

It was then I realized I'd gone the wrong way. Maybe it wasn't surprising after enduring a morning of pure hell. Anyone would be disorientated. When I blinked round at the surrounding houses of dirty red brick I saw I'd entered a neighbourhood I knew inside out. The street to my left led to the house I grew up in. When had I last been there? Probably more years ago then I cared to remember.

What made me do it, I don't know, but I decided to take a look at my childhood home. It was only five minutes away from where I now stood at the little corner supermarket where I used to buy my liquorice torpedoes when I was ten. More than anything at that moment, I wanted to see the redbrick villa with its three bedrooms and garden that sloped down to a stream. I wanted to look up at the small window above the front door and remember what it was like to be a boy. Gazing out, dreaming of how exciting life would be as an adult. How you could then own as many dogs as you liked and no one would stop you. And how you could stay up until way after midnight without anyone telling you to go to bed. The possibilities would be infinite. Only we know better, don't we? As with so much in life the anticipation is far lovelier than actual attainment.

Believe me, I almost ran down that road through all that shooting hail. Just as I turned the corner to enter Alpha Street where we'd lived a sign stopped me dead: ROAD CLOSED. Huge machines squatted in the road. With pneumatic jackhammers they pounded at tarmac, while a bulldozer scooped up the debris and piled it in black pyramid-shaped mounds.

Road closed! I couldn't believe it. Even the place where I'd grown up had been stolen from me. I turned to walk away. My head hung so low I could swear my chin knocked against my chest. Now for the trek across town, back to the room where neighbours screamed or played their music all night. I was a man standing at the bottom of a pit while life hurled rocks down on me. Burying me. Suffocating me.

Dogs barked in the yards – a screaming sound that hurt my ears. My hip throbbed. Cold water seeped through one shoe. My wallet – my empty wallet – pressed against my chest from the breast pocket. A cold, square shape. A little coffin that interred my dead dreams.

I glanced back, saw the old railway bridge, and knew there was another way.

This was the other route home. The frightening, exciting route. I followed it when there were roughneck kids hanging around the end of Alpha Street. Or simply if I wanted to take the unconventional way home. So I did it now. I cut along the dirt track between the houses to where the railway line ran along a high mound as far as the main road. This then was spanned by the railway bridge. When I finally climbed the forty-foot high bank I saw things had changed. But then what in life stands still? The railway tracks had vanished. Sometime, years ago, the rail company must have decided the line was no longer profitable. No trains ran here anymore. At the top of the long, linear mound that curved away beneath cold, grey skies was nothing but a strip of coarse grass dotted with bushes. Even the surface of the bridge a hundred yards ahead had greened over.

Not that this was going to stop me. I walked along the ghost line to the bridge. There I'd cross over to the other side. I'd find the gap in the fence then follow the path down to a gap in a second fence at ground level, then I'd emerge on Alpha Street directly opposite number eleven. My old home.

Only they'd done it to me again. I stood and stared – both angry and frustrated. The old gap in the fence I used to squeeze through as a juvenile had been repaired by a heck of a lot of barbed wire. To scramble over that would slice me to pieces. From the top of the railway mound I could, nevertheless, see 11 Alpha Street through swathes of white hail. From here it looked about the same. A house built of brown-red brick with a rose garden to the front (consisting of little more than pruned stalks at this time of year, sprouting from a bleak oblong of mud). A concrete garage to the side, and trees to the rear that marked the position of the back garden that led down to a stream. A few people walked along the street, their heads covered against the bullet-like hailstones. Above Alpha Street dark clouds boiled in a turbulent sky. Now the sting of hail was getting too much for me up on this exposed hump of earth, forty feet above ground level.

I hadn't the heart to return the way I had come. It would be too much like admitting defeat – and, as God is my witness, I'd had more than enough defeats for one day. So I decided to follow the line of the phantom track a little further to try and find another way down. I'd barely gone a dozen paces when I saw the mound branched off to the right. This branch line, narrower than the main one, disappeared into thick bushes. For some reason I couldn't remember that there had been a fork in the railway track here. But then again I'd always left the railway back at the old gap in the fence to run down the mound to my house. With the hailstones driving harder it suddenly seemed a good idea to get under those bushes where at least the branches should offer some protection. I stooped to walk beneath them, hearing the click of ice particles hitting the wood. Almost immediately, though, the bushes ended as the line of the old railway ran out over an iron bridge. The bridge was only a short one. Perhaps fifteen feet long. What was most peculiar about it was that it ended suddenly in the middle of fresh air, so it resembled a weird iron springboard extending out over a swimming pool. When I leaned over the guardrail I saw that it didn't hang there in space with just one end connected to the earth mound. Steel pillars supported the far end. Probably years ago the bridge had spanned the small river, linking the railway to yet another linear earthwork that ran on through what was now a housing estate. Clearly, the mound had long since been bulldozed out of existence leaving this little iron bridge to nowhere. Even though rusty and overrun with weeds it appeared solid enough. If I walked out on to it and turned south I should be able to see my old home. And from this angle I'd have a view of the back garden where I'd spent so many happy days as a boy.

Along the road at the bottom of the mound a car moved at a crawl. Music boomed from its sound system. My headache beat to the same rhythm. From a building site to the rear of the houses came the scream of power drills. At the other side of the bridge the jackhammers still clattered as they smashed the pavement. The wind blew harder, carrying splinters of sharp hail that felt like spikes being driven into my face. I caught the deeply unpleasant smell of burning plastic. My hip started aching painfully from the blow against the rail earlier. My teeth clicked together I was so cold. And yet still I found myself walking out on that ancient piece of ironwork forty feet above the ground to view a dull brown house I hadn't seen in twenty years.

Ugly, ugly world. I hated the noise – the scream of power tools, the tuneless blast of music from the car. I despised that barren expanse of houses built from cold, dun-coloured brick beneath grim roof tiles. It was so icy it made the exposed skin of my hands and face raw and painful. Good God, a friendless world full of cold; ugliness; discordant, jangling sounds.

I leaned forward, gripping the rust-pitted safety rail in both hands, and at that moment I wanted to scream out to planet Earth how much I hated it.

The music from the car swelled in volume. Hailstones blew out a final flurry as the cloud parted before the force of storm winds. And all the time I stared down at the house where I'd been raised on false promises of a happy future – and I hated it more than I could have thought humanly possible. The April sun finally poured through the rent in the cloud. Sunlight spilled in a flood of gold on to the houses. Brown brick ripened into a luscious warm orange as the light touched it. The music in the car swelled again, resolving itself into a sweeping orchestral piece of melodic beauty and power, while the jackhammers beyond the bridge softened into something that resembled the muffled beat of a human heart. Until then I hadn't noticed the change in wind direction but it had swung to the south immediately transmuting itself into a breath of warm air that carried the scent of wild flowers from the banking.

I'd seen my old home on Alpha Street thousands of times – from north, east, west and south – you name it. But never from quite this angle. From above and the side, looking down on to its roof as if I were a giant. The sun hit the tiles making them shine like precious stones. Bricks shone with a healthy glow all of their own. Trees and bushes were soft pillows of green. The arrangement of windows and door suggested a smiling face.

From utter despair I was transformed, too. A sense of peace, even serenity, flowed through me. Where I'd been cold now I was pleasantly warm. The ache from my bruised side evaporated. Suddenly the world had become a beautiful place. With the swoop of wonderful music from the car came a swell of birdsong that sounded so good to my ears.

And then I realized I was smiling. I was actually standing there on the rusty cut-off bridge, resting both hands on the rail, and smiling a big, happy smile down at the street where I once lived. A car painted a cheerful pink sailed along the road. A large yellow dog gambolled happily on a lawn below. Butterflies danced above lavender-hued flowers.

For how long I hovered there like some kind of angel, hanging suspended above roof top height, I don't know.

Things became a bit vague after that. All I remember was walking up the path to your door. And, still, I felt so happy and relaxed and in such a good mood – which was an impossible mood considering the morning I'd spent at the courthouse.

After telling me about his surreal return journey to his old home he'd said nothing more, merely drank his coffee, while gazing at my dog, which dozed on the rug. I took it he was sifting through his recollection of the experience and left him to it.

At last he turned to me and asked, 'Well, what do you think?'

It would have been insensitive to make some remark about it being a product of acute stress, or asking if he'd perhaps downed a few vodka cocktails after the débâcle at the courthouse. Instead, I answered with a question, 'What do *you* think happened?'

He pondered this for a moment, both hands around the coffee cup, warming his fingers. At last a faint smile flickered across his face as he looked at me. 'A poet once said, *"Behold! I know not anything".*'

'Ah, Tennyson. Wise words. Yes . . . but even if human beings aren't always able to unravel mysteries they are inclined to speculation. Clearly, you *believed* at the time you witnessed something extraordinary.'

'So did I see a mystical transformation of my old home and the street where I once lived? Or is there a more commonplace explanation?'

'That depends on your personality. Any doctor will tell you that an injury will result in the body producing its own natural analgesic to dampen pain.'

'And a psychiatrist would make a similar claim. That if an individual suffers prolonged psychological trauma then the human mind will manufacture some escape from the crisis.'

I agreed. 'Either a retreat into a fugue state or, for most people, the habitual unconsciousness we encounter every night. A good night's sleep is the best cure for stress.'

He gave a grim smile. 'You didn't mention hallucination.'

'Indeed, hallucination.' I nodded. 'And yet there is another explanation. One that is spiritual rather than secular. You'll recall Arthur Machen?'

'Ah, yes. *The Bowman* man.' This time the smile came more readily.

'Well, he experienced something similar after the death of his first wife. He underwent such distress in his state of bereavement that he felt as if his own life was at an end, that he'd never experience happiness or contentment again.'

'I have to say I empathize with the man.'

The experience in court that morning still cast a dark cloud over my friend.

'Machen's spirits were as low as you can possibly get. But then he encountered something that even he couldn't find adequate terminology to express. The best he could articulate was that suddenly reality was transfigured for him; that he encountered "a singular rearrangement of the world". He smelt "great gusts of incense" in the grubbiest of streets. He later wrote that from the depths of depression he felt lifted up until he was "walking on air". In his sitting-room he witnessed pictures on a wall "dissolve and return into chaos". He added that he felt a peace of . . . no, I can't remember the exact words.' I held up my finger as my friend was about to speak. 'Wait, considering what you've experienced this morning it's worth hearing Machen's exact words.' I quickly found the relevant book in my bookcase. A volume I'd read at least a dozen times and regularly dipped into. Quickly, I found the page. 'Ah . . . here. Listen to this. It's important. Machen writes that he was swept by "a peace of the spirit that was quite ineffable, a knowledge that all hurts and doles and wounds were healed. . ." And in the days that followed he fell in love with the world again; in every-day things he once more found "an infinite and exquisite delight. A rapture of life". If that isn't spiritual healing I don't know what is.' I closed the book. 'So how does that compare with what you saw and felt on that old bridge to nowhere this morning?'

He rubbed his jaw, thinking hard. 'I'd say the comparison is uncanny.'

'Machen wasn't alone. These books contain thousands of similar descriptions by writers from different cultures and different ages. This mystical altered state isn't that rare; this sense of one's ordinary surroundings being transformed – *transmuted* – into something extraordinary. Where one glimpses eternity through a sudden transparency of our reality.' I indicated the Van Gogh print on the wall of a cornfield beneath a burning Arles sun. 'Great artists glimpse it, too. See how an energy seems to flow from Van Gogh's sun into the wheat and into the ground itself. As if sun, sky, plants and earth are a conduit for an energy that is as ineffable as it is powerful. Wait . . . aren't you going to finish your coffee?'

He looked at me, his eyes burning with eerie lights. 'I'm going back,' he told me. 'I'm going to see if I can make it happen again.'

'In this weather? It's pouring outside. You'll catch your death.'

'A small price.' His chuckle was a grim one.

'No.'

'Don't you understand? I *need* to go back. I need to prove I didn't imagine it.'

I put my hand on his shoulder, some part of me wanting to hold him down in the chair so he didn't go racing off into the storm, especially not in his exhausted state. Instead, I made the action of resting my hand there on his trembling shoulder a gesture of friendly concern. 'Don't go back there yet. Not until you're rested.'

'But I—'

'Listen. Spend the night here. A good eight hours' sleep will do you a world of good. Besides. I have rack of lamb roasting in the oven, fresh rosemary, heaps of root vegetables and a couple of bottles of Côtes du Rhone that won't drink themselves.'

'But if this is transient? If I'm not back there quickly enough I might never see it again?'

'If what Machen tells us is true, then it will endure far, far longer than any of us. Why not take a large glass of whisky upstairs and have a long hot soak in the bath. I believe I also have a twenty-year-old port in the cellar for later. What do you say?'

He wrestled with the implications. 'What, if when I return to Alpha Street, it's just some plain old street like any other?'

'That's not for us to know.' I poured the whisky. 'But what do you say to this proposition? That both of us go there in the morning? I'm interested in seeing your old home from what is, shall we say, a most singular vantage point?'

For a moment that eerie light blazed in his eyes again and I thought he'd run for the door, but at last he dropped his shoulders with a sigh. 'OK,' he said. 'Tomorrow.'

'Do you see it?'

'No.'

The cold wind cut like a blade. Rain came twisting across the rooftops in veils of sombre grey.

I watched him where he stood at the end of the iron bridge, one hand clutching the safety rail while his intense eyes glared at the house where he'd lived as a child.

'I don't see what I saw yesterday. All I can see are wet houses in a filthy, ordinary street.' With that dark despair in his voice was a barely suppressed rage, too. The man was disappointed beyond belief. He felt cheated.

We'd been standing there on the redundant railway track for twenty minutes. With this depth of cloud cover, the morning had been engaged in a Herculean struggle escaping from night into day. Cold northerlies blew, sometimes driving us back across the bridge toward the forty-foot drop to the river. Now both of us had to keep at least one hand gripped on the rusty rail. Few people had ventured out. One or two cars swished through puddles. Somewhere a power tool droned; a melancholy lost soul sound that did nothing for my nerves. For my friend it must have been a dozen times worse. The good meal accompanied by wine and further embellished by vintage port had helped last night. This morning he'd been eager as a boy jumping out of bed on his birthday. Only now the much-anticipated gift hadn't materialized. And all he could do was stare at the house with those eyes that were so haunted and exhausted and wretched.

'Listen,' I said gently. 'It's there.'

'No. It's gone. Whatever transformed it, it isn't coming back.'

'No, it's *not* coming back.'

'See, I told you—'

'It's not coming back,' I continued, 'because it's still there. That magic; the transformation – that transmutation – however you want to describe it, is just as it was. The only difference is that for the moment you're unable to see it.'

'Not looking from the right angle, am I?' Bitterness rasped in his voice.

'No. Not the right angle. Not a physical angle. But a spiritual angle.'

'Damn.'

For a moment I thought he'd release his grip on the rail and gratefully allow the blast of cold air to carry him backwards across the track and off the edge of the bridge where he'd plunge into the river below. To my friend, death wouldn't be an unwelcome visitor right now. I gripped harder on the rail and placed the flat of my hand in the small of his back, steadying him as the gales shook his body, rippling his coat like a pennant.

'Listen to me,' I said. 'When we are in a bad temper our favourite music becomes a jangling discordant sound that is horrible to hear. We need to approach the music in at least a moderately relaxed state. This is what's happening now. Your mindset isn't receptive to seeing what really exists in the fabric of the street.'

'I'm beginning to doubt if I saw anything at all.'

'Insects can see in the ultra violet. We can not. Imagine just for a moment if your eyes suddenly evolved a new lens allowing you to observe the world in infra red or ultra violet . . . or imagine if you could see gamma rays or X-ray radiation. Imagine how the world would be transformed for you. Something similar happened to you yesterday. Whether it was your frame of mind or Divine intervention we can't say, but just for a few moments the way you perceive the world was miraculously altered. You found yourself seeing not only those houses and bushes and fences down there; you saw the infinite, the eternal. Godammit, man, do *I* have to quote Tennyson at you? Do you remember these lines: "What hope of answer, or redress? Behind the Veil, behind the Veil!" ' I shook him by the shoulder as if trying to wake a sleeping man. '*Behind the Veil!* Don't you see? You've been granted the opportunity to see through the veneer of this world into the next. You are one of the luckiest men alive!'

'Me? *Lucky?*'

'Yes.'

'Are you serious? After the way our so-called legal system wrecked my life yesterday the last word I'd use to describe my present state is *lucky*.'

Furious, he glared down at the road that led under the main bridge. Rain coursed in glistening rivulets down his face. He didn't so much possess eyes but a pair of great open wounds that bled sorrow. Moments passed. The power tool screamed ever more harshly. The wind blew colder. Cloud boiled in great dark waves in the sky. The acres of dull brick houses below were the grimmest of desolate scenes.

Presently, I took a deep breath. 'Maybe we should be getting back to the car, after all.'

He didn't answer. His eyes were locked on his former home. The rain had pasted his hair flat against his skull making it look as if it had been daubed there like paint. His shoulders were shaking.

'We're getting cold,' I told him. 'Come back to my house. At least for the rest of the day.'

He shook his head. A bead of water formed on his eyelashes. Slowly he blinked it away.

'Please,' I said. 'You'll only make yourself ill if you stay here any longer. This rain is getting worse.'

Then, in view of the worsening weather, he said something strange. 'In a moment it will stop.'

'Stop? Look how dark the clouds are. We're in for a deluge.'

I glanced at him . . . then looked again more closely. His eyes were fixed and staring. Uncanny lights flared in the pupils, making them appear as if they were somehow lit from inside his head.

He let out a long breath of air. 'What do you see down there?'

I reeled off the glum list. 'A bridge spanning the road. Water's pouring down the brickwork. The road is half covered by puddles. Lawns are flooding. Pathways are awash. The houses look . . . just look *sad*.'

'Flowers? Blossom?'

'It's raining too hard to see properly. But no . . . nothing.'

'What do you hear?'

'That blasted drill whining away. It's given me one hell of a headache.'

'What can you smell?'

'Smell? Rain. Mud. That's all. No . . . someone's burning plastic or polystyrene. An awful smell. It catches the back of your throat.'

'Don't you see sunlight?'

'No.'

'Can you see roses in full bloom?'

I didn't answer. Merely glanced at him in surprise. And that surrendered to a shudder when I saw the expression transform his rain sodden face. Delight? Happiness? No, more powerful, more biologically visceral than that – rapture. RAPTURE in big, shining capitals. RAPTURE reworked his face into a grinning mask. RAPTURE made his eyes blaze with uncanny fires. Somehow this sudden switch in emotion was more disturbing than I can adequately explain. My stomach squirmed unpleasantly as a hundred shivers dashed down my spine.

'Come on,' I told him while trying to hide my anxiety, 'we need to get away from here.'

He shook his head. Then in a very, very small voice, almost forming the words on a mouthful of air and nothing more, he whispered, 'I can see.' He took a deeper breath. 'Just like yesterday.'

All I saw were rain-lashed houses and a grim suburban street beneath an iron sky. 'I don't . . . nothing.'

'You're not looking properly.' His face told me he gazed on something awesome . . . no, beyond awesome . . . beyond description. 'You have to view the world through an emotion . . . *through* an emotion as if it were a lens.'

'I don't understand.'

Without looking at me he spoke softly. 'When you first fall in love you see the world in a different light . . . through rose coloured spectacles, they say.' He shot me a sudden grin. Then, as if not wanting to miss a second more than he had to of the marvellous landscape, he jerked his eyes down to the windswept Alpha Street. A street that looked nothing but miserable and dull to my eyes.

'Do you see anything yet?' he asked in an awed voice.

'No. Maybe I'm not supposed to see.'

Then he said, 'Close your eyes. Good, that's it; keep them closed. Now cast your mind back to the worst time of your life. The time when the future seemed hopeless and you couldn't see any point in continuing. Have you found it?'

'Yes, it was when my—'

'No, don't tell me! Just keep that memory in your mind. Remember how you felt. How much you hurt. How you despaired. Evoke those emotions. When you feel them again open your eyes.'

For a moment I didn't want to open my eyes. I felt sick to the heart at

135

what I'd just recalled. But at last I did as he asked. I opened my eyes, feeling icy darts of raindrops against my face, blinding me. The power drill was even louder, more nauseatingly raucous. Even when I didn't think it could get worse it did, growing louder – louder, louder. Only as it grew louder it changed. And when it happened I don't know, but I realized it wasn't a power drill at all. It had become a woman singing, in high ethereal notes that swelled then receded on the breeze. A breeze that wasn't as cold as I'd thought. If anything there was refreshing quality to it now. I blinked rainwater from my eyes. The sun had broken through the cloud. It shone on branches and houses and fence posts and the road. The water there must have reflected the light at an unusual angle because it seemed as if a cascade of diamonds had fallen. They covered the neighbourhood in a glittering carpet of dazzling power. In the gardens huge headed roses nodded pinkly. There was blossom after all. I saw it adorning bushes on the railway banking. Luscious lemons, oranges, subtle violets. A wash of gorgeous colours. And now that the sun warmed the blossom it began to exude a beautiful scent that filled my nose. An intoxicating aroma that quickened my heartbeat, making me breathe faster. A sigh of pleasure escaped my lips.

'You see it!' My friend sounded triumphant. 'Tell me! You see it, don't you!'

'Yes . . . *yes!*' I nodded, smiling. The wretched memories I'd evoked of the most miserable period of my life had vanished in a moment. They were replaced by such a feeling of lightness. Of blissful happiness. I wanted to throw my arms around the world and cry out I loved it – and loved everything and everyone in it.

'I'm going down there,' he told me.

'No. This is to be viewed. Not touched. This is as far as our interaction goes. It would – no! *Stay here!*'

But he was gone. Ducking through the bushes, he ran back along the short bridge to where it connected to the mound. Then in a madcap descent he ran down the almost sheer embankment, grasping at shrubs and weeds to stop himself from falling.

Like a drunk going to the assistance of his inebriated friend I followed, determined to help but hardly able to help myself. I was still grinning. I was still bug eyed at the miraculous transformation of what was – what *should* be a drab street on the edge of town. Running back along the bridge, I took my first step on to the rain-sodden slope and fell. As simple as that I shot down on my back as if I was on a snow sled. All the way down forty feet of grass in seconds. A close-boarded fence ran along the bottom of the mound. In that gleeful state (laughing as I careered downward) I saw the best way to stop myself colliding bodily with the fence was to raise my feet and brake myself when I made contact with its timbers. 'Making contact' was more like a crash landing. I didn't feel any pain at the time but I heard a crack and felt part of my anatomy give way in my ankle. My friend had scrambled through a gap in the fence by this time. I could see him through chinks in the boards, running to the home of his childhood. I did my best to follow. And even though there was no pain as such there was an odd numb sensation in my ankle and I found it hard to move quickly. The best I could manage was a slow limp.

Across the street that glittered as if carpeted with diamonds and veined with gold I saw him run. He burst through the gateway to a path that led to the door of his old home. Blossom wafted from the branches by his slipstream, misted the air a delicate pink. Meanwhile, the individual bricks of the house glowed a ripe orange as if they were formed from fresh fruit. Windows shone like friendly eyes; the door as inviting as a pair of open arms.

Even as I struggled to follow him I knew he shouldn't get too close. What we had witnessed was intended to be viewed from a distance. From what I'd read in mystic texts it is plainly no more desirable to physically attempt to interact with this kind of miracle than it is desirable to plunge one's hands into molten glass simply because it appears beautiful.

From an upstairs window a boy gazed out with a happy smile on his face.

My friend turned to me, shouting, while pointing excitedly at the window. *'That's me! That's me when I was twelve!'* He raced up the path to the doorway, raising both hands in front of him to push it open. His hands entered all right. Not opening the door, however, but slipping through *and into* woodwork that glowed with an ineffable light all of its own. He turned to look at me, an expression of wide-eyed shock on his face. Then he seemed to reach a certain understanding. Some secret that had been hidden from him was suddenly made clear. A slow smile spread across his face – one so different from the excited grin on the bridge. This was a smile of acceptance. Satisfaction that the course of events had turned out this way.

He pushed forward with both hands against the door.

As if it was liquid and he was made of dust he began to dissolve into it. I stopped now. Watching him melt. Watching him liquefy. I saw his entire body pass into the fabric of a house transmuted by powers that I can't even begin to understand. I remember so clearly the expression of serene joy on my friend's face as he melted into the door. His essence formed streaks of pink in the door timber. I watched as it expanded, becoming a subtler pink but not vanishing . . . no, never vanishing . . . as it spread like red wine dripped into a large body of water. The ever attenuated pink flowed through the timber frame of the door, growing larger, yet fainter as it spread into brick, then gently flowing across the face of the house, seeping into window frames; then into the panes themselves before expanding across the building to add the faintest pink hue to the gutters and the eaves and the roofing tiles before fusing with the chimney. That tide of pink, so faint that I half suspect I sensed it rather than saw it, flowed into the garden itself, travelling along grass stalks, climbing rose stems to the petals, surging up tree trunks to touch the leaves and breathe a dusting of pink on to white blossom.

It only took seconds. But I saw it all. I saw my old friend's melting release from his cares. I witnessed his peaceful flow into the house and garden that he'd loved as a boy. To become part of it.

Winds shivered the trees. Above me, cloud was breaking, admitting the sunlight into this otherwise commonplace street. A dog barked in a yard nearby. A bus rumbled by, followed by a line of cars.

The magic that had transformed this house and garden was leaving it now. Or if not leaving it, becoming hidden from my gaze. Natural lights were replacing impossible mystical glows. The intensity of the perfumed air was passing. Two boys called to each other as they rode their bicycles toward the bridge.

Pain needled my ankle now. My foot felt tight inside the shoe as the flesh became swollen. I limped back along the road to where I'd parked the car. Then, glancing back at my friend's old home, I saw his face in the window. No. Not quite a face. If anything, a suggestion of a face, a hint, a revenant, as if it were his features reflected faintly in the glass. That image will stay in my mind for as long as I live. I shall always remember that he was smiling as he, or a ghostly image of him, gazed out toward the sawn-off iron bridge. A bridge that is, in one sense, a bridge to nowhere – and yet in a more profound sense – a bridge to everywhere.

7

POND LIFE

This happened when I was ten years old. After thirty years it's easy to fall into the nostalgia trap of talking about the happiest days of your life when you're ten; that summers were warmer, the food tastier, and although television back then only had three channels there was always something worth watching.

At the risk of appearing to don the rose-tinted glasses of nostalgia I'll take you back to a Saturday afternoon in September, just one week after my tenth birthday. I can't remember another day that was just so perfectly sunny. Not too warm; clear blue skies, and with it being Saturday there's the happy thought that Sunday is still to come, which means school on Monday is merely a hazy eventuality in the distance.

So there I was on a sunlit afternoon. If I close my eyes I can picture myself walking across the fields with my best friend Scott Longhurst. If you grow up in the countryside you end up inventing your own entertainment because despite what some might say there's not a lot to do that's fun when you're ten, if all you have is agricultural land surrounding the village where you live. Especially if, like Thorpe Smeaton, that village doesn't boast a shop, a playground or even a park whatsoever. 'Ah, but then there are the fields to play in,' our townie uncles would suggest with a wistful light in their eye. But we'd counter this by saying that you can't play in a field full of cows (there's the stuff they leave underfoot) and arable land is either planted with crops or a ploughed up mud bath awaiting seeding. Besides, farmers have keen eyes and drive children from their fields with all the fervour of driving rats from their barns.

Consequently, village children are often bored. They are so hungry for excitement they take risks.

Now back to Scott and me walking across the field. We carried glass jars in which pink worms squirmed, constantly forming figure of eight shapes with their bodies and threatening to tie themselves into unfathomable knots. We wore jeans, short-sleeve shirts, our shoes might have been black or brown but their original colour was hidden beneath a crust of dirt. These were our 'playing out' shoes so our parents didn't mind the poor state of them as long as they're never brought into the house. Mine lived in a plastic bucket in our garden shed. As we walked we constantly swivelled our heads like a pair of cowboys in Apache territory. We weren't playing anything fanciful. This was a necessity. At any moment there could be a furious, 'Oi, what the bloody hell are you doing!' Then an enraged farmer might charge through the undergrowth.

Scott grinned. 'You're not going to believe what I've found, John. You're going to be amazed.'

'And it's been there all along?' I asked in disbelief.

'It's been there forever. Only nobody from outside has ever seen it.'

'It won't be as good as you say it is.' Some adult-style pessimism touched my heart. 'I bet it's just a bit of marsh with nothing in it.'

Scott held up the jar of contortionist worms. 'You'll need all these. When I saw the pond yesterday it was full of fish.' He laughed. 'Fish soup! That's what it looked like. Millions of fish. When I put my finger in the water they came up and started sucking at it.'

'Really?' A thrill ran through me. 'It really is that good?'

'Just you wait. You're not going to believe your eyes.'

When you're older if things seem too good to be true then they generally are. If a holiday is too happy you suspect ill fortune is lurking just below the surface. Either a flat tyre on a scenic drive, or returning home to find it's been burgled. When you're ten if everything's wonderful then that's just a natural state of affairs – not the quiet before the storm.

Happily, we reached the gap in the hedge without being challenged by an angry farmer. The sun still shone. All the worms in the jar were still perkily alive. We'd both remembered to bring lengths of string that would serve as fishing lines. Let the good times roll.

A cheerful mood filled Scott to the brim. 'Buckers' is just around the corner. Fancy some apples?'

'Yeah, but I don't want to get stung by his bees.'

'It's sunny,' he pointed out. 'They'll all be away from the hive.'

'What if they're not? If you disturb a hive they come out and cover you and sting you to death – everyone knows that.'

An optimism energized Scott. 'It's still worth a try, isn't it?'

I caught that uplift. 'All right then. We can put our shirts over our heads if they attack us.'

Buckers' orchard consisted of about twenty trees that produced nothing but cooking apples. These were huge green things the size of babies' heads, and so sour they'd rip the skin off your tongue. Apart from one tree, that is: a neat-looking tree with smooth bark. Nothing like the cooking apple trees with their shaggy branches and rough bark covering the trunk. The trouble is, the apple tree that produced the sweet apples was surrounded by beehives. They were painted white and resembled boxy gravestones as they stood guard near the tree. This was a tree we'd often discussed because the apples didn't resemble any others we saw grown locally. They weren't red or green but gold. And I mean *gold*. If someone tells you an apple is golden they mean it's a yellowy green. But these apples could have been made out of the gold that makes the rings around your finger. For some reason the bees weren't there to attack us in their thousands. In fact, it was ridiculously easy to walk into the orchard, pull the apples from the tree, stuff one in each pocket, then a third for eating as we walked.

'We should have come here earlier.' I munched at the apple. 'It's the best I've tasted.' And the golden apples were the finest I've ever eaten. No other fruit has come close. They had a subtle, honey-flavour that was sweet without being too sweet. Just like the sunshine everything possessed harmonious qualities. Even the few bees that buzzed back to their hive with cargoes of pollen didn't seem remotely interested in stinging us.

From this vantage point I can look back with hindsight. I want to shout a warning to the ten year old me and to Scott. *'Can't you see? Everything's too good to be true! Don't go any further. Go home . . . go home to your parents!'* But you don't shout warnings to the ghosts of memory, do you? It's too late for that. All you can do is recall what happened next.

'So how do you get in?' I eyed the fifteen-foot-high wall that shone redly in the sun as if it was a veritable cliff face.

'Follow it round,' Scott replied. 'You'll see how.' My friend had a knack of teasing expectation. 'You won't regret going to the trouble once you see how good the pond is.'

We didn't have a publicly accessible pond in our village, merely a grubby little stream that had no fish. So the secret pond that Scott had found became irresistible to me, especially as Thorpe Smeaton bored the children who lived there to the point of insanity. The walled garden lay beyond the extremities of the village at the end of a track nearly half a mile from any other house. Surrounding it were yet more ploughed fields, nothing else. For us kids of Thorpe Smeaton it had always been a mysterious place, forever hidden by its high wall, forever out of reach as the only access gate (also impenetrable) was securely padlocked.

Now Scott had found a way in. Proudly he pointed it out as we rounded a corner of the wall. 'There it is.'

A dead elm tree had toppled at the edge of the track to lean against the wall like an impromptu ladder.

I awarded it a doubtful stare. 'Is it safe?'

'As safe as my little finger with a stick of dynamite tied to it.' Scott grinned. 'Come on, John, take a risk once in your life. You do want to see the pond, don't you?'

' 'Course, I do.'

'Come on, then.'

Walking was impossible now. Instinct drove us to run to the part of the wall where the tree leaned. I had to admit it was conveniently placed. The mouldy trunk leaned at just the right angle for walking up. Even its disease-riddled branches provided handy footholds for anyone wanting to climb it to the top of the wall. *And, dear heaven, did we want to climb it.* My heart beat hard with excitement.

As we stood at the bottom where the trunk had cracked away from the root ball we heard an odd grunting. 'Urrr . . . urrr . . . urrr . . . urrr. . . .'

143

'Oh, bugger,' Scott hissed. 'You know who that is, don't you?'

I glowered. 'Gregory Ripley. What the hell is he doing here?'

Sure enough Gregory Ripley came grunting along the path that followed the exterior of the wall. He was a huge boy for ten, and the only kid we knew who had muscles in his arms like a man. Gregory had been at our school for about a year. Before that he went to some other school that the teachers were coy of mentioning. Everything about Gregory Ripley struck a note of oddness with us. He was the only boy at school to wear short trousers – the cut of the material and the grey colour didn't look right to us either. We had long unkempt hair. His had been cut so short as to be bristly, apart from the very top. Now I'd recognize him as a child with special needs. Back then, all we understood was that he was 'different' – not different in a good way, either. In fact, he scared us though none would admit it. When he first arrived the school bullies mocked his clothes and tried to intimidate him. They didn't frighten Gregory. The boy was uncommonly strong. He never hit the bullies he'd just say with quiet satisfaction, 'Horse bite.' Then he'd grip the bully's shoulder and squeeze with such strength the thugs would sag at the knees as they begged Gregory to let go. Only he tended not to release them for some while. Instead he would intone, 'Horse bite', several more times until the bully croaked for mercy.

On that sunny afternoon Gregory shuffled along the path with a strange mechanical gait and making the grunting sound. 'Urr . . . urr . . . urr. . . .' That wasn't a symptom of any affliction. He made the sound because he loved trucks. Moreover, he had this encyclopaedic knowledge of the component parts of a lorry. His 'Urr . . . urr. . . .' was the sound they made as they lumbered along highways with their heavy loads. As usual he wore grey short trousers and a grey shirt, the same clothes he wore for school. 'Urr . . . urrr. . .' The mechanical steps he took raised a cloud of dust with each jerk forward of the foot. His hands were held out in front of him as if he steered a truck. He didn't show any sign of noticing us until he was just five feet away, then he took his hands off the imaginary steering wheel, put an invisible gear stick into neutral and applied a handbrake neither Scott or I could see.

When he spoke he looked straight ahead. 'Go in, then.'

'Go where?' Scott asked cagily.

'In there.' He nodded at the wall where the tree leaned. 'The pond.'

'We're just hanging around,' I said.

Gregory eyed the jars of worms. 'What's them for?'

Scott shrugged. 'Oh, you know. . . .' And left it at that.

Neither of us had ever been deliberately cruel to Gregory; however his proximity made us uncomfortable. You tended to freeze up when he got close.

'You were going to the pond,' Gregory told us. 'Why would you have worms if you weren't?'

Scott gave the careless shrug again. 'Just worms . . . you know, it's something to do. A laugh.'

'Climb the tree,' Gregory told him.

'Nah. We're on our way home.'

'Climb the tree.'

Scott began to walk away. 'No, like I said, we're off home.'

Gregory pounced. 'Horse bite.' He gripped Scott's shoulder, the boy's expression dissolved with pain.

'Hey,' I shouted. 'Scott's done nothing to you. Leave him.'

'Horse bite.'

'*Gregory*.' Scott dropped the jar of worms. 'You're hurting. . . .'

Gregory's eyes blazed. 'Get up that tree. You two'll get what you deserve in there.'

That was a moment of revelation. Gregory did the horse bite manoeuvre when he was frightened. His only response to fear was to apply that crushing grip.

'You'll suffer in there. It's your turn now after what you've done to me.'

'We've done nothing bad to you, Gregory. Let Scott go.' As I protested I understood something else. Gregory didn't identify individuals. All the kids at school were the same to him. If one threw a stone at him all were guilty in his eyes.

'Horse bite.'

Scott looked as if he'd faint as those powerful fingers dug into his shoulder.

'OK, Gregory,' I cried. 'We're going to the pond.' Then I said the first thing that came into my head to save my friend. 'Come with us. We'll show you how to catch fish.'

The boy's stone-like expression softened. 'Fish?' He released Scott who rubbed his shoulder; there were tears in his eyes. Gregory, however, was still suspicious. 'You're being stupid. You haven't got rods.'

'Don't need 'em,' I responded. 'Look, string.'

He studied both of us. 'You'll catch more than fish in that pond.'

'Why, what's there?'

'Get up that tree. I'll show you.'

Scott was wary of Gregory. 'What have you seen?'

'Not saying. If I do you'll go tell everyone I'm stupid, they'll laugh at me again.'

Scott clearly had a bellyful of adventures for the day. 'I'm not going in there. I'm off home.'

'Climb the tree.'

'No.'

'Horse bite.'

'OK, OK.' Scott picked up the jar of worms from the grass. Luckily the fall hadn't damaged the jar or injured its contents. 'Only, stand back and don't do anything when I'm climbing. OK?'

'Get up there,' Gregory demanded.

Pulling a grim expression Scott climbed the sloping tree to the top of the wall. No doubt he expected Gregory to wait until he was halfway up then grab his foot to make him fall. But all Gregory did was turn to me and say, 'You next. Get up there.'

I remembered the expression on Scott's face as the fingers bit into his shoulder so I didn't argue.

'You'll see what's in there, you two. It's more than fish. And you'll deserve what happens to you after what you did to me.'

Scott whispered so Gregory wouldn't hear. 'But we've done nothing to him. Why's he like this?'

I shrugged. 'Someone said Gregory fell on his head when he was a baby.'

'Get in there. Get to the pond.' Gregory engaged the gears of invisible motors and brummed his way up the tree.

'You don't want to be up on the wall when he gets here,' Scott warned. 'Bugger might push us off.'

For a moment I stood on the fifteen-foot-high wall. Behind me were the ploughed fields that laid siege to Thorpe Smeaton. They were bleak corrugations of soil, a muddy desert that forbade any kind of trespass. On the other side of the wall, however, lay the secret garden, with its equally secret pond. This was a lush, green world of bushes, trees, long grass and flowers that had been allowed to grow wild for years. Through a billowing mass of trees I caught a glimpse of a derelict house. There were no tiles on the roof and I could see blackened timbers.

'Scott,' I marvelled, 'it must have burnt down. Do you think anyone got killed?'

'Bugger that,' he grunted, 'Gregory is nearly here.'

Scott stepped down from the wall on to the timber roof of a shed inside the secret garden. In turn that led to a ladder that someone had propped against the end of the building. Encircled by a halo of brilliant green bushes lay the pond. It glistened there like a huge emerald. A kind of electric green that was the brightest green I've ever seen.

'John?' There was a warning note in Scott's voice.

Behind me the 'Urr . . . urr . . .' grew louder. In a moment Gregory might intone 'Horse bite' before grabbing me by the shoulder, giving it a bone crushing squeeze for good measure, then chucking me from the wall. I did what at the time appeared to be the sensible thing: I followed Scott's route via the shed roof into the secret garden.

Once I'd descended the ladder into the knee-deep grass, the excitement of being in that hitherto hidden world intoxicated me. Carrying my jar of worms, I ran to the pond to stare at it in awe. Its emerald colour was a gift of the willow trees and bushes that encircled it. Dragonflies hovered above the surface; iridescent flashes of electric blue.

Scott joined me. 'Look, did you see it?'

'See what?' Dazzled by all that beauty I tried to take in everything at once.

'Kingfisher. You never see 'em properly. They look like flickers of turquoise.'

'Is there fish in there?'

'See for yourself.'

'Bloody hell.' I gaped. There, beneath the surface, weren't just shoals of sticklebacks there were swarms of them. What's more, they didn't dart away when a human's head loomed over the water. They slowly finned among a multitude of their kind. Not only were these the greatest number of sticklebacks I'd seen in a pond they were the biggest I've ever

147

set eyes on. 'Look at 'em,' I breathed. 'Some as big as your hand.'

'Where's Gregory?' Scott still wore a pained expression when he rubbed his sore shoulder.

'Up on the shed. He's just sat there watching us.' I turned back to Scott. 'He shouldn't have done the horse bite on you. You've never done anything to him.'

Scott shook his head. 'My Dad even stopped to give him a lift home when it was raining, though I told him not to bother.'

'What did Gregory say?'

'He said the car wasn't big enough to drive his lorry into.' For the first time since the horse bite Scott smiled. 'Why do you suppose he really believes he's driving a lorry?'

'Search me.' Then more important thoughts intruded. 'Where's the best place to fish?'

'See the bushes. There's little paths that lead to willows with trunks that go out over the water like piers. Get on one of those, tie the string round a worm then lower it in.'

For the next twenty minutes I indulged my dream of fishing. The pond wasn't much more than fifty feet across and it was as much a secret body of water as the secret garden that concealed it. You reached the fishing spots by following a short path to a willow tree that lay flat on the water; simple enough to walk a few paces out over that liquid emerald, sit astride the branch like you were riding a bike, loop the string round a worm then lower the wriggling blighter into the water. Within seconds I pulled stickleback after stickleback out of the pool. They were so greedy for the worms that once they bit into the flesh they didn't let go. I'd already emptied the worms into a hollow in the wood to keep them safe, so that freed up the jam jar, which I'd filled with water for the fish. They were beautiful silvery specimens with those distinctive needle-like spines that poked from their backs – the stickleback defence mechanism.

Soon I found myself lost in that secret world, the pond absorbed my attention. All I can say for sure is that the sun still shone from a blue sky, Scott fished out of sight on another willow branch nearby, Gregory probably still sat on the shed, and I slowly munched on a golden apple from Buckers' orchard.

'You've seen it. Why haven't you said anything?' Gregory's voice dragged me out of my blissful world of fishing.

'Careful,' I said. 'The branch's moving.'

Gregory took another step out on to the limb of the willow tree where I sat with my feet dangling just an inch above the water. Gregory was built more like a man than a child. His weight made the branch convulse as he moved along it. He didn't respond to my warning, instead he stared at me with that old expression of suspicion he wore at school, when he thought the other kids were making fun of him.

'Gregory, we'll both fall in if you don't go back.'

'You've seen it in the water. Why aren't you saying anything?'

Scott's voice sounded across the water. 'John, are you all right?'

'Gregory is on the branch with me. He won't go back.'

Gregory's eyes had a stone-like quality. Not only cold but somehow dead-looking. 'Why didn't you tell me you saw it in the water?'

'See what it in the water?' I asked puzzled. 'You mean the fish?'

'Not fish. What's lying in the bottom. What did this to me.' He lifted the grey shirt to reveal a huge bruise across his stomach.

'Gregory, this branch won't hold the two of us.'

'First, you tell me what you've seen.' He pointed into the pool.

'Fish, bits of weed . . . what do you think's in there?'

'You look. You tell me.' He edged forward where I sat astride the branch. 'If I say what's there you'll tell the others so they'll laugh at me.'

'Gregory—'

'Horse bite.'

'OK, OK, I'm looking.' Gripping the branch, I leaned out to peer into the pool that reflected the brilliant green willows. 'You've got to give me a clue, though.'

'If I hold you by your feet I can lower you in so you can get a proper look.'

'Not on your life! You'll drown me.'

He inched nearer. 'You'll be safe. I'll hold on hard. I'll bring you back up when you've told me what's at the bottom of the pond.'

Now, this unnerved me. No way would I trust anyone to lower me by my feet headfirst into a pond – least of all Gregory. I called out. 'Scott? Are you there?' I managed to climb to my feet; the branch shook wildly now. Any second both of us would topple into the water.

'Look in the bloody pond.' Gregory's voice possessed a strange flatness.

'Look in. Tell me what's underwater. There. . . .' He showed me the huge dark bruise on his stomach again. 'There's proof if you don't believe me.'

I grabbed another branch that was level with my head to steady myself. As I did so I stared into the water. What had Gregory seen? Maybe someone had dumped an old bike in there? But did that account for the bruise? Yet all I could see were fish and pondweed.

Gregory shuffled closer; a big figure, bristling with menace. 'Look properly. Tell me what it is.'

'Bloody hell, Gregory, I don't see anything.'

'Can.'

'Can't.'

'I'll put your head in the water, then you'll see.'

'Tell me what it is.'

'The robot.'

'Robot?' Then I made the fatal mistake. I laughed out loud. Any other kid who claimed there was a robot in the pond would say it as a joke. Not Gregory, though. He never joked – and no one laughed in his face.

He leapt forward. The branch creaked. 'You knew all along.' The growl became savage. *'You knew and you didn't tell me because you wanted it to hurt me.'* Now our combined weight forced the branch to dip until the end of it struck the water.

All I could do was retreat from Gregory who intoned accusations as he worked his way along the branch. By now I felt like the cabin boy who'd been forced to walk the pirates' plank. Just another five feet of branch left then it was either swim for it or fight Gregory. I saw the muscles bulge in his biceps and I knew I'd end up in the pond one way or another. I stepped over the glass jar that I'd wedged into a fork in the branch. Water slopped as Gregory's movements shook it. I called to Scott wondering what had happened to him.

And constantly Gregory spoke in a monotone. 'You knew it was in there. You let me come in here so you could watch it hurt me.'

'Gregory, there isn't a robot in the pond. Listen to me.'

'You knew the robot was there. Men in the big house made it. When a fire burnt the house down it hid in there.' His dead eyes regarded the pool where the dragonflies darted. 'It waited till I got close then it reached out and grabbed me by the stomach. I had to fight as hard as I could to get away. It hurt me. You wanted it to happen so you could watch and laugh at me. You only got me to come back in here so it could attack me again and kill me, because that's what it said. Now you're going to feel how much it hurts when it grabs you.' And on, and on. . . .

'Scott!' I yelled. 'Help me!'

Then the branch really did began to dance. And what happened next happened so fast it's taken me years to process the sequence inside my head. Scott ran along the willow's limb shouting at Gregory. Gregory shoved me, no doubt wanting me to fall into the pool, but I went head-first into another fork in the branch. My head struck the thick timber. Pain? I'd never known pain like it. It tore through my skull like lightning. The apples I'd eaten tried to charge out through my throat in one sear-ing lump. There were thinner branches at either side of me. They supported my body so I lay flat on the timber just inches above the pond. Gregory pointed into the water; he kept shouting that the robot was coming up; that it would attack us; he could see its iron claws breaking the surface.

At the same time Scott toppled backward into the water. Gregory kept his balance, arms straight out at either side, his dead eyes fixed on the swirl of liquid emerald.

I blinked against the sunlight. Water whooshed. A rumble sounded like empty oilcans rolling across a concrete floor. The sun burnt through my eyes into the back of my head. The pain wouldn't leave my skull. For a moment I thought I sat in the classroom with my head rest-ing on the desk. All the kids were yelling, stamping, alarm bells ringing, Mr Leyland boomed, 'Homework back by Monday, or face my wrath. David O'Connor, you will see me after class.' Why couldn't I lift my head from the desk? I felt so dizzy I seemed to be permanently toppling over.

With a huge effort I raised my head.

'The robot,' Gregory said. 'See it, you two. I told you. It's going to hurt you like it hurt me.'

And there it was. I raised my hand to shield my eyes from the sunlight as the robot reared out of the pool. Water sluiced off it, along with the black muck that lies in the bottom of ditches and ponds everywhere. I could smell its stink. The robot cut a dark silhouette against the sun. It seemed to be made of interconnecting cylinders; its torso could have been a petrol tanker standing on end, while from its barrel-sized head twin eyes blazed at me like a car's headlamps.

Gregory chanted in monotone. 'It's coming for you now. It's going to hurt you . . . it's going to squeeze you hard. Horse bite, only worse. You're going to scream it's that bad.'

The robot loomed over me its metal pincers reaching out. It had lain in the pond for so long weed grew from it to create a green, shaggy brute of a thing. Water snails formed a rash of black spots across its inhuman face, and that stink of pond slime . . . I gagged on it. My mind spun as vertigo dragged at me, and my head hurt like all the bones had shattered in my skull.

'See how you like it,' Gregory's monotone bored through my brain. 'See what it's like to be hurt so bad you stop sleeping. It's going to break you into pieces.'

The robot stooped over me. Then in a metallic whisper it breathed my name in a foul-smelling miasma. *'John. . . .'*

I howled in terror.

'John. I'll get you. . . .'

In blind panic, I searched the branch for a weapon. If only I could rip a piece of wood away to use as a club. All I could find, however, was the jar with the sticklebacks. With vertigo nearly toppling me, I snatched it up. But what use is a glass jam jar against a huge robot?

'John.' It breathed my name again as its weed-covered visage loomed toward me. I swung the jar in my fist. I aimed for the barrel of a head but my blow landed lower. Instead of a clang of glass against steel I only heard the sound of the jar shattering.

Dizzily, I scrambled along the branch. When I looked back I realized the robot was far smaller than I first thought. It stood waist deep in the pond. For a second my mind blanked. When I opened my eyes again that water, which had been the loveliest emerald I'd ever seen, had turned red. A deep, deep red that spread out across the pool. I'd killed the robot. I must have, because it had gone.

As I regained my mental equilibrium after that stunning blow I saw only Scott. He stood waist deep in the water. It should have been laughable because he was festooned with pond weed; mud smeared his face. Only he didn't move. He merely stared with bright, glassy eyes. One hand clutched the side of his neck. Blood streamed from a wound in his flesh. It fed the pond with more red, transforming it into a vat of crimson that reflected the disc of the sun.

Somehow I made it past Gregory, who remained like a statue on the branch as he stared at Scott. By the time I moved back through the willows Scott finally began to sag until he lay flat in the water. Gregory remained perfectly still as he watched the floating body.

Nothing is clear in my mind after that. Only climbing into bed that night as my mother called up to me, 'John? Scott's mother's here. She's worried about him. Have you seen Scott today?'

And my reply, 'No. Not at all.'

On the Monday everything was different at school. There were no lessons. We had prayers in the hall. After lunch we sat with our books but nobody was in the mood to read. Some of the kids were crying. Only Gregory took an interest in his book, a big photo-history of trucks. He studied every page in minute detail. Presently the headmistress came into the class with two policemen in uniform. They whispered to Mr Leyland for a moment, then they crossed the classroom floor toward me. I waited for them to say my name. When they uttered it I knew I'd shout out – it wouldn't be words it would be a terrible yell. Their footsteps grew louder. I stared at the page of the book. The print slid in front of my eyes; a smell like stagnant ditchwater filled my nostrils.

Then one of the policemen spoke. 'You were at the pond with Scott on Saturday, weren't you?'

Mr Leyland murmured apologetically, 'He doesn't always understand straight away.'

The policeman repeated his question,. 'Gregory, you were at the pond with Scott on Saturday, weren't you?'

Gregory gave a slow nod. His face bore no expression whatsoever.

'Gregory,' said the teacher, 'don't be frightened. These policemen want you to go with them.'

The boy with the dead eyes stood up, closed the book, then walked silently out of the classroom. The policemen followed. Whatever happened to Gregory I don't know but he never returned to the school.

Now I spend my free time sitting at the edge of the pond. Whether or not there really is a robot lying in the silt at the bottom is neither here nor there. What really matters is that one sunny afternoon thirty years ago this secret garden robbed me of my best friend and my capacity to enjoy life. So until a robot emerges from the slime, or hell freezes over, or pigs decide that this is a good time to fly, my peace of mind will forever be held captive by those cold emerald waters.

8

SHE LOVES MONSTERS

- Or the quest for lost *Vorada*

1   EXT. FOREST – DAY
LONG SHOT. A silver BMW speeds along a deserted forest road. The prestige car and the confident driving is the consummate expression of its owner's personality: **I come. I see. I conquer.**

CUT TO:

2   INT. MONTAGE – DAY
UNASSIGNED CAMERA. Camera drifts fluidly through rooms and along corridors decorated with marble statues to find CHRISTOPHER LAKE lying on his bed. Silence – as in a tomb. He stares at the ceiling. It appears we find him moments after his death. An audience APPLAUDS and CALLS out. The EERIE NOTES of an ACCORDION introduce the song AMSTERDAM by Jacques Brel. The MUSIC comes from a laptop computer. On its screen colours oscillate to provide a visual response to VOICE and MUSIC. CHRISTOPHER LAKE slowly blinks to break the appearance of death. He doesn't move, but continues to lie there, staring at the ceiling. The camera glides away to exit the room, enter the corridor then drift along, as if this is POV of a spirit visitor. It approaches a window that has views of trees and evening sky. There it stops as the music swells.

CUT TO:

3   INT/EXT. CAR/FOREST – DAY
During following CUT between exterior and interior of JACK
CALNER'S BMW. MUSIC OVER, continuing seamlessly from scene
number 2. AMSTERDAM grows in VOLUME and quickens in pace as
JACK CALNER pilots the car along the road as if it's a missile. The
epitome of self assurance – this is a man on a quest. Ahead, a sign for
a cattle grid. He brakes, not violently, but enough to allow the car to
cross the grid in safety. . . .

ONE

This is the first time I've hit a woman before.

She asks for it. I mean, she *really* does ask for it. In fact, I can't even
stop myself. *Pow!* She's sprawling in the dirt. She's rolling over, her arms
flung out, hair spilling wildly. And did I tell you she's naked? Not a stitch.
Not a thread. Nothing on her bare body but scratches and a bruise the
size of an open hand on her gleamingly nude hip.

That's the first time I hit a woman. It happens as I'm driving to a house
that's been mine for ten months, but I've never clapped eyes on it, never
mind set one foot across its expensive threshold. It's the biggest asset I
own. Thank you, Dad, for putting it just beyond reach. Look up the defi-
nition of 'tantalize' in the dictionary and you'll know the mood I'm in
when I strike her down.

I'd been driving for six hours. After passing through the mountains
and forests of Cumbria, one of the rare wilderness tracts of England, I'd
just had my first teasing glimpse of Montage with its spires, green domes
and red chimneys – my Montage; bequeathed to me in my father's last
will and testament. The sun was setting. I could see the red light reflected
in the windows like the house – *my house* – was filled with fire. A sign
told me a cattle grid lay ahead, so I braked. A second later the woman ran
from the trees on to the road and – **BANG!** I saw her naked body roll up
over the bonnet of the car. Her bare hip struck the windscreen, turning
it into a spider's web of radiating lines.

SO THIS HAPPENS NOW: I climb out of the car with the intention

156

of walking back to where she's lying on the road. She's on her side with her back to me. She's a slim woman with long legs and longish brown hair that's splashed out across the blacktop. Even though I see the scratches, EVEN though I see the bruise on her hip, **EVEN** though I see she's not moving, I'm angry. I feel searing rage. I mean, my God, what a crazy thing to do! I don't give a damn about her running through the countryside so she can expose her nakedness to the elements, but couldn't she at least ensure there's no traffic when she cavorts into a road?

The woman's maybe thirty paces from me. Still she's not moving. Now there's just a whisper of a possibility that she might be dead. What do you do with a nude corpse? How do you report such a find to the police? How do you convince them that you haven't killed her for the fun of it?

Ten paces from my car and some twenty-five from the woman, my mobile phone rings. That's a good reminder. Call an ambulance. This nude marathon runner isn't my responsibility.

I slip the phone from my belt. A glance at the screen reveals it's my business partner. No doubt he's keen for a progress report – more specifically: *Jack, do you have your hands on the film yet?*

'Not now, Steiger,' I say by way of greeting. 'I've just killed a woman.'

'You've done what?' Steiger's normally placid tones rise in shock from the phone's speaker.

I'm still angry and continue in a no-nonsense way, 'She ran out of the trees. Straight into the car. And just wait until you hear this, Steiger: she's not wearing a stitch of clothes.'

'Jack, come on. You're in a bar, and you're telling me all this crap because you're stinking drunk and think it's hilarious.'

'No. Steiger. Listen to me. She slammed into the car. I thought she'd come right through the windscreen into my face.'

Steiger's voice rips from the speaker with enough force to make me hold the phone from my ear. 'Don't do anything stupid, Jack. Don't hide the body. Call the police. Tell them everything. And that means the truth!'

'You think I've a reputation for lying?'

'You've a reputation for being ruthless, so don't—'

'Wait. Steiger, she's moving.'

'Thank God for—'

I stop taking an interest in what Steiger's shouting from the phone as I say the first thing that comes into my head. And it's nothing to do with putting the accident victim's needs first. 'What the hell were you playing at? Have you seen the damage to my car? Hey! I'm talking to you. *Hey!*'

The sun's so low that the light's in my eyes, while the woman appears to lie in a vale of shadows. She doesn't so much as stand as move forward on all fours – a feline movement, a girl panther slinking away from the scene of its kill. That's the impression that darts through my head.

'Jack? What's happening? What's she doing?'

I don't reply as I break into a run after the woman. I don't want to console her, or ask if she's hurt. I want to give the idiot a full-blooded shaking while I yell 'You lunatic! Why the hell did you run into my car!' But like a panther she just sort of breezes away into the trees. By now she must be running on two legs rather than all fours. When I reach the section of road, where her nude body had lain sprawled out with that hand-sized bruise on her hip, there's nothing much to see. I catch glimpses of her as she sprints away through the trees, her hair fluttering out. Wicked little snatches of bare buttocks, gleaming legs, lithesome torso.

'You idiot. You stupid, crazy idiot!' I roar these words after her. 'Hey, listen to me. You're a lunatic. You should be locked up!'

'Jack!'

'You've wrecked my car! You've got to pay! Do you hear? You stupid, little—'

Panther-girl has vanished back into the wilderness. I stand there panting. I wait for a the flash of naked skin to reappear.

'Jack!' The voice of my old friend shrills from the speaker. *'Jack! Whatever you're doing to her, stop it! Leave her alone!'*

I stand there feeling my heart thump in my chest. What a way to end a journey. Six hours of monotonous driving then this happens. Naked woman strikes car. Naked woman runs away into wilderness forest. Naked woman vanishes.

'Jack? Jack!'

At last my friend's voice registers. I lift the mobile to my ear. 'Steiger?'

'Jack? What've you done to her?'

'I know what I'd like to do to her.'

'Jack?'

'It's all right, she's run off. Listen. I'm a couple of minutes from Montage. I'll give you a call then.'

'If they let you in, Jack.'

'Oh, they'll let me in, all right.'

'You do realize they're not going to welcome you in with open arms?'

I feel the smile on my face. 'You know me, Steiger.'

'Yeah, only too well, Jack.'

'Speak to you later.'

'Get there safely . . . and good hunting.'

'I don't think I could catch her now.'

'I'm not talking about naked strangers, Jack. You know what I mean.'

'Don't hold your breath, Steiger. Treasure hunting takes time.' I return the mobile phone to my belt clip then walk back to the car. I'm scanning the forest all the time for the beautiful creature that made such an impression on my car's bodywork.

There's nothing. There isn't even any traffic. I haven't seen another car or truck in ten miles. After five wasted minutes of waiting for the naked runner to magically reappear I climb into the car. I find a piece of the crumpled windscreen I can see through and drive in the direction of Montage, the finest piece of real estate I own. Yeah, remember to look up the word 'tantalize' – and 'tease' while you're at it. As a poet might say, 'So near, yet so far away.'

TWO

For the entire six hours of the drive to this wilderness I'd expected to be turned away. Oh, yes they were expecting me. They know who I am. They've been told Jack Calner's on the road to Montage. All the more reason, then, to lock all doors and untie the hounds.

Sure enough, there's a man waiting at the gate. This is it, I tell myself. By the hairs of his chinny-chin-chin he's not going to let me in. Only instead of turning me away the man can't wait to welcome me. He advances through the open gates while waving me through. He's about sixty with hair that's shines like chrome rather than silver. On his face, along with wire-rimmed spectacles, is the beaming smile of an avuncular monk. He doesn't appear to notice my crumpled windscreen or dented bonnet, or he doesn't care. Everything's nice by this man. For him the world must be an eternally happy place.

I scroll down the window with a clipped, 'You know who I am?'

'Mr Calner, yes. Miss Lake asked me to wait for you, so I can direct you to the house.'

'I've just gone and found it, haven't I? Correct me if I'm wrong, but it's that geometric object with doors, windows and a dirty, great roof. Aren't I right, Jeeves?'

'Oh, my name's not Jeeves.' The man's smiling so broadly I'm surprised he doesn't do himself a mischief. 'I'm called Bunny.'

'All butlers should be called Jeeves. It saves having to remember their names.'

'I'm not a butler, Mr Calner, I'm—'

'Look. I'm not interested. I've been driving all afternoon. As you can see my car's taken a beating. I want a drink, then I have to call out a garage to replace my windscreen that some lunatic tried to dive through – hey, leave the car alone, you're not going to be able to fix it. Did you hear me, buddy? Hands off.'

'It's not *Buddy*, sir. My name's Bunny.'

'OK, Bunny. Take your fingers away from my car.'

'But this was wrapped around the wiper, Mr Calner.'

Bunny smiles happily all through this exchange of pleasantries (and if you know me, these are pleasantries as far as I'm concerned). Now he holds out strands of hair that he's unhooked from the bent wiper.

'Uh-ho. Souvenir,' I tell myself, rather than this grinning boyo. She's left some of her mane behind. After taking the hair from him I allow the evening breeze to take the long wisps from my fingers. Strangely, the moment they float away I wish I'd held on to them. Why? I don't know. Suddenly it seems important to preserve them. Recollection of the naked woman running away into the forest still blazes bright as a chunk of the noonday sun between my ears. As I debate retrieving them the mobile rings. My accountant. I bark into it: 'Not now, Harry! Call me back in the morning.' Instead of chasing through bushes in pursuit of the girl's tresses I turn my guns back on to Buddy, Bunny, Jeeves – whatever they call Mr Happy here. He's leaning forward to smile into the car; his face is as shiny and as pink as a baby's. Must be the neighbourhood idiot.

I warn him, 'If you don't want me to run over your foot, keep back.'

He smiles, dips his head, nodding. 'Follow me up to the house. Mr Calner.'

160

'Follow?'

'I'll show you where to go.'

'Hell. I can see the bloody house. It's right there. Fifty yards away. I'm hardly going to take a wrong turn into Death Valley, am I?'

'Miss Lake was concerned for your safety. She asked me to wait for you and guide you in.'

'Dear God.' I can't stop laughter bubbling out of my mouth. I do try but despite the six hour journey, despite nearly killing a naked woman, despite Loony Tune here I've got to laugh out loud. 'Guide me in! Is there some complex docking procedure when I reach the house?'

'No, sir.' He chuckles happily with me. His blue eyes are alight with merry twinkles. 'No docking, sir. But just behind the lilac there's a bridge over a stream and it's seen better days. If you don't drive along the main timbers your car might go through the planking.'

'You are joking, aren't you?'

'Why should I tell you something that isn't true, Mr Calner?'

'All right. I believe you, Jeeves.'

'It's Bunny, sir.'

'Start walking, Jeeves. I'll follow.'

The man still smiles as he begins what I can tell is an important task in his mind. He's guiding me to Montage. He's going to do everything in his power to prevent my lovely, but wounded car falling through the bridge into the stream. He's there to keep me safe from danger. What a hero! What an adventure! I can't wait to tell Steiger about this. Once more I'm laughing as I ease the car forward in Bunny's footsteps.

But here I am at last. This is Montage. My house. My biggest asset. I want it back in my hands. And if I don't extract what I need from the parasites that live here that's exactly what I'll do.

In the growing darkness I follow the pale blob that is jolly Bunny. He makes little waving motions with one hand as I crawl the car forward. It's as if he's gently encouraging me: Come along, Mr Calner. Don't be frightened. Keep moving. *I'll get you safely there.* The idiot. I imagine what it would be like to floor the accelerator and allow the car to surge over him, breaking every happy bone in his body. 'Will you be smiling then, Mr Happy Bloody Bunny?'

Spanning the stream, a timber bridge that's barely longer than the car itself. The mere trickle of a brook lies about two feet beneath the timber supports. Jeeves, goes to a lot of trouble to inch me across the bridge as he points to the boards I should follow ... so the car doesn't plunge through. Note to self: once I reclaim possession of the house, replace bridge. Rustic stonework would be more impressive than timber.

The phone rings again. I check the screen as I inch the car forward over Danger Bridge (feel free to insert sarcasm icon of choice). I switch off the phone, lob it into the backseat. 'Not tonight, Rebecca. I'm taking care of business.' Then I lean out of the window to call, 'Are we nearly there yet?'

Flashback: Being driven through this county by Dad when I'm six years old. I'm asking the man in the driving seat the same question: 'Are we nearly there yet?' And he replies, 'That we are, Jack. See the field over there? That's where I'm going to build our house. I'm going to call it Montage.'

Montage – a little bit of everything. Italianate, Moorish, Gothic, English Elizabethan, American post-modern. An architectural potage.

'You built the house, Dad, but we poor schmucks never got to visit. You handed it over to your loony friend.'

Smiler is now waving me forward to park on the gravel turning area at the front of the house. The only other vehicle there is a truck with the words LOCATION CATERER TO THE STARS just visible through a plague of rust on its side.

That one-mile-per-hour creep makes my right foot ache. It's a relief to press the pedal down and roar the last few yards to park outside the front door. Bunny hurries up as I climb out of the car.

I ask him, 'Where will I find Christopher Lake?'

'Oh, he'll be asleep by now, Mr Calner.'

'At eight o'clock? The sun's only just setting?'

'Miss Lake asked me to show you to your room.'

'Don't you mean guide me to my room?'

He carries on smiling like I'm the loveliest guy in the world. Not someone hell-bent on making him homeless – if I don't get what I want.

'Once you've freshened up I'll take you down to meet Miss Lake.'

I grunt. 'I'll be able to find the lounge by myself. Unless there are any dangerous bridges indoors to cross?'

'No, nothing like that, sir. But it is a big house.'

'Glad to hear it. At least my father did one thing right.'

'Sir?'

'Never mind. Lead on, Jeeves.'

'My name's Bunny, sir.'

And after all my sulphuric comments the man's still smiling.

'Just show me my room.' I pull my weekend bag from the backseat. When I see the depression in the bonnet created by the woman's naked body impacting the car it's enough to send the blood blazing through my veins. 'Find me a glass on the way. I've a very nice single malt. I don't plan drinking something as expensive as that from the bottle.'

THREE

Bunny takes me to the guest room. It lies beneath the dome in one corner of the house. He never stops smiling. Bunny's either the happiest man in the world, or his doctor needs to prescribe something a little less powerful. I mean, surely this guy has to be gorging on some powerful pharmaceuticals to make him so unrelentingly cheerful? At the door of the room I glance back as he stands at the top of the stairs. With the electric light shining on that abundantly silver hair of his he appears more like a saint than a genial monk now. If wincingly cute little bluebirds alighted on his arms I shouldn't have been in the least surprised.

'Everything you need is in your room, Mr Calner.'

'I doubt everything,' I tell him as I step inside. 'Be back here at nine on the nail. I'll see Miss Lake then.'

He utters words I don't catch as I shut the door in that genial face. The dent in my car still infuriates me. So, first things first, I pull the whisky from my bag then pour a meaty slug into the glass on the bedside table. Once I've rolled a mouthful of that wonderful single malt across my tongue, and swallowed with a grateful sigh, I take more notice of my room here in Montage. As I said, it's under the bronze dome that thrusts up with phallic splendor from the corner of the house. '*Dad, I've got to ask, did you ever read Freud?*' The ceiling echoes the curve to create a rising vault above my head. The room is richly furnished. There's a large bed with an ornate iron frame that sports finials, which resemble lotus flowers. Beneath my feet there's an antique Persian rug. Before I leave I'll make an inventory of the furnishings. I probably inherited those with the house. The walls are painted sunflower yellow and the lantern hanging down from the convex ceiling is a Moorish style lamp in polished brass. Mine, too.

I check the bathroom. Dated, but it'll banish road dust.

Another swallow of whisky and I take a look out through the window. It's nearly dark now. I don't see any lights from other houses, an absence that suggests there are no neighbours for miles. What I can see of the road is deserted. This is the ideal rustic retreat. What sticks in my throat is that it's become a lunatic asylum for one. A solitary madman. Dad left me holding the baby. That's the phrase that lingers irritatingly in my head.

I gaze up at the ceiling as I raise the glass of malt in a toast. 'I'm here, Dad. I've made it to Montage. Cheers.' I take a deeply satisfying swallow. Those Scots got something right when they called their liquor 'the water of life'. It energizes. I smile at my reflection in the wall mirror. I've got the same shaped eyes as my late departed, gone to the hereafter, father. But they're not soft like is. They're hard. Hard as tungsten. And I tell you now that is a feature I'm proud of. If Dad's loopy friends don't co-operate they're going to learn the hard way that, for once, the maxim 'Father like son' won't run true.

FOUR

After a brisk shower I dress for power not for comfort. A charcoal Armani suit, white shirt, a narrow necktie in dark blue. Shoes are important. From my bag I extract black leather brogues that have been buffed until they shine like gunmetal. Bunny knows the meaning of punctuality. On the stroke of nine he escorts me downstairs to meet Miss Lake in a lounge that's cavernous enough to double as a Zeppelin hanger. This room is in the classical Greek style with marble columns and statues of Gods and heroes armed with spears. They stand along the walls, guarding Montage against intruders like me. On the ceiling a painted Zeus is hurling lightning bolts across a turbulent sky. Enemies are well and truly smited. The place smells of garlic. I hate garlic.

'Mr Calner,' Bunny intones with a beatific smile. 'Miss Lake won't be a moment.'

'I'd rather hoped she'd be here to meet me. This isn't a social call.'

Bunny doesn't so much walk out of the room but withdraws backward from it with a smile and a slow bobbing of the head. It irritates that the Lake woman isn't here waiting; however, it gives me a chance to examine the statues. They've got to be copies; nevertheless, they'll still be valuable. By the French doors is a naked goddess with a rear that is nothing less than Olympian. Now, there's a bottom that should be the Eighth Wonder of the World. With a smile I move on. I'm examining the carving of Apollo, standing with his chin up, adopting a noble stance in his warrior's helmet, when I hear footsteps on the mosaic floor.

'Mr Calner.'

I turn to see woman . . . no, a girl. She approaches me with all the confidence of a fawn approaching a grizzly bear. She's slim with dark hair tied back into a pony tail. An orange flower is pinned above her left ear. Her eyes are brown and so large that they accentuate the thin face – the kind of face some fanciful people might describe as elfin. She's made an effort to be decorous even, though she's not displaying any jewelry, whatsoever. She's wearing a bright turquoise dress with electric blue swirls. It reaches below her knees and buttons halfway up her neck. Women calibrate their fashions with their peers. This woman – this girl – clearly has no peers. She lives out here in the wilderness and copies fashion designs from magazines that have been lying under a sofa for decades. Anyway, to cut away the fudge of superfluous descriptions: here is a shy girl with an apprehensive smile dressed in peculiar hippy fabrics. I can't wait to see Mr Lake, if the daughter's anything to go by.

'Mr Calner?' she repeats.

'Yes.'

'Hello. I'm Venus Lake.'

'Venus?' I frown. 'You're not Christopher Lake's sister?'

She smiles nervously. 'Yes, I am.'

'You're younger than I expected.'

'Thank you.'

'It wasn't intended to be a compliment.' I mentally review my facts. 'According to my father's papers you're thirty-seven.'

'That's right. Oh, I'm sorry to hear about your loss, Mr Calner. Jeremy was such a nice man.'

'Yes. He was nice wasn't he?' I can't help rendering the word 'nice' as

165

if it's as derogatory as the descriptions 'soft' or 'meek'. Then Dad was an easy touch. I'm standing in the proof right now.

'Your father loved to drive here through the mountains. He called them the Aspirin Hills, because every time he saw them his headache would disappear.'

'Really.'

'What he liked best was to help Bunny in the garden. They'd mow the lawns and tidy the flower beds. The last time he was here he sketched out a bridge to replace the old one. He said it would be our Japanese bridge like you'd find—'

'Miss Lake. As I stated in my letter this wouldn't be a social call.'

She gives one of those awkward, shy smiles that weak people favour. 'Sorry. Yes. You wanted to discuss my brother's work.'

'And the house. I inherited Montage from my father. The production company passed to me, too. What there is of it.'

'I hope you're going to start making films again. The last film of your father's was beautiful. I'm hoping I can afford a player so I . . . oh, please sit down.' She perches on the edge of a sofa. If anything she appears even more nervous.

I remain standing. 'I've been driving the best part of the day, so being on my feet's preferable. Now, to get to the point, I've a lot to do this weekend.'

'Of course, I apologize for . . . you know . . . we don't get many visitors.'

'You do understand why I'm here, Miss Lake?'

'Yes . . . well, I think so.'

'My father's records show there are two people living here. Yourself and your brother, Christopher Lake.'

'That's right.'

'And the man who calls himself Bunny?'

'He lives in the summerhouse in the garden . . . it's not really a summerhouse, more of a cottage. There's electricity and—'

'Does he pay rent?'

'No. He helps out here. I don't know what we'd do without him.'

I click my tongue. 'There's no record of him signing a tenancy agreement.'

'Oh, that's OK. Your father knew all about Bunny. He said it was all right for him to live in the summerhouse.'

'Miss Lake, it's not all right. If he's not signed a tenancy agreement then he might claim squatter's rights, which hampers my right to do what I wish with my property.'

This makes her flinch. She's maybe had a sneak preview of her future. 'Mr Calner, your father promised we could stay here.'

'My father is dead, Miss Lake. Regrettable though that loss is for both you and for myself, the fact remains that ownership of Montage has passed to me. It's customary for a tenant to pay rent on a property they occupy. I know for a fact you never paid a penny in rent to my father . . . nor to me.'

'I'm sorry.' Flustered, she's more apologetic than defensive. 'My brother had an agreement with your father. They decided that they would have equal shares in the profits of the films. In return my brother would live here.'

I sigh. 'But that never happened, did it?' With that I sit in the large armchair that faces her. I draw a cigar from my pocket. Her eyes follow me with all the concentration of someone watching a surgical procedure as I use gold cutters to amputate the sealed tip of the cigar. Maybe she doesn't want me to smoke. Oh dear, oh dear, oh dear, oh dear . . . My house, missy.

To smoke in someone else's home is to stake a possessory claim. Just like a male dog cocking its leg against a tree. The symbolism isn't lost on her.

I lock eye contact with her. For a moment I say nothing. I'm demonstrating I dictate the pace of this meeting. Then: 'Miss Lake. Listen carefully. I'm a businessman. I take my money and property seriously.'

'Your father was very proud of you. He liked to—'

I talk over her. 'I'm going to tell you what I've been able to learn from the office files about my father's business relationship with your brother. When I've finished add any facts I might have missed. Correct any misapprehensions. Then I'll make a financial proposition that your brother will agree to in a written contract.'

'That won't be possible.'

'There are no *possibles* or *maybes* or *equivocation* whatsoever, Miss Lake,' I tell her. 'Come what may, I'll be leaving here tomorrow with Mr Lake's signature on that document.'

'I'm really sorry, Mr Calner.' Her brown eyes are big and frightened. 'It's impossible.'

'Believe me . . . in this matter, you don't have the right to say what is or is not impossible. Do you understand?'

'I understand. And I am sorry.' Tears aren't far away. 'But before you get angry with me, Mr Calner, I'd like you to come with me and see my brother.'

FIVE

So, I follow her upstairs. It's now so dark that she has to switch on the lights in each section of corridor in this sprawling house. It's completely silent. The smell reminds me of a museum; the trigger is that evocative odour of old wood and floor polish; maybe a subtler whiff of lives frozen in time, too. When she reaches a door at the end of the corridor she gently taps on the panel.

'Christopher? It's only me.'

She opens the door in that tentative way of hers, as if afraid of what she'll find on the other side. I follow her into a room that's as frugally furnished as a hermit's cell. Perhaps the only concession to the modern world is a laptop standing on a bedside table. The moment she switches on the light I see the bed with a bearded guy stretched out on it. With the beard and long hair he resembles one of those old portrayals of Jesus. His brown eyes are open. They stare at the ceiling.

He's dead, I tell myself in surprise. He's stone dead. She's left him here to rot. I picture a million squirming maggots. Only no sooner does the thought go skipping through my head than he comes to life. He sits up in bed and begins to pull off his T-shirt.

'No, Christopher.' Her voice is gentle. 'It's not time to get up yet.'

There's no emotion on his face. He doesn't acknowledge our presence. He just stares at the wall as if he can see through it into the distance. The guy's clean. Well nourished without being fat. The nails on his hands are evenly shaped as if they've been manicured. The man, however, is clearly absent from reality. He tries to climb out of bed again with a mechanical slowness. There's no spark there; it's merely an automatic process.

'Christopher.' His sister puts her hand on his shoulder to signal to him that he should remain there. 'It's not morning yet. Stay in bed.'

He regards her with dead eyes.

'Christopher. This is Mr Calner. He's Jeremy's son.' No response. The man's zombie expression doesn't even flicker. 'Look. Christopher . . . *look*.' It's like trying to show a baby a visitor. 'Look, this is Jeremy's son. He's come to see you.' She makes waggling movements with her fingers, in front of his face. When his eyes at last lock on to the fingers she moves her hand so as to draw his captured gaze to my face. 'This is Jack Calner . . . You remember Jeremy talked about his son? Jeremy showed you a photograph of the graduation. Remember the cap and gown?'

For a second the man's dead eyes rest on my face. They don't focus they simply happen to gaze in my direction.

'Put your T-shirt back on, Christopher. That's it.' She helps him with it. 'Go back to sleep now.' She has the soothing voice of a mother settling a child. 'Make yourself comfortable. There, let your head rest back on the pillow.'

He obeys in that mechanical way. A moment later his eyes stare up at the ceiling.

'See, Mr Calner? My brother isn't capable of signing any documents.'

'He's always like this?'

She nods.

I click my tongue. 'For how long?'

'Twelve years this July.'

'I'd been told that Mr Lake had become a recluse after his breakdown. I didn't expect this.' I turn to the thing on the bed that my father had once described as a genius. 'Mr Lake. Do you know where you are?'

Lake doesn't respond. He lies on his back as he gazes at the ceiling with that blank, zombie expression.

This is a setback, I tell myself. This is a problem. Thank God, I'm one of those men who feed on problems. Conflict fires me into over-drive. Good! Make this treasure hunt difficult. It'll prompt me to perform even better. Obstacles – not an easy ride – are the real keys to success.

'Miss Lake. A moment ago I said I'd outline what I know about my father's contract with your brother here. Tell me if I've got this right. Your brother was a film-maker. In his early twenties he produced three feature films that are now considered by people, who like that kind of thing, as classics.' Crisply, I reel off the titles. '*Triangle, Octagon* and

169

Ellipse.' Venus Lake appears daunted by my knowledge of her brother. She nods in that timid way of hers, while I continue without hesitation, 'Together they sell a million copies a year in DVD. The commercial rights to the stills alone turn over five million per annum. I'm correct, aren't I?'

She nods. 'But we don't make any money from them. Nothing.'

'I know. You were stitched up by the studio's contract. Your brother made the films for a flat fee without securing a share in either gross or net profits.' I move on swiftly. 'Then fifteen years ago enter my father, Jeremy Calner. He agrees to finance Christopher's fourth film. I was fourteen years old at the time. I remember him being very excited about the deal. The money meant nothing in his eyes. All that interested him was that he'd be working with a film maker whom critics described as the new Orson Welles.'

'But he wasn't—'

'No, Christopher Lake wasn't a new Welles. My father told me he was a Lon Chaney, H.P. Lovecraft and Tod Browning rolled into one. The names meant nothing to me until I researched them a few days ago. Whether or not those individuals were geniuses or charlatans I don't know, but I do know they are marketable. I also learnt that my father funded your brother's fourth and final film. A production entitled *Vorada*. Subtitled: *I Am Your Death*. He began it fifteen years ago. Thirteen years ago he screened portions of it to a private audience. Then with my father's consent Lake moved here to Montage to complete it. As I say, that was thirteen years ago. I'm entitled to fifty percent of *Vorada*'s gross profits. And so here's my question to you: Where is the film?'

'I'm sorry, Mr Calner, I don't know.'

'Don't know? Or won't say?'

'I've not seen the reels in ten years.'

I turn to the man in bed. 'Mr Lake, where's the film? Where do you keep it?' No response. '*Vorada*. Come on, you must know where it is?'

Venus Lake is frightened but she forces herself to speak. 'Mr Calner, please don't try and talk to Christopher. He doesn't speak to anyone. He hasn't for years.'

'What's wrong with him?'

'He went into a decline when he was making the film. He told me he'd nearly finished it when he suffered a breakdown. He'd exhausted himself.'

'But he screened some excerpts? My father saw part of it.'

'Yes, but Christopher became very anxious about the film.'

'Anxious? Why?'

'I don't know. When he came back here after showing parts of the film he continued work in the editing suite, but he wouldn't let anyone see it. He even locked himself in the room with it. When I asked if I could see it he refused; he said the film wasn't right.'

'Those exact words? "The film wasn't right"?'

'Yes.'

'What did he mean by that?'

'I don't know.'

'Come on, Miss Lake, you must realize what your brother was inferring. "The film's not right". That means it's not finished, or not good enough. Or "not right" in a moral sense?'

She shrugs.

I press the point home. 'After all, "the film's not right", could mean that it will could be condemned as being sadistic or pornographic, or even downright evil.'

Venus Lake doesn't answer.

I push the interrogation. 'So, the situation is this: your brother had finished the film here in an editing suite in the house. Other than a few clips at a private screening it's never been seen in its entirety. Your brother told you the "film wasn't right". Then the reels vanished?'

She nods.

'And your brother became a recluse here and suffered a mental deterioration to the point we see him today. Uncommunicative to say the least.'

She gives that pained nod again.

'Good.' I smile. 'It makes the hunt interesting, anyway.'

'I'm sorry, Mr Calner. I don't know if the film exists anymore. He might have destroyed it.'

'The bottom line is this,' I tell her. 'Either I find *Vorada*, which as you know will be worth millions to both of us, or I'll consider your brother's contract with my father void. In that case, I'll require you to vacate Montage within twenty-eight days.' My smile broadens at her wide-eyed expression. 'That's right, Miss Lake, the truth is finally sinking in. I either drive away tomorrow with the film – or I'll have my house back. Thank you very much.'

171

SIX

The pounding on the door brings me out of bed before I'm fully awake. I'm cursing because I can't find a light switch in the unfamiliar room, but I do find the door handle and wrench it open in a rage.

Venus Lake is standing there in white cotton pyamas that simper innocence and beauty. *'Help me!'*

She's barely got the words through her lips when she turns and runs along the corridor. I go after the woman, wondering what fun and games she's got planned for this time of night. As I follow her mad dash downstairs she cries out to me, 'It's Christopher. He's set fire to the house!'

God Almighty. The one-time genius is crazier than I gave him credit for. 'Venus!' I drop the Miss Lake in view that it's *my* house burning down. 'Venus, where's your fire extinguisher?'

'There isn't one.'

She disappears into the living-room. When I smell acrid smoke I move faster. And when I enter the living-room with its statues and mosaic floor this is what I see. Christopher Lake is sitting in an armchair. And that armchair isn't just alight it's spewing flames. I mean jets of flame like it's been hit by napalm. The lights aren't on but the fire is so brilliant I have to shield my eyes as I run forward. Venus is screaming at her brother to get out of the burning chair. But all he does is sit there. His forearms are supported by the arm rest. Same zombie expression on his face. The dull eyes stare into the distance. I lunge at the madman. Now I'm closer I see he's wearing a leather flying jacket. Other than the chair blazing to high heavens he could be some idle schmuck lazing in front of the TV.

'MOVE!' I don't wait for him to obey. I grab him by the front of the jacket and lift him out of the chair like he's a rag doll and throw him away from the flames. 'Venus! Open the French windows.' I'm gambling the doors I've ordered her to open do exit outside. It's too late now. I've got to go for it. The flames are bursting from the sides of the chair. The headrest is still untouched, so this is the part I grab then start pushing it across the floor on its castors. Within seconds I'm running with this chair that's rapidly becoming a ball of fire. I feel my face smart from the heat of it. The black smoke shrouds me. It's in my eyes and throat. The fumes reach my lungs. It hurts so much it's like rats gnawing inside of me. A hundred sharp teeth crunching through lung tissue.

I yell at her, 'Get out of my way!' I see enough of the open doorway to charge through, shoving the burning chair in front of me. Then I'm outside, gulping down cold night air. Finally, I kick the armchair across the patio, so it's well away from the house. There it burns like a torch, like a great bloody torch. The kind you get in medieval castles. It spits burning plastic on to the stone slabs. The flames are a tower of light jetting into the night sky. I turn away from it. My eyes are streaming, I'm coughing. By the time I get back indoors I'm roaring at the man lying there on the mosaic floor of dolphins and fish swimming through a surreal ocean.

'You idiot! You could have burned the house down! You nearly killed us!' I glare at the man who reclines there like a child mildly surprised by nothing more than a window banging in the wind. Venus is crouching beside him. She examines his hands, no doubt checking to see if he's burnt his mindless, arsonist self. I continue my rant, 'You should be in the nut house. Do you hear me? You should be locked away!'

'I'm sorry,' gulps his sister. 'He's never done anything like this before. I don't know ... he's ... I'm sorry. Look ... Please don't hurt him.' She's so shocked she hardly knows what she's saying as she examines him in a trembling way, her hands shaking.

I take a breath. My heart's still pounding. Adrenalin's taking me on a real rush. A sky-high, nerve-spangling rush-a-roo. Even so, my voice is coming down a notch or two. 'Is he hurt?'

'The jacket protected him. It's scorched but he seems OK.'

'OK? Venus, for a pyromaniac "OK" is debatable.'

'I don't understand.' Then she repeats the statement, 'He's never done anything like this before.'

'You mean he's never tried to burn the house down?'

'I haven't even seen him strike a match in ten years.' She's aghast. For a moment she dips her head in defeat. She's shaking her head and her long brown hair tumbles forward. The pyjama top is loose around the collar. Part of it slips off her shoulder. A bright red scratch on her skin runs from the back of her neck to end in a whopping purple bruise on her shoulder. She senses I'm looking at her. Quickly she stands upright while adjusting the neckline of the pyjama top to cover the injury. She pulls her long brown hair down over her neck to hide the scratch, too.

For an instant her big, dark eyes flick up into mine, then glance away – that frightened deer look again.

Forcing herself to speak she asks, 'Are you all right?'

'Never better.' I flex my right fist. A tightness in my fingers tells me I've scorched them.

'You've burnt your hand.'

'Lightly toasted. It's nothing.'

Venus finds it hard to look me in the eye. 'I'll find some antiseptic.'

'It'll be fine.' But she disappears so quickly it's as if she's flitted away like a bird. I go to check on the burning armchair. 'That better not be valuable,' I say aloud as I look out through the doorway. There it is: a sad skeleton of burning wood. One thing's for sure it's not going to damage anything now it's isolated from the house. It can burn itself out on the patio.

When I hear a footstep I turn round. 'Venus?' Instead of the woman it's brother Christopher who stands beside me. The leather flying jacket is burnt black in parts but it clearly saved the lunatic's bacon. I tell him, 'You might as well enjoy what's left of your pyrotechnics. Just promise me you won't try setting fire to my house again?'

He gazes at the burning bones of the chair, his face lit by the yellow flame. Then his wide eyes suddenly narrow as if for the first time in years thought has entered that hollow head of his.

His lips part, his teeth catch the firelight in golden glints. There's an inward rush of air through his mouth. A second later with the exhalation come words. They're understated. So quiet I have to strain to hear them.

'Find my film,' he tells me, as he stares at the burning chair. 'She took it from me. Destroy it before she can use it.'

SEVEN

Venus is back with the salve before I can question the man further. Christopher Lake, meanwhile, retreats into himself. Staring vacantly with that zombied look again, he utters zilch. He does nothing but stand there and gaze at the remains of the burning furniture.

'Mr Calner? I have the cream. I'll put some on for you.' After switching on the table lamp she sits on the sofa. I go sit beside her. I'm still shooting glances at Christopher. His words have taken me by surprise. *Find my film. She took it from me. Destroy it before she can use it.* How does that equate with one of his last cogent statements ten years ago that Venus repeated to me: *The film wasn't right.* Question mark? Not just any question mark. This is a huge symbol of the mystery that punctuates the atmosphere in this mausoleum of a house.

I'm sure Venus hasn't heard Lake's plea to me, so for the time being I decide to say nothing about it. Now she's squeezing antiseptic cream from the tube on to the tip of her slim finger. A clock on the mantelpiece chimes 2 a.m.

As I sit beside her she takes my hand, rests it on her pyjama-clad lap, and gently begins to smooth the cream into my scorched skin. Her fingers are cooler than the salve and the movements gentle as she can make. Christopher still stares out at the burning chair.

'I've been thinking,' she says. 'We can start looking for the film in the editing suite; there are more cans of film in the garage as well.' She applies another blob of cream to my reddened knuckles. 'As far as I know, Christopher had finished shooting all the material he needed for the film. And he'd decided on the title. *Vorada.* I'm sorry.' Venus flinches because she's found the burn has raised a blister on my little finger. 'I didn't mean to hurt you.' As if handling a live butterfly she carefully dabs more salve on to the blister. 'There's local anesthetic in the ointment. It should stop hurting soon.' Then she returns to the subject of the film. 'The first cut of *Vorada* ran to eight hours. I know Christopher spent months in the editing suite to pare it down to four hours. Then he became ill. . .' The memory pains her even though she forces a tiny smile on to her face that suddenly has a fairy-tale beauty in this muted light. 'It was his mind. He'd worked too hard on the film. Chrissie started hiding himself away in the garden . . . behind walls or lying under bushes. There's even a cave in the grotto where he. . . .' She bites her lip. 'Anyway. He finished work on the film. Then he just stopped functioning. He hasn't talked for years. Not a word.' She turns her face to me, meeting my eyes for the first time that evening in a long unblinking look. 'How long do you plan to stay?'

My eyes fix on hers, holding the gaze. 'Venus? Why did you run out in front of my car today?'

She shakes her head, then whispers a very tight-lipped, 'No.'

'So how did you get the bruise on your shoulder – and the scratch on your neck?'

Again that shake of the head. She looks away from me as if in shame.

I raise my voice. 'Or did your brother use you as a punch bag?'

She whirls away from the sofa. A second later she's rushing in the direction of the hallway door.

'Venus! Why did you run into the front of the car? Why were you naked!'

EIGHT

The instant I wake up I make a decision. I want Venus Lake. And I don't intend to wait long. For a moment I sit on the edge of the bed beneath that bronze domed ceiling, the birds are making a racket outside, the breeze is blowing scents of a countryside in spring through the windows. It's not a pretty perfume of fruit blossom, it's that prickling odour of stinging nettles. With that is an underlying mustiness of wild hemlock. I'm drawing in that smell and I'm thinking where I'd like to touch Venus Lake, her of the slender waist and large brown eyes that are so soulful. Frankly it surprises me that I'm taken with the woman. She's timid, she's nothing more than a full-time nurse to an empty pot of a brother. Maybe it's the challenge? She seems beyond the range of many a man's hunting prowess. It's that old case of: *because I can't have that's exactly what I want.* I WANT Venus Lake. And I repeat to myself under my breath it's only lust, not love. Love's a treacherous and unpredictable force.

There's also another element to the attraction.

I murmur the words for the pleasure of saying this revelation out loud, 'Venus Lake runs through the woods naked.' I know she's the individual who crashed across the hood of my car yesterday and shattered the windscreen. Last night I saw the scratches and bruising. With her brown hair loose around her shoulders it made her resemble the naked figure I saw in the gloom. It's strange to say, but I'm impressed the way she bounced off half a ton of German steelwork then seconds later raced away into the trees like a panther. It's as if being knocked down hardly fazed her.

Briskly, I shower, treat myself to the closest of shaves, then dress in an open necked lemon-hued shirt and chinos. After the businessman's uniform of last night I can afford to dress down for the treasure hunt today. Especially now I know Venus can do nothing to prevent me from searching for lost *Vorada*. I'm not interested in the film's story-line. Go on, strike me down, but I haven't even bothered to ask what it's about. What's important to me is that the theatrical, DVD and stills rights will form a constructive arc of my investment portfolio (as will this house before very long). That's what I find compelling – not screenplays, nor actors' performances and all the precious activity that goes with movie-making. When I get my hands on the film reels I'll be calculating *Vorada*'s ability to generate revenue. Dollars, pounds sterling, euros, yen, pesos. You can disregard art, religion, science . . . and you can even turn your nose up at politics. The truth is, my friend, money is the engine that powers the world.

It's 6.30 a.m. The early sunlight slices through the windows in dazzling rods of gold. There's no one about. All I can hear is birdsong. My view consists of garden, meadows, woodland and hills.

My thoughts are drawn back to Venus Lake. After I identified Venus as the woman who'd bounced merrily off my car yesterday she didn't admit or deny it, she simply rushed from the room. No matter. That's a minor issue that can be cleared up later. Along with another issue of peeling away the rest of her defensive layers. The thought produces a tingle in my scalp. I hum softly to myself as I go downstairs to find the kitchen. At least the Lakes don't dine exclusively on cracked nuts and fruit. I find coffee and cereals. That's ample breakfast for me. After I've eaten I take a walk. Now, at last, I can take a good look at Montage in the daylight. First of all, of course, I pass the film caterer's truck that's clearly reached the end of its useful life. And then my car that still bears signs of the impact of Venus's naked body.

As for Montage, I get to appreciate its mix of architectural styles properly for the first time. Some windows are oblong, some narrow at the top into pointed arches in a Moorish style. A couple of the walls are bare stone while the rest are rendered either in pale green or yellow. The property is enclosed by post and rail fencing. Beyond that are fields that roll away to forests and hills. As I walk I flex the hand that suffered a lick of flame from the burning chair. Apart from one small blister on my little finger there's no damage to speak off. At the back of the house I cross the patio by a small mound of ash. That's all that remains of Christopher Lake's act of pyromania.

In the sun slanting through trees I see a figure standing at a pair of double gates set in a garden wall. He's tugging at them without much success.

I stroll across to him. 'Having trouble getting in, Bunny?'

Bunny casts a benevolent smile back over his shoulder at me; his spectacles catch the sunlight in peculiar little heliograph flashes as if he's signalling a concealed message. 'Good morning, Mr Calner.' He tugs at the gates again. They are heavy-duty things in wrought iron. They wouldn't look out of place in a prison.

'What do you keep on the other side of the gates, Bunny? Gold bullion?'

'Mr Lake was very interested in keeping the barn secure.'

'Barn?' I step up to the gates to look through the bars. Beyond a stretch of lush stinging nettles that occupies the intervening space like a green pond I see a single-storey timber building with a red tiled roof. 'What's the fascination with that? It's derelict.'

'Oh, it's in fair order, sir.' Bunny has no luck opening the gates, but it doesn't stop him tugging at them. The hinges are rusted solid. 'It just hasn't been used in a while.'

'A long while it looks to me. Here, you take the left-hand one. No, stand further to the left so I can get hold.' We stand side-by-side as we grip the vertical bars. 'OK, Bunny. On the count of three pull. And I mean really pull. Don't just play at it. One, two, three.'

We both tug hard. Bunny's no muscleman but he gives it everything he's got. With a piercing screaming the gate judders open.

'Now for the next one.' We do the same. It opens as if begrudging the favour. Flakes of rust cascade from the hinges. 'If I were you,' I pant. 'I'd oil them from time to time.' Now we're faced with that barrier of stinging nettles that are as high as my chest. It's probably these venomous beauties that I smelt in my bedroom. 'Well, that's the gates open. But you're going to give yourself some pain walking through those nettles.'

Bunny smiles. 'And there are brambles grown up over the door as well. I'll cut them down with a scythe.'

I brush the rust off my palms. 'It passes the time, I suppose.'

Bunny shakes his head. 'Miss Lake asked me to clear a way to the door for you.'

'For me?'

'In there.' He points at the barn. 'It's Mr Lake's place where he worked on his films.'

'The editing suite?'

He nods his grey head. 'Miss Lake says you need to look inside.'

'Bring another scythe, Bunny. I'll give you a hand.' Now I'm keen to see what's in there. I'd joked about the gold bullion, but if *Vorada* is beyond those nettles then that ramshackle building might as well be Aladdin's cave.

In a minute the man's back with a couple of scythes with handles that are as long as I am tall. Soon we're working side-by-side, slicing lush nettle stalks that leave a smear of green juice on the blades. We make good progress through the swathe of plants that extends twenty feet or so to the entrance of what served as Lake's editing suite. By this time I'm aware that Venus Lake stands on the patio watching us work. When we reach the door and cut down the last of the nettles and briars that bar our way to what I hope is the treasure house, the woman walks down the lawn to the gate. She wears a purple skirt that reaches her calves, and complementing that a white blouse. This morning I find myself noticing the curves of her body and the texture of her smooth skin on her face. Longing becomes an ache that creeps into my body. Oh my Lord, I didn't plan this. I find myself smiling.

'Good morning,' I say brightly.

She nods. I sense a wariness. 'Good morning, Jack. Did you sleep well?'

'Perfectly.' She calls me by my first name. Before it was Mr Calner, never Jack. Maybe when we saved the house from burning down last night we both crossed some kind of threshold. Partners in the face of adversity – that kind of thing.

'I've brought you the key to the barn.' She holds it up as she steps forward.

I shout at her: '*No!*' She stops with a startled expression on her face. 'You're wearing sandals,' I explain. 'We've chopped down the nettles but they're still ankle deep. You'll get stung if you try walking across.'

'Oh.'

I lean the scythe against the wall. 'Stay there. I'll carry you over.'

Will she permit me getting that close? For a moment I imagine her running away from me and back to the house.

Venus is pliant. She allows me to pick her up. Then like a new husband carrying the fresh bride over the threshold of their home I lift her with one arm under her spine and one under the backs of her knees.

Shyly, she looks down so she doesn't have to make eye contact as I bear her across the rug of fallen nettles to the door. She hands Bunny the door key who has to wrestle with the padlock for a moment before he can unfasten it. It gives me plenty of time to hold her. She's as light as air in my arms. A faint, pleasant scent rises from her body.

'There you go, Mr Calner.' Bunny pushes the door open. Again old hinges squeal like they resent being woken from a deep slumber. And into the dusty interior I carry the woman that I intend to hold again very soon.

'This is an editing suite?' I look round. 'It'd pass for a junk yard.'

I set Venus down on her sandalled feet as she gazes round the chaotic interior. 'Before Christopher's big breakdown he became very disorganized.'

'Is this the viewer?' I touch a contraption that's the size of a refrigerator with a TV size screen on top and a pair of spindles where I suspect the spools are placed.

'It's the editing machine,' she explains. 'These hinged metal plates are the splicer. It's used to cut the celluloid and reattach the ends. You can still see drops of glue on the bench that Christopher used to splice it together.

'Is this part of the film?' I point to a rack against one wall from where strips of celluloid hang down in brown strands.

'They're out-takes from his earlier work, not *Vorada*.'

'How do you know?'

'He was most particular about that film, Jack. He never left so much as a frame of *Vorada* out on show. When he wasn't working on it he kept it in the safe up at the house.'

'So we're not going to find the film here?'

In the gloom her eyes are large glittery orbs as she shakes her head.

'Then why allow Bunny and me go to all the trouble of clearing the way to the editing suite?'

'You'd have wanted to check here for yourself.'

'So, next stop the safe?'

'If you like. It's empty.'

'OK.' I give a philosophical shrug. 'We search the house. Any ideas where to start?'

'As I told you yesterday, Jack. I haven't seen the film cans for years. It's likely my brother destroyed them.'

'Like he nearly burnt the house down last night.'

She assents with a shrug.

'So why do you run naked through the woods?'

Her frowning glance at me reveals that she hoped I'd wouldn't be so impolite as to raise the bare marathon stuff again.

'I'll go back to the house and start lunch.' She makes a decision. 'I'll tell you then.'

With that she turns and runs through the cropped nettles. The sandals are secured to her bare feet by the thinnest of straps. Her nude toes, feet and ankles must be badly stung by the venomous plants but she gives no indication of noticing the pain.

Why do I find myself thinking that Montage is a house full of secrets that are just itching to break out? A vessel full to the gunnels with mystery? A building awash with skewed perspectives? Forgive my purple prose. But this is just the kind of place that provokes melodramatic notions. Strange house. Strange, *strange* inhabitants.

Bunny smiles through the doorway as he wipes away the nettles' poisonous juices from the scythe with a rag. 'You'll like Miss Lake's cooking.'

I tell him straight, 'That's not all of hers I'm going to enjoy.'

The monk-like Bunny continues smiling at me. I can't see his eyes behind his spectacles. Instead I see an image of myself reflected in the lenses. I notice an expression of yearning in my face. I want Venus Lake. I know I've got it bad. That surprises me. But it's not a problem. Everything that life tosses in your direction you can turn it to your advantage. Learn to do that, and the rewards are there for your taking. Fail . . . and you're doomed to a life of hell on earth.

NINE

A sense of tantalizing promise hangs in the air. Not only the search for *Vorada* or Venus's impending elaboration on her nude roving across the countryside, but I have that taste in my mouth. You know the one. The taste you get when you're close to breaking through someone's defences, and either clinching a business deal, or taking a woman in her bed. And that taste, my friend, is the taste of conquest.

Before lunch I've time to telephone the only garage in forty miles. With it being Saturday morning they can't replace the windscreen until Monday. So I'm here for an extra couple of nights. That's no hardship. Something tells me there'll be entertainment aplenty here. I make calls to my business partner and accountant to postpone a Monday morning meeting until the Tuesday. I have to tell them that I haven't got my hands on *Vorada* yet, Lake's famous lost film that critics and fans alike have been baying for. But I'm close. I'm very close. Here's what I've figured out so far: Lake is mentally ill. He'll be insanely possessive of the film, so he won't have destroyed it. Also, remember his words from last night. Seeing as he hadn't spoken in years his plea: *"Find my film. She took it from me. Destroy it before she can use it"* are potent ones indeed. This is where the proverbial slack-faced dummy asks: 'What's all that about then?' But the mentally dissipated Christopher Lake's three sentences are lucid enough to me.

First sentence: *Find my film.* If Lake wants me to find the film – undoubtedly *Vorada* – then the film is capable of being found; therefore, it still exists.

Second sentence: *She took it from me.* The only 'she' for miles around is the man's sister, Venus Lake. He believes Venus seized possession of the film reels. That means, despite her pretence at ignorance, she knows full well the whereabouts of the missing 'masterpiece'.

Third sentence: a most mysterious and provocative sentence: *Destroy it before she can use it.* What do you infer from that? That not only is the content of the film dangerous in some way, but Christopher Lake is terrified that his sister will 'use' the film. For commercial gain? To expose a dangerous secret? As a weapon? This, I tell myself, will be a fascinating mystery to unravel.

With two hours to kill before lunch I decide to explore. Inactivity irritates me. There's nothing worse than sitting doing nothing. Now I'm certain that Venus knows where the missing film is hidden there's no point in me making a play of searching for it. Better to hear its whereabouts from her own lips. In fact, it will be satisfying to manoeuvre that revelation out of Venus's very attractive mouth. So I head out into a sunlit morning to follow the boundaries of what, after all, is my property. There's a freshness in the air I like; a crispness that makes me think of chilled champagne. Bunny doesn't rule the garden with a firm hand. The lawns are ankle deep in places, more like meadow. The green open spaces are speckled with golden dandelions. There's not much in the way of formal flower beds; planting is fairly haphazard – a clump of roses there, raft of red tulips here. A mass of violet lavender runs alongside a stretch of lush mint and lemon balm that's been allowed to grow wild, like the tresses of a fairy-tale hag. As I walk down through the garden toward the boundary fence rabbits lope off into the bushes in front of me. Not in a frightened away, but quite relaxed as if in these parts it's only a formality for the wild life to avoid humans. Again, the sense of isolation is a strong one. There are no neighbouring houses. The only road is deserted. There aren't even any jet trails in the sky. Not that I mind: this kind of retreat from civilization comes at a premium. It adds cash value to this real estate that passed to me when my father died last year.

Marked by a post and rail fence, the boundary guides me downhill into a hollow. The forest I'd driven through yesterday extends a wooded finger into the garden itself by about a hundred paces or so. Soon I enter a shady stand of oak. There's not so much as a path but a series of interconnected clearings that form a route through the copse. Presently the ground folds up at either side so what passes as a pathway descends into a gully. As I follow it, the sides are transformed from earth banking topped with trees to boulders that form an artificial grotto. It's probably some folly of Dad's from when he first built the house. Now, brambles and stinging nettles grow between the boulders. There are broken statues and stumps of pillars. No doubt it's intentional to create the appearance of an ancient Roman ruin. Here the light is greenish due to it being filtered through the leaves. The grotto forms a gloomy underworld. Vines, ivy, brambles, moss, plenty of moss; it combines to form a jade skin on the boulders. Even though I'm outdoors this is an enclosed world. The steep boulder sides are perhaps twenty feet high. Above me, at ground level, huge oaks form an ever shifting canopy of branches that, every now and again, admit a pencil-thin ray of sunlight.

Just as the sense of peace here becomes so intense I can almost reach out and touch it, a sharp snap of a sound splits the stillness. Five feet from me chips of stone burst from the boulder.

'Hey! Watch out!' I've enough wits to realize that someone's just let fly with a firearm, and the bullet's knocked a chunk out of a boulder not far from my head. 'If you're hunting rabbits they're the ones with the long ears.' I tug one of my own ears. 'Don't you recognize a man when you see one?'

I don't see the hunter, but the next shot follows within seconds of the first. This time I hear the pop of the bullet as it rips through the air near the ear I've just pulled. The bullet ricochets away down the canyon with a whine.

'*Hey!*' My yell echoes back at me.

The next shot is even closer. The rush of its slipstream tugs my hair. Whoever it is they're not hunting rabbits. I know that now. So I run forward through the grotto. A couple of shots follow in quick succession. As I run I glance up. About twenty feet above me a shadowy figure moves along the top of the canyon. They have to weave around trees and bushes along its edge so it spoils their aim. But there's no doubt who their target is.

I keep moving at a sprint. All the time I'm scanning the rock sides looking for a place to shelter. I feel like a rat scurrying inside an old bath tub. There's nowhere to hide. And I'm limited to where I can run.

Although I don't take the time to idly gaze up at my pursuer I have an impression of a hooded figure, either masked or with a scarf over their face. They appear to carry an automatic rifle. The chunky magazine protruding beneath it suggests that they're not going to run out of ammunition in a hurry. Beyond that I'm not dallying to check on detail. Another shot explodes the earth in front of me. I race forward. There's got to be shelter ahead I tell myself. A fake cave, or rocky overhang. I don't plan on taking a slug in the guts, and reclining here in the dirt to watch the life ooze out of me.

'Bastard!' I yell. My God, I want to get my hands around their neck. I push myself faster. If they have to match my speed over that rough terrain up there then that's going to spoil their aim. Good. I don't want to make it easy for that piece of human filth.

A couple more shots peck chunks out of Dad's folly. They must be out of breath because the bullets fly wide of me by ten paces at least. 'Useless piece of crap!' All here, take note. Berate your assailant rather than be a victim, fleeing in silence.

Then it goes wrong for me. The gully closes off into a dead end. There's a mock temple, however, with stone columns and a crumbling roof. It might afford protection if I could only reach it but it's built ten feet up into a cliff face.

Only there's a miracle ... a great, flaming God-given, Christ-spon-sored, archangel underwritten, miracle. Leaning against a boulder is a pump-action shotgun. My attacker's running along the top of the cliff. He's having to watch out for tangles of tree roots, so he's glancing down at his feet to avoid tripping. Now's my wonderfully juicy opportunity. I grab the shotgun. I slide the loading mechanism. A round enters the chamber with a satisfying *snick*. Steadying my breath, I raise the shotgun, and aim at the guy as he stops directly above my head. He points the rifle muzzle down at me. It's pleasing to see him jerk back a little in shock. He's seen I'm armed now. A warming glow of pleasure spreads through my stomach. Nice to provoke that reaction. Of course he's going to fire the moment I pull my trigger, only ... only he has trouble with the gun. A jammed round? The mechanism isn't cocked? He takes the gun away from his shoulder so he can see what the problem is.

I settle the stock against my shoulder. Aim. Directly at the head. I squeeze the trigger. Because I'm surrounded by rock on three sides the shotgun blast sounds like an artillery piece discharging a five pound shell. Venting cordite gases rip leaves from the vines that cling to the rock.

What it doesn't affect is my attacker. I chamber another round and fire it at the masked figure. It doesn't even flinch. The aim is true. Only the shot doesn't hurt him. I fire again. No burst of blood and stinking guts; no scream of pain. The guy stares down at me through the slit between scarf and hood.

'Bastard!' I yell. I chamber another round then fire it directly into the cliff face. The moss ripples. I see tiny pieces of paper stick to the blast area, but no harm done. 'You bastard!' I yell again. 'You're a real joker, aren't you?' I shake the shotgun over my head. 'You left this for me to find, didn't you? And you left it loaded with blanks! Why'd you bother with blank cartridges? Why not just leave it empty? What went wrong with your life? Did you get bored pulling wings off flies!'

Now the body language of my attacker shines with confidence. He's tricked me. He must be laughing inside until his ribs crack. Slowly now, he's in no hurry, the guy cocks the rifle, and then raises it until the muzzle points down at me. With a roar of anger I hurl the shotgun aside. 'OK. You win!' I nod with a perverse satisfaction. 'Don't you get into a sweat about getting a clean shot. I'll make it easy for you.' I rip open my shirt to expose my chest. 'Hey, stupid. You'll find my heart just here. At the end of my finger.' I touch my chest with my middle finger then flip it upright at him. If this is my last moment on Earth I'm going to use that sixty seconds to tell my assassin to go shove it.

There's a pause. Silence oozes into the grove. Though the hood is drawn over the head, so it conceals the face in shadow, I sense the guy staring at me.

I find a smile tugging at my mouth. 'Hey, stupid. If you've forgotten where the trigger is, it's that iddy-biddy bit of metal sticking out of the bottom.'

My murderer's deciding what to do. If there's such a thing as a moment of significance I figure it passes us by. Because a second later he raises the rifle, so the muzzle is pointing skyward, then he steps backward from the lip of the cliff and vanishes.

'Yeah,' I shout. 'Tell all your friends that you hunted a man for sport. A better man than you! Have a laugh about it. Because next time . . . do you hear me? *Next time I'll rip your head off!*'

TEN

So, this is the meal. The one that Bunny told me I'd enjoy so much. Now, despite whatever I might want to do, I find it difficult to take my eyes off Venus Lake as she ladles bright green soup into two earthenware bowls. Describe the crockery as Third World chic and you have it. Venus is dressed in a flowing skirt in white cotton. Very nearly see through. A little voice yattering away at the back of my head wishes it was completely transparent. Fortuitously, she's wearing a purple bodice of a flimsy material that's sheer enough to allow me teasing glimpses of her breasts. So what happened to the shy sister that's very much her brother's keeper? This version of Venus today is teasing me with glimpses of her body beneath that Gypsy-cum-hippy confection.

We're dining in the kitchen. It's ramshackle, old fashioned, but clean and homely. There's a dresser displaying bright blue plates. The kitchen is cavernous and full of roast meat smells from the huge iron oven. There's a trace of spice hanging on the air. I've already taken my place at the farmhouse table and I'm hungrily anticipating the feast.

There's a terrific topic of conversation I can open with. Someone tried to murder me this morning. *And just for a joke they left me a gun loaded with blanks. Isn't that the most deliciously witty jape you've ever heard?* But, no. I don't mention it. I'll save that revelation for later. Because I'm watching the way she walks. My intentions are purely wolfish. To confess a gunman tried to blow holes in my heart will be an ideal tool to win her sympathy this evening when the time is right. Did I say wolfish? Yes, I lust manfully after her. No doubting that. She's beautiful.

'How are your fingers?' she asks.

'Fine.' I glance at the reddened skin with the singed hairs. She's looking, too, with concern on that pretty, elfin face. I add, 'You're confident your brother won't try and burn us all alive in our beds again tonight?'

'I've locked him in his room.'

'Oh.'

'Bread?'

'Just a slice.'

She cuts a piece from a gargantuan dome of golden brown loaf.

I add, 'And confiscated all his matches and firearms?'

As she sits she glances sharply at me. 'He doesn't own any guns.'

'Glad to hear it. Interesting looking soup.' I nod at the bowl of brilliant green liquid.

'It's made from nettles.'

'The same ones Mr Happy Bunny and I cut this morning?'

'Why waste them? Nettles are good for you. One of the most mineral-rich vegetables you can eat.'

187

I peer into the bilious green and see my reflection gazing back. 'Then you can have them carve *She Fed Him Poison Weeds* on my gravestone.'

'Cooking destroys the poison.'

'An old country recipe I suppose.'

'I found it on the internet. Gently fry the nettle tops in oil, add vegetable stock and seasoning, and then liquefy in the blender.'

I eat a spoonful. 'Not bad. Tastes a bit like spinach.' I glance up as she breaks her slice of bread in two. There's a kind of energy in the woman that was absent yesterday when she was as timid as the proverbial mouse. It's as if she's found the dial to her internal rheostat and cranked up the voltage. So why the change? I lean sideways a little so I can see one of her bare feet against the stone floor. Her toes are puffy. The skin is mottled with pinks and whites. 'Venus, you stung your feet badly down at the barn this morning. What made you walk through the nettles?'

'Last year I broke my ankle. The poison in stinging nettles is a remedy for conditions like rheumatism and arthritis. Its anti-inflammatory properties have been used for thousands of years. You can also treat snakebites and asthma with preparations made from them.'

'So you deliberately sting yourself? Masochistic, don't you think?'

'From time to time my ankle still aches and I find nettle stings stop it hurting.'

I have to smile at this. 'If it works for you.' There's a pause as we eat then I ask, 'How many nettles would you need to treat a broken neck?'

'I'm sorry, Mr Calner, I don't understand.'

'Don't go back to Mr Calner. Call me Jack.'

'Jack.' She nods, accepting the invitation to use my first name.

I press on, 'I was curious if nettles would cure major injuries because yesterday you nearly wound up with a broken neck when you ran into my car. Why did you do that?'

'I run because the exercise is good for me.'

'You mean you always go jogging in the nude?'

'It's attaining parity with nature. To me, that's important.'

Expansion on a theme. Elaboration of the facts. If I'd been expecting Venus, pretty fawn-eyed Venus Lake to get all evangelical about the merits of dashing through the woods in her birthday suit I'm mistaken. Instead she fires back a question at me. Her tone is pleasant, she's smiling, but I sense currents of fire in her veins now.

'Jack, what are your plans for my brother's film?'

I feign ignorance. 'If I find it.'

'If you find it,' she nods, while holding my gaze.

'Christopher Lake fans have been waiting for years to see it. It ranks alongside Lon Chaney's *London After Midnight* as one of the legendary lost films. So. . .' I set down my spoon beside the bowl. 'It will be worth millions. I plan a theatrical release worldwide. There'll be a collector's edition DVD to follow. A coffee table tie-in book. I'll exploit the photo library stills from the film for use in commercials, clothing and whatever merchandise I deem appropriate.'

'And "appropriate" means anything that will turn a profit?'

'Absolutely.'

'My brother sacrificed his health for that film.'

'With the intention of earning money from it. Even Da Vinci and Van Gogh painted with the intention of reaping cash from their art. Christopher is no exception.' I smile. 'Think of *Vorada* becoming an epidemic of flu. It's going to infect the cinema-going public. It'll saturate the TV-watching and DVD-collecting world. Everyone will see your brother's masterpiece. And when the theatre prints are worn out I'm going to slice them, mount them and sell them frame by frame to the fans. This is really satisfying soup, by the way.'

'You have Bunny to thank for it.'

'Happy, smiling Bunny. Why is he brimming with sheer bloody joy all the time?'

'Because forty years ago he saved the world.'

'Bunny's a super-hero? My-oh-my.' This brings a smile to my own face. 'Go on, Venus, break it to me. How?' I bite off a chunk of bread.

'He killed his family,' she says before spooning that audaciously green soup into her mouth.

I suspect a leg pull. 'Bunny bumped-off his family? So you're harbouring a murderer?'

As if recounting a banal event she shrugs. 'When he was nineteen he killed his parents in their sleep, then he set fire to the house.'

'In the lunacy stakes that is spectacular.'

'No. There weren't any symptoms of mental illness. None of the malaise or distorted perceptions associated with schizophrenia, or any other indicators of psychosis. Neither were drugs or alcohol involved.'

'Why'd he do it then? For the inheritance?'

'Bunny told me that on his nineteenth birthday he became convinced that his parents were infected with a virus that would decimate the human race.'

'So he barbecued Ma and Pa.'

She nods.

I continue spooning the soup into my mouth. 'Like I said: nuts. Has to be.'

'Psychiatrists couldn't diagnose a mental condition. They said he was sane so the judge sent him to prison. Bunny was a model prisoner; they released him on licence ten years ago.'

'Let's get this straight.' I'm still amused by the notion of the mass-murderer harvesting nettles for my soup. Talk about adding a certain *je ne sais quoi*. 'Bunny convinced himself his mother and father were plague carriers. That to save the human race he must destroy them and the bug, so he slaughtered them and burnt their bodies. Then he spent the next thirty years of his life behind bars?'

'Yes.'

'Then why the devil is he so infernally happy all the time?'

'Don't you see? In his heat of hearts, Bunny believed he saved the human race by destroying a lethal virus.'

'But there was no bloody virus.'

'Bunny believes that there was. And though he knew he couldn't convince the authorities that was the case, he knew he sacrificed his liberty for the good of humankind.'

'And to this day Bunny thinks he saved our skins by incinerating his parents?'

'Yes. That's why he's happy. He had the courage to risk everything in his life to spare the world from plague. In his eyes he succeeded.'

'Wow.' I say this in an understated way to show her I'm not living in awe of Bunny's accomplishments.

'Jack, I know I can't make you understand how Bunny feels,' she tells me. 'but Bunny has this supreme . . . *absolute* self-confidence. Bunny knows he has the power to save the world. How many of us can claim we're able to do that?'

I finish the last spoonful of soup. 'That's not power, that's self-delusion. Delicious bread by the way. I'll bet it's home baked. Did Bunny's superhero fingers knead the dough?'

'I've roasted lamb for the main course.'

'I had you down for a vegetarian.'

'Then it proves you know nothing about me, Jack.'

She stands and collects the bowls from the table. When she reaches out for my spoon beside the bowl I close my hand over hers. 'Venus, you and your brother will make a lot of money out of the film. You know that?'

At that moment I want to grip her so hard in my arms that it makes her gasp. I picture myself kissing her lips. That sheer naked *wanting*. It's so powerful that my heart hammers. The same moment I imagine myself kissing her I also see her rejecting me. It's an agony-ecstasy moment. What if she is physically repelled by me? The idea is so unnerving. So unusual. I've not experienced anything like it before, but at that instant I shudder with fear. I am terrified of being rejected by her. Even the film I've fought to take possession of seems unimportant. For me, that's heresy to turn my back on the opportunity to make money. But: *I want Venus Lake*. The truth is as simple and as stark as that.

It can only have been seconds, yet it seems I've been resting my hand on hers for whole minutes. With those fawn-like brown eyes she looks into mine. I can't read what she's thinking from her expression. Her face is a mask – a beautiful mask – but she's not allowing any emotion escape the armour plating. In that painful, suspended moment, where time slips away through the window to be replaced by this painful longing in my chest I hear a rising surge of applause and voices calling. I glance toward the doorway. The eerie notes of an accordion wind through the corridor and into the kitchen. On the heels of that comes a male voice singing in French. The song rises in volume until it takes possession of the room.

Venus slips her hand from beneath mine, then moves away to put the bowls and cutlery in the sink. As the resonant voice surges through the house, singing a song that appears to quiver with profundity, Venus tosses words back to me over her shoulder. 'That's Christopher's favourite song . . . *Amsterdam* . . . the singer's Jacques Brel. There's potatoes and spring cabbage . . . is that OK?'

'I'm fine with anything. As long as there's no garlic: I hate garlic.'

Things are changing. Venus telling me Bunny is a parent killer, who thinks he's saved the world. My feelings . . . *no* . . . my desires for Venus. My fear of her rejecting me. The song that's . . . well . . . so haunting . . .

191

so incredibly haunting. All that is transforming not only the environment I find myself in, but I feel different inside myself. Fear? Lack of confidence? No, I never experience those states of mind. But in the last few minutes I sense I'm different inside. It's hard to put my finger on it. I'm more tentative. Instead of firing off the usual string of authoritative statements that is my norm, I'm considering what to say before I open my mouth. For a moment back there I planned to stand up and kiss Venus. A full, passionate, searing kiss that would have signalled to her what my intentions were.

Now?

Well, now I sit at the table in this rustic kitchen with the song gusting through the fabric of my father's house like it's a cavalcade of ghosts. I say nothing. Venus moves to the oven to lift out a sizzling leg of lamb. The smell of roasting meat has an intensity I don't remember experiencing before. And the song starts again. The same song. Jacques Brel's *Amsterdam*. My heart's beating hard. The music is insinuating itself into my mind. I can't take my eyes off Venus. Her calves are so slender beneath that skirt. Yesterday, she'd hurled her naked body into the path of my car. Wait a minute. What did I say just then? What was it? Because it wasn't true. I described this as my father's house. No. Correction. My father is dead. Montage is my house.

Venus sets the steaming leg of lamb on the table. The brown meat bubbles with aromatic juices. After that she puts a large knife in front of me. 'You can carve while I finish the vegetables.'

So as Venus moves back and forth from stove to sink, draining greens and adding butter to potatoes, I carve thick glistening slices of lamb. Meanwhile, the Jacques Brel song still ghosts through the house. A hymn to sailors, to dancing, bloodshed and to the whores of Amsterdam. All this and a glimpse of the eternal, too. Or so Venus tells me as she drains the cabbage.

You're going to have to do something about finding the film – and do something about Venus. This is what I tell myself as I cut the meat. And I know I've got to do it soon. Because I suspect that Venus Lake has developed plans all of her own.

ELEVEN

I'm sitting in my room The one beneath the bronze dome. The sun is incredibly bright as it piles in through the windows. When I shield my eyes I can look over the lawns to the meadows, forests and the hills in the distance. I've not had alcohol with the lunch Venus prepared. The meal's been satisfying, perhaps so satisfying I feel sluggish, yet my fingers and face are tingling. I find myself repeating the same banal thought for no particular reason. '*Vorada* will require a cinematograph.' And again: '*Vorada* will need a cinematograph.' But what is a cinematograph? Some mechanical device employed by a cinema I suppose. But it's that word. CINEMATOGRAPH. An odd word full of lumpy syllables. I imagine Orson Welles's deep, rumbling voice enunciating the word through clouds of cigar smoke. 'Mr Jack Calner,' Orson says to me. 'Jack, if I may call you Jack? Let me tell you, Jack. When you find that lost film it will be necessary to employ a Cinematograph.'

I chuckle. 'Cinematograph.' My face tingles and I rub it vigorously. 'Nettles. Nettle soup.' My head shakes. 'The nettles are stinging me from the inside.' My head is so heavy ... it's weighed down by the word CINEMATOGRAPH. All those syllables like so many lumps of iron.

The weight of it all draws my face downward so I'm staring at the pattern in the rug. Suddenly, it seems a long way off. It's all random swirls and blocks of colour. I see a face in a clump of tangerine-coloured blotches. It's an earnest face. The face of a young man. The expression suggests that the owner of the face has some vital message to impart to me.

I lick my lips. They're tingling too. A rumbustious tingling. Prick, prick, prick. The face in the rug locks eyes with me. The lips move but I can't hear any sound.

'Hello,' I say, as if faces appearing from rugs happens to me every day and twice on Sundays. 'What have you got to tell me?'

'*Get out!*' The face dissolves into a stream of tangerine light rays.

'Hmm.' I lick my lips. 'Hmm. Nettle soup.' My eyes tingle. 'I think I'm allergic.' My hands are so numb that I rub my fingers together as if trying to remove a sticky juice from the tips. 'I don't feel ... hmm.' Now I'm distracted by my hands. The backs of them are too big. The pores have become a series of pits in the skin. Hairs bristle with the thickness and blackness of sea urchin spines. '*Rest.*' With an odd abruptness I throw myself back from my sitting position on the bed to lying flat on the mattress.

The sunlight grows more intense. It's as if the room cascades with molten gold. Its brilliance goes beyond magnitude. The light has been transfigured. The tingling I experience in the irises of my eyes dances along the optic nerve to scintillate and coruscate amid the roomy, billowing, delicious folds of my brain. When I close my eyes the light isn't diminished. It grows brighter . . . brighter. . . .

Funny this . . . Not funny ha-ha. . . . Previously, I believed I had an excellent vocabulary. But now I know those words were like buds on a plant. As I lie here I realize the tightly budded words are blossoming into their full meaning. My native tongue was, hitherto, a foreign language to me.

TWELVE

The instant I wake I look at the clock on the bedside table. Six o'clock on the nail. The evening sun floods the room. With insight blazing through my head I know the truth. That meal I ate: Venus Lake spiked it. There have been times I've drunk so much whisky that it's all but wiped clean my mind. What I experienced before I fell asleep this afternoon was nothing like being drunk. There was no diminishment of intelligence. No slurring or staggering. Instead, perceptions altered. My hands had appeared the size of table tops. The rug on the floor had seemed a hundred yards away before the human face had grown out of it. That, my friend, was hallucination for sure. I was seeing things that simply did not exist in the real world. So what else do I know as I sit here, staring at the clock? Venus has slipped a drug into my meal with a specific purpose in mind. All part of her master plan. But what plan is that? Venus possesses the lost film. She pretends she hasn't. Her insane brother knows she has it, too. He urged me to find it before 'she can use it'. Venus, however, has drugged me so she can move *Vorada* to a new hiding place.

Whereas I should be punching the pillow while cursing Venus Lake for dropping LSD into my soup I also know another fact – that great big glittering not-to-be-denied fact. And that fact is: I long to get hold of her. No, not to do her a violence. But to hold her. To say sweet and gentle things to her. The truth is I've never responded like this to a woman before. This state of mind should trouble me. The thing is when I picture her I'm filled with a warming goodness that is so alien to me.

I clench my fists. What now? I can't just drive away with a forgiving smile splashed all across my face. There are questions to be answered. I've got to confront her and hear from her lips why she drugged me – and learn her intentions for the film. 'Ask her what the hell is a cinematograph, too.' The line I speak aloud makes me pause. I study my hands – both backs and palms. The lines in the skin are deep as creeks. Fingernails are as broad and as glossy as polished window glass. My lips tingle.

I breathe deeply. 'Take it easy, Jack. You're not clear of it yet.'

For a moment I'm compelled to examine my hands. They have an allure that's both monstrous and beautiful. They repel me but I'm driven to keep staring at these blood filled extremities as I rotate them, so I can see them back and palm. I bite my lip. 'You've got to give it to her, Jack. She's spiked you good.' The tingle spreads along my arms. 'Hmm. Cinematograph.' I give a savage shake of my head. 'Don't start that again, Jack. Don't you dare.'

I stand upright and move to the open window as if I'm carried through the air. There's no sensation of walking. I've not used drugs before. This must be one of the effects. There maybe more. I must be on my guard. A second later I'm at the window where I inhale deeply. Fresh air might dispel the narcotic from my veins. At the second lungful of air I see a figure run across the sunlit lawn. With the sun shining in my eyes I have to shield them with my hand.

It's her. Venus Lake. Running once more. Slim legs a blur. Brown hair fluttering. Naked body shining.

'She's at it again.' I murmur. That nude cross-country run fetish of hers that brought her in bruising collision with my car.

Then the insane idea. No, not idea. This mad compulsion. Run after Venus Lake. Stop her. Grab her by the shoulders. Don't let go until she tells you why she drugged you. Get her to confess where she's hidden the film. *Force her!*

That lightness in my body makes running effortless. I fly for the bedroom door that dilates from *Gulliver* huge to *Alice Through The*

Looking Glass miniscule. Shouldn't have poisoned you with that muck, Jack. She's no right to trick you into eating acid . . . trippy, dippy, hippy acid. . . .

The door swells into normality as I reach it. A moment later I'm through it. I don't stagger. I'm not clumsy. My mind isn't cloudy. This sensation isn't like knocking back a potful of booze. My thoughts are sharp as a razor. Only they're stretched into different shapes. Perspectives are skewed. The light possesses different qualities. Dimensions have been rearranged. As I speed toward the stairs. I hear applause.

For me.

Cheers.

They're my adulation.

Then I know what it is. Venus's mad hatter brother is playing his music again. It's the same wheezing call of the accordion. Jacques Brel sings the opening verse of *Amsterdam*. The volume swells as I zoom downstairs without seemingly making contact with the risers. Then as the voice grows in passion, and those French words about love and death and obsession blow through my head, I hurtle through the hallway, through the living room with its mosaic and marbles statues of gods and monsters and heroes. And then I'm through the door on to the patio. There's the burn mark where I kicked out the blazing chair last night. Way off to my right I glimpse the silver head of Bunny – smiling, mass-murdering Bunny, the gardener. He's wiping the blade of the scythe. Then he returns to slaughtering a whole family of nettles. Just for a second he pauses as he watches me run across the lawn in pursuit of his mistress. After that, he returns to his rhythmic work. As measured as a metronome. Sweep, cut, swish. The curving blade fells a dozen nettles in a stroke. The green blood of the plants drips from sharp steel.

Jacques Brel's song fades slowly as I race away from Montage. I glance back to see Christopher Lake standing in the window of his room. The man's empty stare follow me across the lawn. Then I look forward again as I zigzag past bushes in my hunt for that strange guy's naked sister. The sun is much lower. It's brilliance dazzles. She was here. This is where I saw her from the window. My pace slows to a near standstill. Her perfume haunts the spaces between the trees. In my mind the scent takes the shape of her beautiful figure. I step into it to envelop myself in that sweetened atmosphere.

A desperation takes hold of me. I'll never see her again. She's gone. That sense of loss is almost overwhelming. Just as I believe I'll crumble to the earth there and then I catch a glimpse of her behind a line of poplars. Once more an unnatural energy fires me up. I'm running before I've even thought about doing so. My feet don't seem to touch the ground. This is an effortless glide just above the grass. Ahead of me I catch glimpses of her silhouette. The sun is dazzlingly low in the sky. All I make out is the flick of her long hair. That and the pale flash of the bare soles of her feet.

I call out. 'Venus!' She doesn't seem to hear. 'Venus, stop! I need to talk to you.'

Stop. Talk. Conversation. A civilized exchange of statements. But it doesn't feel like that now. This is a chase. I'm the hunter! It's The Powerful versus The Powerless. A formidable strength fills my body. That energy drives my legs. In my arms is the power to uproot trees and topple mountains.

It's the drug. You knew it could have more effects. You're running. The narcotic is moving faster through your bloodstream. Beware, beware, beware. . . . *Don't do anything that will cause harm.* These words resonate. Because that's the feeling . . . that's the TASTE in my mouth. I have become dangerous. DANGEROUS.

In my drug altered state . . . my mind is reconfigured. The word DANGEROUS has a dozen new definitions. Didn't I tell you that until now words had been tightly budded things with a constricted meaning? Now the words are opening. Blossoming. Their meaning is expanding all the time. Take DANGEROUS for instance. It's become a magic word. I am dangerous. That means I can perform acts that no other man can. Danger is the key to giving me what I want. Danger is power. The power of danger has the ability to destroy old boundaries, it can smash moribund ideas and annihilate redundant systems. With this dangerous, destructive power I can obliterate the old and build anew.

Hunt her. Catch her. Hold Venus by those lovely naked shoulders. Tell her exactly what will happen to her.

THEN DO IT!

THIRTEEN

We're running along the boundary of the property. I catch teasing glimpses of her bare skin. But most of the time she's concealed by bushes . . . another time she's running through open ground. Only the grass there's so tall it comes to her shoulder blades. The bruise on her shoulder is plain to see. The one dealt to her by smacking into the front of my car.

Venus. Venus. Venus. In my mind her name is fire. Its heat drives through my flesh. And I'm gaining on her. We've run around the perimeter of the grounds. Her arms, legs, head and back are a blur. The bare skin is a shining miracle. I have to touch it soon. Very, very soon. Not just touch either. Grip. Clutch in my strong fingers.

Rabbits hop aside as she runs through a group of them. Birds fly from branches near her until sometimes it seems she's haloed by the flapping wings of white doves. Then she's moving through the trees again, along the path that takes her into the finger of woodland that penetrates the garden. I've been here before. I know it. I know where it leads. That gully. The steep-sided valley of boulders with no exit. The sheltering oaks. What I describe next is contradictory, but it's nothing less than a metaphor for my experiences here at Montage. Even though I can fully see her body I don't see her in entirety. The dappling shadows, the spots of sunlight, they simultaneously illuminate her and hide her. It's a light that has the power to transform her once again. The first time I'd seen Venus after the car had struck her and she'd raced away into the forest I'd fancied she'd become part-panther. Now she becomes almost feline; a beautiful, supple figure that moves with undulating grace through a confusion of light and shade to glide deeper into the forest.

I know this place only too well. I've been here before. This is where the gunman tried to kill me. Then the terrifying thought: what if he's lying in wait again with his rifle? This vivid sculptured piece of woman flesh. Gorgeous, lithe, with the fawn-like eyes beneath a wash of brown hair. What value would he award to a target such as that? What will he do when he sees a beautiful woman racing toward him without so much as a scrap of cloth to cover her nakedness. I imagine him drawing back the rifle bolt with a gloating smile.

'Venus!' Her name is thunder on my lips. 'Venus! Don't go down there. It's dangerous!' But aren't I the danger? Aren't I a thundering, raging bull of a man who is the sole threat to this vulnerable human being? 'Venus.' I pause to bellow, 'STOP!' But I've paused too long. She's escaping me. Within seconds she's vanished into the deep-sided gully.

In no time at all, I run into the man-made valley; the sound of my feet pound back at me from the rock sides. I've been a mere moment, I've been so quick. So why is it she's vanished from the face of the earth?

That drug . . . that mutilator of reality . . . is still polluting my bloodstream. Down here in the gully my perception of the world is mangled out of shape. The stones slabs that form the path appear to undulate like the scaled back of a long, sinuous boa constrictor. Boulders swell to the size of trucks. The valley sides could be a mile high at either side of me. Above them, tree trunks soar up into leafy branches that now form a ceiling that's nothing less than an incandescent green. I can smell the moss so strongly it becomes an electric current running through my nostrils into my head to tingle the nerves in my brain. And amid this psychedelic hub-hub of shifting colours and coalescing shades of green where is Venus Lake? The naked beauty who poisons men's food. Narcotic inveigler.

I look at my hands again. The fingers are as long and as thin as bamboo canes. Yet the joints are bulbous mouth shapes with shouting lips. The veins beneath the skin are purple highways. I fancy I see blood platelets scurrying through them, each one being piggy-backed by molecules of the narcotic. Little parasites. Dirty little parasites. As I rub the palms of my hands against my hips I feel an object in my pocket. My mobile phone. Quickly, I drag it out and switch on. Uncanny. The cane-like fingers still possess their old dexterity. On screen the directory throws up my business partner's name. I thumb the call button. And I'm standing there in the wash of jade light. At both sides of me rise the rocky cliffs to the emerald heaven above.

'Where have you disappeared, Venus? Where have you gone. . .' I'm singing the words under my breath. 'Watch out, watch out, there's a man-shooter about.' This is funny. Laughter bubbles from my mouth. A ring tone is merrily tooting away, then a voice in my ear.

'Jack. I've been trying to phone you for the last ten hours. Where the hell are you?'

'Steiger—'

'Do you have the film? Because I've got some guys from Hollywood chomping on the bit. They'll pay a million finder's fee over and above the rights sale. Did you hear that, Jack?'

'Steiger . . . Steiger. Listen. She's poisoned me. Isn't that just so brilliant!'

'You're talking about Venus Lake?'

'She put some stuff in the soup . . . Lord, it was the greenest soup I've ever seen in my life.'

'She's poisoned you? Hell, Jack. Don't do anything. I'll get the police and an ambulance. Just wait there!'

'Steiger. Isn't that wonderful? The woman spiked my food.'

'Wait until you get medical help.'

'And then this morning a guy tried to pick me off with a rifle. I'm standing here in the forest and I'm looking at where the bullet went – SMACK! – into a rock. Look, I can put my finger in the hole. That would have blown my head all over the place.'

'You're still at Montage, right?'

'Absolutely.'

'I'll get help to you there.'

'No.'

'What?'

'No, don't you dare, Steiger. No police.'

'Jack you said you'd been poisoned. Jack, if this is a joke it's not funny.'

'Venus Lake shoved acid . . . LSD? It must be LSD; she shoved it into my food. I'm high. Everything looks weird. Either too big or too small or out of shape . . . or things like trees seem to be lit from the inside. The light is blinding. But I can think clearly. I'm lucid.'

'You don't sound lucid.'

'I'm fine. My mind's a razor . . . I've never known it so sharp.'

'But if she's tried to kill you—'

'Not kill me. She'd have done something else . . . arsenic, or Bunny. Maybe the burning chair. You know, toxic fumes.'

'Jack, look for God's sake listen to me. What you're telling me isn't making any sense. Go lie down. I'll phone the police from here. Then I'll drive up to Montage with a couple of the guys.'

200

'Do nothing.' I take a deep breath and rush the words out before he can speak. 'I can use this, Steiger. Venus Lake could end up in jail for doing this to me. This is my lever. I'll get her to bring the film to me. And then I'll renegotiate the contract. Currently, we have to split the proceeds fifty-fifty with Christopher Lake. I'll get her to sign a rider to the contract altering the profit split seventy-thirty in our favour.'

Poison. Shootings. Drug trips. That's all well and good, but just you talk money to Steiger – that's when his mind really begins to focus. 'OK, Jack. As long as you know what you're doing. If they try anything else on you call the police. Got that?'

'Don't worry, my funny little friend.' The endearment tickles me. I have to clamp my hand over my mouth to stop laughing out loud. 'I can do joined up writing now . . . I can tie my own shoelaces. I'm big enough to look after myself.'

'OK, but watch your back. Did you hear me? *Watch your back.*'

I switch off the phone and slip it back into my pocket.

'Oh, Steiger. I forgot to tell you one thing.' I murmur these words under my breath as my heart slams against my ribs. 'I like Venus Lake. She's amazing . . . Never ever met a woman like her.' And, don't you know it? The only ears that hear my once in a life-time confession are fixed to the heads of furry woodland animals.

I move forward again. The valley walls close in. I glimpse fragments of stone lintel and columns that convey the fantasy that this is the site of a ruined temple. Now stone arms are outstretched from the rock. Whitely gleaming marble with delicate fingers. They reach out to touch my face as I pass. That drug. It's trickling hallucinatory thoughts into my head again. Now I see the carved head of a woman jutting from the moss level with my own face. Her eyes are closed but all of a sudden her mouth drops open as if to call at me. A curse? A blessing? A warning? There's no human voice. It's the same sound as a seashell placed against your ear. Only louder . . . far louder than you've heard before. It rises to a wail as blood begins to pour from the yawning mouth.

How long will this drug stay in my body? What will it make me see next?

By now I've reached the end of the gully. There's no way forward. And no way up to the top of the cliffs which hem me in at both side as sheer as prison walls. There's the mock temple again. I see the black smudge on

201

the boulder where I fired the shotgun blank this morning. Up there had stood the rifleman. The big tease. He pretended to make a play of shooting me then scuttled away. My gaze travels up the moss covered rock face to a million tree roots bursting like monstrous tentacles from the earth above me. And there are the tree trunks. Above them, the branches that make a sizzling sound as the evening breeze stirs the leaves. And it's green . . . all so very green . . . Vertigo tugs at me. I'm lightheaded.

Then it's her. As if she's been there for the last hundred years. For decades she's remained rooted there like one of those trees. And yet all along . . . all down through those waiting, watchful, just-biding-her-time years . . . she knows I'd come walking along his gully to find her there, haloed by an emerald radiance.

She must still be naked. With the light behind her all I see is her silhouette. Her hair flutters. Those soft doe eyes glint from the shadow and I know . . . I KNOW . . . she's watching me.

'Venus.' I meet the gaze head on. 'You've got to come down here.'

She says nothing. Golden dust motes glide with aching slowness on green rays of light.

Louder I say, 'Come down here where I can I talk to you.'

'No, Jack. That won't be a good idea.'

'Why?'

'Call it intuition, but I sense you're liable to do things now that you wouldn't dream of doing at any other time.'

'Come down here. You can trust me.'

'Not until the acid's worn off. It's working on the barriers inside your head, Jack. For the next couple of hours you'll be capable of anything.'

The woozy sense of floating through the forest is being replaced by a burning need to have my questions answered.

'Venus, you put something in my food. What was it?'

'The "what" is less important than the "why".'

'You wanted me out of the way for a few hours so you could move the film to some place I couldn't find it. Isn't that right?'

'No.'

Still she doesn't move during this surreal conversation. Me, at the bottom of a gully adorned with mock temple ruins, addressing the naked woman in tantalizing silhouette at the top of the cliff. Only the knowledge that she is – for the moment – beyond my reach exerts a corrosive effect on my nerves. For the first time since waking this afternoon an edginess unsettles me. I realize I've lost control of events here at Montage. I came here to see the house that my father left me, and to lay claim to Christopher Lake's famously lost *Vorada*. Knowing that Venus has out-manoeuvred me, prickles my ego to say the least.

'So why did you decide to spice up the broth with a narcotic?'

'To remove inhibitions. When you hear what I'm going to tell you next I want you to absorb the information differently to how you usually do.'

'OK, you're going to tell me something amazing. Come down here and share it with me properly.'

'Jack, right now you're capable of committing acts that you wouldn't dream of. That will soon pass, but until it does you'll be a danger to me.'

'You can trust me. I'm still lovable Jack Calner.'

'You've never ever been lovable Jack Calner.'

'So why put your dirty drug in my food, then?'

'Creative destruction.'

'Did I hallucinate what you said right then? You did say creative destruction?'

'Does it mean anything to you?'

'It means crap all.' Suddenly the lights are greener; the cliff face taller. The moss is fascinating beyond words. I must stare at a turquoise and sea green phosphorescence spiralling through it. It's a fact. I'm not free of these chemicals yet.

'Creative destruction,' she says matter-of-factly. 'That's an academic phrase coined by the Austrian economist Joseph Schumpeter. Put another way, it's evidence for every cloud having a silver lining. In order for civilization to advance conventional ideas, machines, technologies, social models become obsolete, they are regularly destroyed, and are replaced by something newer and better. Look at the financial news: over ten per cent of all companies in America vanish every twelve months. It affects biology, too. More than ninety-nine per cent of all species that have lived on this planet are now extinct. Creative destruction is what makes progress possible.'

'This is weird.' I shake my head as the vertigo returns. 'You're up there lecturing to me – naked; I'm down here – not understanding.'

'Jack, society is stagnating. Progress is slowing down. It's because we as nations in the Western world have contrived to get ourselves in a rut.

When there are wars – and I'm talking about major conflicts here – technology leaps forward, society goes into a state of melt down, but then emerges in a new dynamic mould.'

'For example?'

'Before World War One nearly every household had at least one maid. After the war only the rich employed servants. When World War Two started we had piston-engined biplanes that took off from cow pastures. By the end of the war the old flying machines were being replaced by jet aircraft that could see through fog and darkness using radar. They landed on concrete runways. Soon they'd be breaking the sound barrier. Ten years after that, ordinary men and women could board passenger jets to fly the world over.'

'You're saying that if it wasn't for the world wars we'd still be hitching our crusty old mule to a cart?'

'And today we ride around in cars. But even the latest models employ stagnant technology now. Progress is becoming sluggish. There should be a cure for cancer, only we're losing the will to find it.'

'You know, Venus, you weren't at all like this yesterday when I first met you. Apart from the clothes thing, of course.' I catch a glimpse of gleaming, naked hip. 'You played dumb, didn't you? So I'd underestimate you?'

'It's not only wars. When individuals that the public adore are killed they become martyrs. That in turn empowers people. They achieve the impossible to honour their martyred hero.'

'Like?'

'President Kennedy. Do you think his promise to land a man on the moon in less than a decade would have been fulfilled if he'd lived? He'd become just another retired politician playing golf all day. When Kennedy made the promise he was only trying to raise the public's spirits. Even he didn't believe a moon landing would happen.'

'But he died – and it did.'

'Yes.'

'Hmm. Now let me get this straight. You tricked me into eating a potful of drugs so you could give me this lecture. Me down here – baffled; you up there – naked as the day you were born. I'll tell you this, Venus, I'm feeling pretty wacky on this stuff at the moment. You know … hell … talking statues, gooseberry skies, marshmallow stones.' I squeeze a boulder with my fingers. For me it's rubbery rather than rigid. 'I know I'm hallucinating . . . but come on, you can tell Jack your master plan.'

'The drug reduces the patterns of resistance you've built up inside your head since childhood. Everyone develops these systems of "disbelief" to protect them from radical new ideas. If I explained creative destruction without the chemical in your bloodstream you would have processed this information in your habitual way. Which would have been negative and disbelieving to say the least.'

'Who says I believe you now?'

'You won't immediately, but the facts will side-step the mental barriers that resist radical, and therefore troubling, ideas.'

'Excuse me, Venus, for pointing this out, but I don't recollect you telling me any earthshaking ideas.'

'No, this is it. This film of Christopher's—'

'*Vorada* . . . originally called *I Am Your Death*. Cheerful title. Cheerful as body bags.' The greens of moss and leaves are turning very green again.

'*Vorada* has certain qualities.'

'Go on.'

'Some people watching it will come to understand the necessity for creative destruction. They'll realize that it will be ultimately beneficial for humankind if they start a war. Or kill a prominent public figure. A death that will create a martyr. Just as Lee Harvey Oswald made a martyr of Kennedy.'

'Venus. My lovely, lovely Venus. You've lived in isolation for too long. That can play tricks on people, you know?'

'If you promise to help me, I'll give you *Vorada*.'

'It's mine anyway.'

Her voice softens. 'You can have whatever else you want, too.'

As I look up at the silhouette against the emerald splash of leaves she steps forward into the light. Then she moves back into the shadows again.

But I've seen her. I've set my eyes on every inch of her shining nakedness. The beauty of her body winds me. I stand there breathless for a full minute. Thoughts whirl inside my head. Possibilities. So much is within reach now. I only need the courage to reach out and take it. A thought occurs to me. If I run back along the gully now, can I catch her before she makes it back to the house?

So, this is it. I race along that crease in the woodland floor. My drug-enhanced senses revel in its greenery of the vines, grass, plants, lichens, moss – so much velvety, jade moss – the trees and marble debris of mock temples. All that and the marbled whiteness of ancient gods and goddesses. Colours, scents, sounds are so much more vibrant. When this drug leaves my system will the world seem a poor, grey thing in comparison? Now the sound of birdsong swells – the excited piping, shrills, whistles, hoots and love calls. It fills the forest. Just as I think the sound will overwhelm me it suddenly collapses into silence.

Standing there in front of me, blocking my way, his eyes locked on mine is a figure with a gun.

I stop dead twenty paces from the man. 'So . . . you've come to finish what you started?' I see Christopher Lake standing there. He's wearing a brown leather jacket over a naked torso. His lower half is clad in faded denim jeans. He's barefoot.

'What is it with you Lakes and clothes? Or rather the lack of them?'

The automatic rifle he holds is the same model as I saw this morning. A chunky magazine extends downward from beneath it, no doubt packed full of nice, shining high-velocity ammo.

'What are you waiting for, Christopher? Still haven't got the guts to shoot me in the head?' I extend my arms in a crucifixion pose. 'Why not start at the fingertips? Then, blasting merrily away, work in toward the centre. That's where the lungs and heart are. Understand?'

I look over his shoulder in case Venus has noticed that her brother's on one of his nutty frolics. But she's vanished back to the house. I turn back to meet Christopher's eye. This cult film director . . . a living legend for critics and fans alike is panting. He's unsure of himself. There's an edginess there as if he's only holding it together with a supreme effort of will. He's gripping the gun by the barrel close to its muzzle with one hand; the other's at the end of the stock. The rifle's pointing upward. It looks alien to him. I tell him, 'You did a better job of handling that weapon this morning, didn't you? What went wrong? Afraid it might bite?'

Twitchy, he flicks a glance back at the house.

Then the great, shining bells of revelation ring out for me. 'That wasn't you this morning, was it?'

He turns to me, tremors run across his face. 'What?'

'You weren't the one trying to kill me. You can't even hold a rifle properly.'

With a jerky abruptness he moves the rifle. It's not pointing at me. But it's getting close. I keep an eye on his trigger finger. It's still curled around the rifle's body.

'You, Christopher, were locked in your bedroom. No. It was Venus who was playing games with the rifle this morning. Isn't that right?'

He nods. There's a scared expression on his face. His body language is edgy. He's expecting to be discovered . . . or even attacked.

'So what's your sister doing taking pot shots at her house guest? I'm only trying to make the pair of you rich. Because you haven't got a penny between you, isn't that the truth?'

He advances toward me with the rifle pointing dangerously in my direction. As he walks, however, he stretches his arms out to hand the gun to me.

'Here you are.' His eyes are terrified. 'Take this. Go use it on Venus.'

This takes me by surprise. 'You want me to shoot your own sister?'

'You've got to.'

'If you hate her so much why don't you blow her head off? Why ask me?'

His lips twitch. 'Because I can't use it.'

'You're a genius film director. You shouldn't have any trouble in figuring a gun out. You point it, then yank the trigger.'

'I can't . . . here.'

He pushes the gun at me. It seems a wise idea to take it before he attempts an experimental tug or two on the trigger.

In a spray of saliva he spits out these words: 'Now kill her. Please. Before it's too late.'

I check the safety's on before lowering the rifle, so its muzzle's pointing down at the earth. 'Christopher.' I speak matter-of-factly. 'It's about your film again, isn't it? Last night you told me to destroy it before she could use it.'

'Yes.'

'She told me how the film works. That *Vorada* is all about this thing she calls creative destruction.'

He nods. The agitation is becoming more pronounced. I realize he's frightened of us being discovered here. Little Sis terrifies him.

'Does this film brainwash people?' I ask. 'Is that how it works? Subliminal images or something?'

He rushes the words out. 'It does what great film does. It manipulates the viewer's thoughts and emotions. Go see – go see D.W. Griffith's *The Birth of a Nation*, or Riefenstahl's *Triumph of the Will* . . . their message is evil – but for a moment as you watch you'll be captured by the film-maker's art. For a few seconds they will have brainwashed you . . . *yes, yes, yes*! Brainwashed you into believing their message. It doesn't matter how wrong, or how downright evil. Once the filmmaker's inside your head you believe.' The speech leaves him breathless.

'For someone who hasn't spoken in years you're doing a fine job,' I tell him.

'Venus told you I'm insane and that I never say anything.' He shoots a nervous glance through the trees in the direction of the house. 'That's what she tells everyone. OK, Calner, I had a breakdown. That's true, I did. Because I knew what I'd created could result in murder. People would see the film, and it would implant in their mind a suggestion: an – an irresistible suggestion that the world would be a better place if you created a martyr. Imagine if you are Catholic – a devout Catholic – you figure out for yourself that if you kill the Pope you won't destroy the Church, will you? You will have created a saint. You will make the Catholic Church more powerful and more influential.'

'Wait a minute . . . this film is about killing the Pope?'

'No, you idiot! Its theme is about elevating a human being into that magical, powerful, wonderful creature known as a martyr. A martyr becomes immortal. A martyr is more than human. They're like a god. People will commit extraordinary acts in their name. Listen . . . my film will make ordinary people draw the inescapable conclusion that they will be helping humankind by killing another fellow human being that they respect.' He wags his finger. '*To kill an individual in power that they respect*. Not hate. That is the crucial element. Kill a good man or woman, not a dictator.' He steps back, moving away all the time as he speaks. '*Vorada*. See it and you'll understand. You'll realize that to motivate humanity to find a cure for AIDS, or to rid the world of famine, or make your nation greater you must murder the Secretary-General of the UN,

208

or the Pope, or the Dalai Lama, or a president. You'll yearn . . . are you listening? You will yearn to sacrifice your life and reputation in order to create something much greater. A martyr whom humanity will rally around. Who will empower them. Who will make your people greater tomorrow than they are today.' His eyes are blazing. He's energized by his words. 'But you're smart enough to understand the human cost, aren't you?' His eyes blaze. '*Aren't you?*'

The lights are bright here in the glade. The drug reconfigures my senses. The trees are the epitome of tree-hood. Greens are the greenest. The universe is revealed. Its truths are like Russian dolls. You know the sort, those toys shaped the same as skittles. They have faces that reveal their inexplicable contentment at containing a series of smaller replicas secreted within them. And so life's truths are concealed one within the other. You learn one, and then find there is another truth deeper inside. These revelations spin lazily through my mind. I'm feeling it . . . a sense of wonder. . . .

Christopher Lake is thirty paces away when he calls out, 'You know what you've got to do, Calner. Use that gun on my sister. Then destroy the film. . . . *Burn it!*' With that he runs back to the house.

FOURTEEN

I find myself walking across the lawn in the direction of Montage. With this stuff flowing in my brain the architecture is even more extravagant – and exaggerated. The green bronze dome appears larger than before, minarets tower above the garden. Battlement walls are threatening to become dragon's teeth that will savage lumps out of the sky. Has there been an interval between Christopher Lake's demand that I kill his sister? Or was it just seconds ago? Because the drug that's working inside of me distorts my perception of time, too. After he'd left me there in the glade with the rifle in my hands I might have stood there for ten minutes or even an hour. I was processing what Venus had told me in the gully. That tantalizing offer of hers. '*I'll give you* Vorada . . . *You can have whatever else you want, too.*' Then I needed to digest Christopher's revelation. Did I believe this film had the power to persuade people to assassinate a president, or some great, iconic human being for the betterment of humanity?

It's the drug. But the segment of my mind that makes judgements on issues such as these stands outside its usual framework. The narcotic has tinkered with my mental apparatus ... and tinkered spectacularly. Greens are greener. Triangles are no longer limited to three sides. Fact is malleable.

By now I'm moving toward the house to find Venus. And you know something? The rifle feels good in my hands. The same sensation as slipping into a hand stitched suit. It notches up the personal power quotient. The great unwashed are going to show you respect. A man with a gun walks differently to one unarmed. The body language sings a different song. *Come on, let's rip it up.*

Through the evening sunlight I see Bunny ambling toward me. The red light reflects in his glasses; it even lends ruby tints to his silver hair. He's carrying the scythe, its blade is stained green with nettle juice. The man who slaughtered his own parents must notice I have the rifle but gives no indication he's seen it, or, come to that, isn't remotely concerned that I should be carrying a firearm.

He smiles. It's not the beaming I'm-so-gloriously-joyful-about-life grin of old; it's a more subtle, knowing smile.

When we're ten paces apart he says to me, 'She loves monsters.'

'Do you consider yourself a monster?'

Bunny's smile widens. 'I'm no monster. Society said I was.'

'That was a monstrous act, Bunny. To kill your mother and father then burn them in their own home.'

'It was a terrible decision to make, Mr Calner. But if I hadn't the country would have been devastated by plague.'

Self-delusion. That's a drug too. It's the most potent mind medicine of all. This white-haired man has been high on self-delusion for years.

'You said, she loves monsters. Does Venus love you?' I watch him carefully as he makes his reply, because just asking Bunny that question twists my stomach with jealousy.

'She loves me with the same conviction as she loves the rest of humanity,' he replies. 'Venus Lake is blessed with a mission, Mr Calner. Before she leaves this life she is determined to help humanity take a step forward.'

'So what do you think of Venus Lake, Bunny? Monster or saint?' Without waiting to hear his reply I rest the rifle across my shoulder and continue my walk to the house. It's time to confront her – this woman: she 'who loves monsters'.

FIFTEEN

I encounter Venus Lake in the hallway. She wears a silk gown, something like a Japanese kimono in black with a pattern of silvered infinity symbols. Circles within circles within circles. She's brushed her brown hair. Her eyes watch my face in that interested way, which suggests the woman wants something from me. She's endeavouring to read my expression for clues that will reveal if her wishes are to be granted.

'So, Jack?' Her dark eyes flit across my face. 'Are you here to kill me?'

'That wouldn't be polite, would it?' I feel a smile curl my lip. 'Murder my hostess?' I click my tongue. 'It just isn't done. Besides' – I fix my gaze on hers – 'when you were firing this gun this morning you weren't aiming to hit me, were you?'

'So, you have been talking to my brother.'

'And, despite the little white lies you've been spinning me, your brother is capable of being vocal.'

'For you only, and no one else.'

'When you were blasting those bits of rock near my head this morning, and leaving that shotgun where I'd find it, you were testing me. Why?'

'You're going to be dealing with the business side of distributing and marketing Christopher's film. I needed to know if you had a killer instinct.'

'And do I?'

'You fired the shotgun straight at me. If I hadn't loaded it with blanks I'd be dead now.'

'So you needed to know that deep down I really am a monster?' I keep my eyes locked on hers. 'Am I a monster?'

'If a human monster can be defined as someone who is prepared to take whatever action is necessary without a conscience.'

'I'm impressed, Venus.' And no way am I being sarcastic. I AM IMPRESSED. Write it LARGE, say it OUT LOUD. 'Truly, I'm impressed. No one's ever gone to such lengths to test me to breaking point. You're a remarkable woman.' My voice softens on the last sentence. She picks up on the change in tone from businesslike to something like intimacy.

211

'Thank you, Jack. After the way you showed me your heart this morning I know you're a remarkable man.'

'I showed you my heart as a target, don't forget.'

There's a moment where we're communicating by glances and body language alone. That's the province of two people who are either going to fight each other or become lovers. Either way. The realization excites me.

Her smile now is a warm one. 'Jack, if you don't intend using the rifle on me, then perhaps you'd like to step through into the lounge. I have something to show you.'

I follow her through the doorway to find her brother there. He's sitting slumped down on a sofa. His arms hang limp across his legs. For all the world, he resembles a teenager deep in a sulk. Head down, chin almost resting on his chest he stares with unflinching resentment at the floor. *Did your sister scold you, then? Who's been a naughty boy?* Those thoughts flick through my head. I find myself shooting her a smile then glancing at Christopher as if to say, 'Just look at old grumpy boots.'

A similar glance from Venus would confirm that we are becoming allies. Before she can respond, however, Christopher's head snaps up. 'You've got the rifle, Calner. Do it while you can.'

'You don't really believe I'm going to blow holes in your sister?'

'More's the pity, Calner!' He spits the words. 'There's not only you who'll regret it if you don't.'

'The film again?' I rest the stock of the rifle on the floor and hold the muzzle in one hand. '*Vorada.*' I glance from one to the other. They are more alike than I thought. Two sets of eyes beneath dark archways of eyebrows burn at me with an unusual intensity. Viper eyes, I find myself thinking. You do not blink. 'You've both explained to me about *Vorada* . . . that just like a computer virus invades a hard drive to reprogramme software so this film will reprogramme an individual's mind. That it'll compel them to assassinate a President, or strangle the Pope, or bump off a Prime Minister.' I know I'm smiling. That smile makes their glare even chillier. 'Isn't the biggest danger here, is that the audience who sees *Vorada* will amble away to bars and restaurants afterward saying to one another, "Wow. That was a great film. Wonderful lighting. Brilliant camera angles. Dazzling editing. Consummate production values. . ." all that movie-speak – jabber, jabber, jabber. But are they going to be infected by this burning need to go out and change the world by creating a martyr? Or . . . and, yes, this might be hard for you both to take . . . or will they just acknowledge that it's entertainment, and nothing more?'

'That,' Venus admits, 'is in the laps of the gods. We won't know how effective it is until you do your job, and make sure that when it's distributed it'll eventually reach every cinema in the Western world.'

'See?' Christopher clenches his fists. 'You know what she plans to do with it, Calner. In her hands it's a weapon that will—'

'Chrissie, shut up!' she snaps. 'You intended the film to have this result *exactly*. You told me it was your God-given opportunity to make the world a better place.'

'But it could result in a war.' Anguish twists his features. 'How could anyone predict the film's effects?'

'Creative destruction. You can't make an omelette without breaking eggs.'

'Damn it, Venus! Millions could wind up dead.'

I break in, 'Millions? We are talking about a bit of filmed drama here. Not nuclear bombs.'

Christopher's suddenly on his feet. 'Why do you think I had that breakdown! I screened the entire film to my crew. They came to me in the days afterward and said they couldn't get this notion out of their heads that they wanted to create a martyr; they were obsessed by the idea; that's all they could think about. They said it all made such perfect sense! If they could only murder someone loved enough by the public, then the world would be a better place.'

I'm angry with him, so I bark back, 'OK! So you show this to an audience of a hundred people. Ten of those become "infected", as you put it. They're infected by the film's message. They become obsessed by a compulsion to kill a president. But how the hell is some kid from the Acacia Avenue going to put a bomb under the president's bed? Even if they get hold of a machine-gun they'll never get anywhere near the president with all the security and armour plated cars. They'll just be another maniac with a gun and a one-way ticket to the nut house.'

'You never understand what I tell you!' Saliva sprays from Lake's mouth with the force of his passion. 'But you're right about one thing: *Vorada* won't affect everyone. Not everyone will read between the lines and understand its subtext: that is, to create a martyr will advance us

213

toward social utopia, or it'll lead to a quantum leap in technology, or inspire scientists with the passion to work flat out to develop a cure for cancer. We're talking about one per cent of its audience that are smart enough to draw their own conclusions.'

Now Venus steps in as if suddenly she's on her brother's side, 'And you have to ask yourself who will be in the audience. This is a film that anyone with a passing interest in cult cinema has been waiting to see. Just imagine for a moment, Jack.' Her voice becomes silky as those fawn-soft eyes hold me. 'Imagine when the film is playing in Washington DC there's a member of the security service, a bodyguard, or a marksman assigned to providing that security umbrella for the president. Those security servicemen are selected for their intelligence and integrity, as well as their complete and utter commitment to safeguarding the most powerful individual in the world. Before they see the film they can't think of a higher purpose in their life. They are instrumental in protecting that most special of VIPs. In the battle between good and evil they are prepared to sacrifice their life. That is their purpose. Now imagine if the film suggests to them a *higher* purpose. That they can personally raise their fellow human beings to a new plateau of greater happiness. That it is in their power to endow a renewed sense of security, and reap a harvest of increased national prosperity. And that they come to believe they can achieve all this by creating a martyr who will be revered throughout history. For a personal bodyguard in an opportune location it will only take a moment.' Venus's smile lights up the room. 'Whoever makes the martyr doesn't even have to be armed. After all, the Emperor Romanus was drowned in his bath by his own aides.'

I watch her face. Whatever she introduced to my food hasn't left me yet. Her smile illuminates my world. Even her words are blossoms of the most intense colour imaginable. They're unfurling one after another inside my head.

Christopher takes a step toward me; he's pleading. 'Calner, you can see what the film did to me. As soon as I understood its power I knew I could never let it go into the world. The pressure of that knowledge tore me apart.'

'So why didn't you destroy it?'

'It was too late. I couldn't make that decision. My willpower was all gone. I was a wreck. It was like a paralysis of not just body but mind, too.

All I could do was lock myself away here with the film, and then pretend to your father that I was still working on it to make it perfect.' He gulps as if the words have swollen in his throat so much he can barely get them out. 'Your father had faith in me. He trusted me to finish the film. I wanted . . . I didn't know if. . . .' As his voice ends in a croak he turns away. He's rubbing his temples as if the pressure inside there is so great he fears it will erupt through the bone. As for me? I'm in the grip of the chemicals in my blood again. Maybe this is its last surge of mind-altering magic.

'Jack?' Venus smiles – pure honey for my soul. She grips my forearm in both her hands. I feel her body press up close to mine. 'We're nearly there, aren't we? Doesn't it feel as if we're just a step away from something marvellous?'

Christopher's haggard eyes fix on me. 'You've got the rifle, Mr Calner. You only have to stick it in her face and pull the trigger. You'll save the world so much heartache if you do. What's the use of a martyr anyway?'

The setting sun floods the room with red light. Suddenly it seems as if the walls are drenched in blood. Crimson is splashed on those marble statues of Greek gods and goddesses. Apollo's face has the appearance of being carved from raw beef.

It's that little pill that Venus melted into my soup I tell myself. It hasn't stopped casting its spell yet.

'Calner.' Christopher Lake speaks through gritted teeth. 'You must stop Venus. This could be your last chance.' He punches down on the table. 'Kill her!'

Venus snaps, 'Save your breath, Chrissie. Can't you see Jack won't be using that gun on me?' She rests those slender fingers on my arm again, 'You could never hurt me, could you, Jack?'

I shake my head. A solemn shake. This provokes the man to act. With a howl he snatches a glass figurine from the table top. I see it happening. I know what he will do with it. But this drug has put me in a place outside myself. It's as if I'm watching all this happen to a stranger . . . not to me. So there's no burning need to react.

Venus shouts. I track the sweep of his arm with my eyes. The foot tall statue of a Greek huntress glitters with cranberry lights in the setting sun. I feel nothing but tranquil detachment. At some point during this swirl of movement Lake dashes the figurine into my forehead. There's no pain but I'm falling back on to the floor. Venus is there, helping me to my feet. Once more I'm impressed by the understanding that I can't tell how much time has passed between being clubbed by the glass ornament and a slow motion rise to my feet with Venus's anxious face looking into mine. As I stand I realize that the automatic rifle is no longer in my hands; it has made the short but crucial journey into those of Christopher – he of cracked mind. These thoughts are surprising, yet expected; surreally funny, yet alarming. That blow he delivered to my skull was harder than I thought. Venus is having to exert herself to keep me upright.

Christopher Lake backs away until he's a dozen paces from us. The combination of the drug and the crack across the head with the ornament leaves me detached. I see all this happening as if I'm perched high in the minstrel's gallery at the end of the lounge. However, in reality I'm standing room centre, supported by Venus in her rippling silk kimono. Her lunatic brother is fumbling with the automatic rifle. His movements are fast. To my mind they're exaggerated as his fingers pull at levers on the rifle. He's trying to find the safety catch. I know he is. Because he's tugged at the trigger at least five times without successfully firing the rifle.

And Venus is shouting, 'No, Christopher! Put the gun down . . . listen to me, put it down!'

I'm saying nothing. I seem to have more in common with those marble statues. Right at that moment a stone-like quality is preferable to anything of flesh and feeling.

'Christopher . . . Chrissie, please don't do this. Put the gun on the table, then go back to your room. I'll bring supper. You can listen to your music. . . .'

'Venus . . . I'm not an imbecile. Listen to me! I'm going to stop you.' The clouded expression of confusion on the man's face suddenly brightens into one of wonder as at last he manages to slide the safety catch into fire mode.

My senses return in a rush. The mental image of Venus and I being torn to pieces by high velocity ammunition hits me with brutal force. 'You won't do this, Christopher. Give me the rifle.'

The expression of wonder on his face that appeared as he realized he had a killing machine in his hands evolves into one of grim determination. 'I'm sorry. But you know why I've got to kill her. You know what she's planning? She's wanting to set the world on fire. Creative destruction? It'd lead to nothing but total destruction. There'd be carnage.' Lake swings the rifle muzzle to point it at her. He holds it awkwardly; he's not familiar with firearms. I know, however, that at this range he can not miss. Venus stiffens as she realizes he really does intend to open fire.

The blast comes like a roar of thunder. Venus flinches. Her body snaps against mine. I search her face for an expression of agony. With all my will-power I pray she won't die. Yet, as my eyes fix on her, I realize she's turning to stare at her brother. I glance back to see him lurching backward with his arms outstretched. The rifle tumbles from his hands to the floor. A second later his body slaps down on to the mosaic. There he lies. On his back, with his arms flung outward. Blood trickles from his mouth. More of the stuff seeps through his shirt in a crimson mass that engulfs the entire area of his chest.

That gust of pure fear has flushed the drug right out of me. I'm ME again. Jack Calner. I'm clear headed. The world is as it always has been. Colours and perspectives are normal. I still have my arm around Venus's shoulders as I glance back to see Bunny standing in the doorway. He holds the shotgun to his shoulder; it's still aimed at the few cubic feet of air that, until a moment ago, were occupied by one deranged filmmaker by the name of Christopher Lake. Auteur of long lost *Vorada*. Blue smoke oozes from the muzzle of the gun. Whereas the room had been filled with what seemed like an explosion, along with a shriek of lead pellets tearing the air, and the impact of Lake against the floor – all of those rolled into one avalanche of sound – now there is profound silence.

Forty years after Bunny murdered his parents he's gone and killed all over again. For a while, the tableau remains just like that. I stand with my arms around Venus. Bunny poses, motionless, in the doorway with the shotgun, his eyes locked on to his victim. Christopher Lake lies dead on the floor.

Despite the smell of spilt body fluids and the reek of cordite being powerful ones, I'm noticing other things now. The song of birds in the evening sunlight reaches me through the open window. I can smell stinging nettles again.

It seems to touch Bunny, too, who relaxes with a sigh. He lowers the shotgun so it dangles harmlessly in one hand with its muzzle pointing down at the floor.

217

'Miss Lake.' His smile returns, yet this time it's sympathetic. 'I'm sorry I had to do that to your brother. I know how much you loved him.'

She takes a deep breath to steady herself. 'You did the right thing, Bunny.'

'I'll wait until the end of the week. Then I'll report what I've done to the police.'

She nods. 'Thank you. That'll give us time to announce to the press about the release of the film before my brother's death becomes public knowledge.'

I feel as if I'm having to run hard to keep up with the thread of this conversation. 'Venus, Bunny has just killed your brother. You need to—'

'I need to put my plan first, that's what I need to do, Jack.' She steps forward to gaze down at the corpse then glances back at me. 'And don't stare at me like that. I'm not a heartless bitch. We need to collect the film then get it to the distributors as quickly as possible. When news of Christopher's death breaks there'll be plenty of publicity we can use.'

'And I thought I was ruthless.'

Suddenly she's businesslike again. 'You'll get what you want, Jack. Money; lots of money; more than you can ever spend. And I'll get. . .' Her voice fades as she fully appreciates the enormity of events.

I finish her sentence, 'You'll get your martyr.' I glance at Bunny who smiles fondly at her, then I turn back to her. 'You really do love monsters.' I can't resist saying this. Talk about bad-timing and insensitivity, but. . . . 'Bunny killed his parents to stop a plague wiping us out. Now he's killed Christopher who planned to stop you releasing his film. *Vorada*'s going to create your martyr, and that martyr will elevate this world to a better place.' I address Bunny. 'It's becoming quite a habit. You've saved humanity all over again. Well done.' A sarcastic note adds a sour tone to my voice. Bunny doesn't notice. Or he doesn't give a damn. Either way, his heart will be bursting with heroic pride.

Venus locks those big brown eyes on me. 'Jack. We're both going to get what we want from this film. So you're not going to try and stop me – are you?'

SIXTEEN

Now it is dark.

Expedient. This word can sting the conscience like those stinging nettles we cut earlier can prickle your skin. Expediency isn't for the weak. Many a time in the past I've done what is expedient – or necessary, if you prefer that word – with a reasoned disregard for morality. I'm a businessman, after all.

Now this is expedient. In its own way it's moving, too, just in case you think I've a heart beaten from solid brass. In the hour since Christopher Lake was shot dead in the living room here at Montage I watched this happen.

Refusing help from either Venus or myself, Bunny carried Christopher's body upstairs to his bedroom. With tenderness, love and utter respect, this white haired man who'd murdered his mother and father half a lifetime ago sets Christopher on his bed. Venus follows them into the room. She presses a button on the laptop. The applause recorded in a Parisian concert hall fills the room. It's followed by the eerie notes of an accordion, and once more Jacques Brel thunders his hymn to sailors carousing in the Port of Amsterdam against a backdrop of the eternal. From the foot of the bed, she watches as Bunny adjusts her dead brother's limbs until it appears he lies there dozing, not dead. He makes a beautiful corpse. There, I've said it. It's a strange observation, yet true. Christopher Lake could be posing for a painting of a fallen warrior.

It's tranquil in the house now. There's no panic. Everyone moves in an unrushed way. Our voices are relaxed; no one speaks loudly. I pack my clothes and put the bag in the car. The night is still. A new moon shines down. Lights burn inside Montage. Through its open windows drifts the sound of the male voice singing in French. The mood of the song is tidal. At times it creeps along in a melancholy way before surging upward in floods of triumph. Venus told me it's a song about a sailor drinking hard, getting into a brawl, and then dying in a dockside bar. At that moment, as the music pours out over the moonlit garden, it becomes a rhapsody to life's conquest of death.

Then I'm back in the house again. Bunny is mopping blood from the mosaic dolphins in the living room. Venus Lake sits on her brother's bed. She's holding his hands while she gazes at his face in genuine sorrow. The music's still playing, but quietly now.

'When we were young,' she begins, 'we'd build sandcastles. Then we'd pretend that we gathered all the frightened and vulnerable people in the world together, and put them in the castle. Christopher would tell me it was the strongest castle there ever was, and now the people inside would be safe. Nobody would ever be able to hurt them again. When he grew up his films became his sandcastle. *Vorada* was going to be the biggest and the best. But he lost his nerve.' She stands before gently kissing him on the forehead. 'Goodbye, Christopher.'

SEVENTEEN

We're driving away from Montage. Even though the sound of Jacques Brel's music fades from my ears I can still hear it play on inside my head. Venus sits beside me. Of course, I haven't had a chance to have the cracked windscreen replaced. Venus Lake's naked body shattered that glass. I marvel over this fact more than once as I watch the road through the crazed pattern of white lines. But then she has constantly surprised me from that first encounter with her when she raced from the forest to smash into the front of my car. When I spoke to her initially she appeared naïve, but I realize now that she was simply wearing that naïvety as a disguise. In all of this she's been in control. The car's headlights slice through the darkness in front of us. At that moment there's also the searing beam of insight cutting through the inside of my head – my still aching head. I mean, just look at what Venus Lake has done:

Naked, she ran into my car. An accident? Now I wonder.

Duped me into thinking she was a simple woman of limited intelligence.

Enticed me into desiring her . . . no, it's more powerful than that: Venus Lake succeeded in making me fall in love with her.

She made me scuttle around that woodland folly like a frightened rabbit as she fired off the rifle.

She put drugs in my soup. Just like I swallowed everything she told me I swallowed those, too.

After that, she lured me out of the house to chase her as she ran naked through the trees.

Then, when my mind had been turned inside out by the narcotic, she tells me that *Vorada* will radically alter the civilized world. And this is the method: its storyline will suggest to certain individuals that progress – both social and technological – is accelerated either by a world war, or by the death of a public figure beloved by all, who will become a martyr in the eyes of the masses. With me so far? Good.

Because now I feel a tingle down my spine. Understand this, Venus is exceptional. She calculates that her actions will achieve the results she wants. If everything she has done since her brother completed *Vorada* has been a logical step-by-step process in her quest to change the world, then . . . listen to me carefully now . . . then I must reach a conclusion that the film will successfully complete her meticulous strategy. Venus will create her martyr. The world changes.

These thoughts loop round inside my head as I drive. It's near to midnight now as the car surges along the forest highway. It'll take around six hours to reach my house in London. For a while, we've been chatting in a friendly way. If I'm reading the signals right she'll be giving me more than reels of film. In a matter of hours we'll be sharing a bed. The images that spin in my mind quicken my pulse. I want her. That's the long and the short of it. I want her so much I ache. And it's one of those absurd universal truths of life that most men are prepared to undertake a heck of a lot of uncharacteristic activity if there's a chance of an amorous encounter at the end of it. Such as serenading their heart's desire with a guitar beneath her window; writing long love letters; or driving across country to make that all-important rendezvous, or . . . in my case . . . yes, in my case, doing everything in my power to make sure that the film her brother, now lying bloody and dead in his bedroom, made all those years ago will finally be released to a world-wide audience. That's it, isn't it? I'm doing this for love . . . a puppy-eyed, head-over-heels, madly-truly-deeply, forever and ever without end kind of love.

Thoughts like these . . . and their piggy-back images of sizzling, erotic sex push me to drive faster. I power the car along the road; its lights splash against bushes and trees. The moon is high above the hills.

After what we've been through together over the last forty-eight hours

I'm sure she'll confide in me now.

'So,' I begin as I accelerate out of a bend, 'now you can tell me where you hid the film.'

Venus looks at me without answering. There's a Mona Lisa smile ghosting on her lips.

I continue, 'It can't be back at the house, can it?'

'I know better to leave thousands of feet of priceless celluloid lying around in a garage or an attic. Years ago I took it to a safety deposit vault where humidity and temperature are controlled. It's cost a hell of a lot to keep it there, but. . . .' She shrugs as if the end of the sentence is obvious.

I agree. 'Something that valuable deserves the best.'

She nods.

'So when do we collect?' I ask.

Her smile broadens. 'This is the plan. I'll arrange a press call at a hotel in London. You'll read a speech I've prepared, which talks about cult director Christopher Lake, the history of *Vorada* and your plans for its release. I'll collect the film, and for dramatic effect I'll wheel it in for the media to photograph, and no doubt carry its reappearance live on news channels the world over. At the press conference I hand the reels over to the distributor who will take them away; make the necessary copies. At the same time you take care of the business side. Promotion, marketing, rights deals and so on.'

'You've got this all covered.' On the road ahead rabbits scatter in the car's lights. They avoid death by inches. 'But what about the fact Bunny killed your brother?'

'It's a tragedy I didn't foresee. Until tonight Chrissie was never violent. Anyway, we can't turn back time. Bunny knows what I plan to do, and that we need a couple of days to get everything in place before he goes to the police. Bunny won't implicate us. He'll confess to shooting Christopher.'

'And as he's murdered before the police are hardly likely to doubt Bunny's confession.' I nod. 'Does Bunny know where the film is?'

'No. Only I do.'

'You won't share its location with me, Venus?'

'There's no need at this stage.'

'You've really got this all planned to the letter, haven't you?'

'Yes. Because it's the most important thing I've ever done in my life.'

Her face is illuminated by the dashboard lights. 'You've never had the conviction that you were born in order to fulfil a destiny?'

'I've had ambition for personal gain. Never destiny.' In her face I can see that single purpose in her life. It shines there. It's unquenchable. Nothing else matters. If she has to sacrifice her own life to make sure that *Vorada* gets seen by even more people then she'll do it.

It's been an extraordinary forty-eight hours. When I first drove through this forest toward Montage I wouldn't have believed the film I was hunting had the power to change the civilized world. Christopher Lake even said it might trigger new wars. I wouldn't have believed any of that – not for one, lousy moment – but this woman beside me has the power to work a new kind of magic. It's a magic that has the power to transfigure minds. Without a scrap of doubt I know the film will achieve everything she claims. Oh, it'll make me even wealthier in the process. Even if it does cost the life of one famous, iconic human being. Go on, read your history books. Martyrs change the world, although there is a risk that such an assassination might lead to the deaths of thousands of men, women and children. I guess that's what they term 'collateral damage'. And so . . . Venus Lake asks if I've ever had a sense of my own destiny. This has provoked a whole slew of disparate thoughts. I recall Christopher Lake's pleas to stop this. I'm struck that I've never even asked what *Vorada* was about. Brel's song is in my head. Life beats death. Ultimately, it always does. Maybe at this precise second I'm not thinking clearly. It occurs to me that my brain isn't clear of the drug after all. And even now it's shaping the way I think. Maybe this isn't noble at all. That the sense of destiny that fills me at this instant might be nothing more than another chemical-induced hallucination.

But, God help me, this seems to be the right decision.

As I press the pedal to the floor and the car hurtles along this wilderness road I close my eyes. I keep them closed. I keep them tightly shut even as Venus Lake shouts my name and tries to grab the wheel.

I keep them closed . . . I'm keeping them closed . . . I'm keeping—

'Jack! I know what you're doing. It won't work!'

The car leaves the road. For now, there are no obstructions. It rolls in the air.

Venus speaks. There's no fear. Only the pure note of destiny that resonates. 'Jack. I lied. Bunny knows where *Vorada*—'

223

94   EXT. FOREST – DAY

Seasons change. Summer has gone. Now winter blows in. Trees are bare. It's a monochrome landscape of black trees and white snow on the ground. Deep in a gully out of sight from the world is JACK CALNER'S silver BMW. Its bodywork is crumpled, the windshield is missing; vines climb over the roof. Strapped in the front seats are the two decomposing corpses of VENUS and JACK. FADE IN APPLAUSE and CALLS from an audience as Brel's AMSTERDAM begins. Ghostly notes of the ACCORDION rise in volume. Views of car, boulders and trees as if POV is becoming detached from the tragedy that unfolded here ten months ago. CAMERA drifts away from the car to wander through the frozen forest in search of other lives.